The Horse Who Walked Through Time

Other books by Lisa Maxwell:

The Horse In The Mirror

Truthseeker

The Horse Who Walked Through Time

Lisa Maxwell

Published by Lisa Maxwell
2017

First Printing: 2017

ISBN 978-0-9987421-1-3

Sugar Creek Publications

www.frenchclassicaldressageforall.com

For Dan Palmer,
my best and longest friend.

Chapter One

The two horses picked their way down the forest-clad slope following a steep deer track. Their riders sat as silent as the shadows under the old-growth pines through which they rode. The horse in the lead was a towering eighteen hands tall, solidly muscled and proud. His liver-chestnut coat matched perfectly the color of the pine needles underfoot. He carried his neck arched, his mane and the feathers on the backs of his legs rippling with each ponderous step. His hooves were the size of dinner plates, his legs like pillars and yet there was nothing of the dullness of a draft horse about him. His eyes shone with intelligence as he bore his rider with care and grace.

By contrast the stallion's rider sat hunched and inattentive on his back, grief drawn about her like a cumbersome cloak. Dark hair spilled in uncombed tendrils from beneath her hood, almond-shaped eyes cast down as though watching the trail in front of her, but she saw nothing.

The horse that followed was much smaller, less than fifteen hands tall, as fine boned and petite as the stallion was massive. She picked her way among the roots and rocks with the wisdom of a horse accustomed to steep and difficult terrain. Her dappled bay coat and black mane blended with the dappled shadows, and her large eyes shone with intelligence in her finely chiseled face.

The mare's rider fought the grief and shock that threatened to overwhelm him, aware of the danger lurking in these woods. His gaze swept the forest to either side, in sync with the rhythm of his horse's gait. Too many things could go wrong in an instant. His sand-colored hair fell in a ponytail down his back, revealing a round face that was better suited to laughter and friendliness than the grief and worry it held now. Dressed in the skins of wild animals, he was almost as hard to pick out of the shadows as his horse.

He was well equipped to handle some of the dangers they might face. He was Hluit, a horse herder –.born to the wild. As a boy, Petre had traveled these lands in a small tribe and later alone as a scout. He knew the land, the animals, and the risks, but what he faced now was beyond those simple and direct things. He was responsible for keeping Isadora and the stallion safe but he was not the leader. He would follow where Isadora and Lark led for they would take him – if they were successful – to a place he could never find on his own no matter how well he knew the land.

Somewhere over the next several ridges lay their destination, Amil's cabin. Petre knew it only as a ruin – a few stacked bricks that were still recognizable as a chimney, scattered mounds of fieldstone overgrown with vines, inhabited by mice, and lizards when the weather was warmer. Petre tried to banish that image from his mind. Where Isadora would take them, if she could, was Amil's cabin when it had been new and whole and inhabited by a man. Amil had been a scholar in the Alliance before he had become an outlaw hiding from the Alliance, as Petre and Is were hiding from the Alliance now.

The ability to get to Amil's cabin in its original state was beyond Petre. He could only get them to the right *place*. Isadora had to get them to the right *time*. He looked at her slumped, grief-stricken form and worried. She seemed barely aware of her surroundings, hardly caring of her own survival. It was not fair that the survival of all of the tribes of Hluit rested on her. Yet Petre was secretly glad that there was something driving her to stay alive. Without that she would have sought to die as John had died.

Sorrow moved Petre to reach out and stroke his horse's mane as though to reassure her. This was John's mare, Celeste, whose presence sometimes made it hard to believe that he would never see John again.

Petre had grown up with John. They had been best friends as boys; John, Petre, and John's brother Ondre had been inseparable. As young boys they had gotten into trouble together trying to race the brood mares they were supposed to be watching. As adolescents they had tried more daring adventures – climbing Deadman's rock, shooting White Eagle Rapids in a handmade canoe. John was always the instigator; always sure the impossible could be done. John. It was impossible not to be swept up in his energy, infected by his idealism, impossible not to love him. Now all of their hearts had to pay the cost for that love.

It was no surprise that John had chosen for himself the most dangerous occupation a Hluit could have – spying inside the Alliance. For a time Petre and Ondre had followed John even there, leaving their wild homeland to infiltrate the huge concrete cities of the Alliance. In time Petre and Ondre had been drawn home to the open grasslands, the horse herds, and nomadic life but John had stayed on in the Alliance penetrating to the top levels of secret Alliance research.

Petre's fingers stroking Celeste's mane were stopped by a knot – a knot that would never have been there when John was alive. The Alliance had caught John spying and had done to him the very sophisticated equivalent of cutting out his tongue. When the Alliance was through with him, John could not communicate in speech, writing, or sign. He had escaped, but was unaware that his captors had arranged for him to steal certain provisions that were poisoned. If Isadora hadn't found him soon afterward, he would have died.

Is had been an outlaw herself, fleeing from the Alliance troopers, hiding from other outlaws and the Blueskins who inhabited the Boundary Mountains. Even though it was a big risk, she had tried to help John. Although he must have often seemed more than half crazy, for any attempt to communicate would throw him into a fit of hysterical laughing or crying, Is had come to trust him.

She had once told Petre that her trust in John was because of the gentle way he treated his horse. He rode Celeste without bridle or bit of any sort, the way all the Hluit rode their horses, but back then Is had never heard of the Hluit. The bond of trust required by that sort of horsemanship intrigued her. Petre half smiled at the thought. Is, who had trained the magnificent and deadly war stallions that awed his people had wanted to learn this gentle love-based horsemanship. Is, who had suffered so much abuse at the hands of the Alliance that she had finally been driven to steal one of the stallions and flee, had still been able to recognize in John, as crazy as he appeared, the kindness and love she needed to heal. It was no wonder she had fallen in love with John. Petre worried at the knot in Celeste's mane and thought of the first time he had seen Isadora on her stolen war stallion, returning with John when everyone had thought John must be dead. Even in the joy of that reunion it had been clear to Petre that Is had a special connection with John. It was also clear that under her brave exterior she was terrified of people and social situations. Petre had spent enough time in the Alliance to know how badly its citizens were treated, especially the women. Is needed help adjusting to Hluit society. She needed someone to explain things to her, and John could not do that. Petre had meant only to befriend her.

The knot refused Petre's attempts to undo it. He would have to cut it out with his knife later. Right now his attention was needed on the trail which seemed to be taking them too far west, but he couldn't be certain wending through the trees as they were. He needed an open vista to get his bearings.

He was playing with the thought of stopping to climb a tree when they came upon a sudden break in the forest. Is stopped Lark short before he could step into the open. Petre rode up beside her. An avalanche had cut a swath, wiping out all trees and vegetation and leaving behind a clear chute with only a few stray boulders, stripped like bone and left to stand sentinel.

Petre left Is and the horses in the protection of the trees and made his way out into the open using the rocks for cover. He could not let himself be seen; there were too many people looking for them. Alliance troopers wanted to take Is and Lark back to their territory where Lark would be used for some purpose that would further the Alliance's dominion over its people and Is would be punished or executed as a traitor.

The troopers weren't the only ones looking for them. There were also the Blueskins and possibly bounty hunters searching for them.

.Crouched low, Petre made his way to one great slab of rock that leaned out over the valley below. Its cracked and fissured surface supplied plenty of hand and toeholds. When he got near the top he lay on his stomach and inched his way out to the very edge, careful never to let himself be silhouetted against the sky.

To either side of the avalanche chute the forest fell away below him – evergreens, tall and dense, making a secret of what was happening beneath them. Even the sounds he should hear if anyone were down there would be muted by the pine needles. The sky above was blue, the sun bright, and the air so clear it seemed he could see every needle on every tree. It was a perfect fall day, the kind that Petre would normally have enjoyed to the utmost knowing there would be few enough days like this before winter set in. But today the beauty seemed at odds with the danger that faced them. This could be the last autumn his people would ever spend free on the land, at peace with their horses.

Near the base of the chute, all the boulders carried by the avalanche had come to rest. A shadow moved in that maze of rocks and broken trees. An instant later a horse and rider broke from the cover of the forest and flowed into the cover of the boulder field. The rider was bare from the waist up despite the cold. The bluish cast to the rider's skin was unmistakable, as were the feathers and strips of animal skins tied in his horse's mane. The Blueskin glanced behind him, guiding his horse with his knees as he disappeared from sight among the rocks.

In his wake came more quick-stepping little horses streaming from the woods, their barebacked riders, legs dangling long, wearing full war party regalia. Naked from the waist up except for orange and black paint, they were armed with anything from sharpened sticks to sophisticated blasters taken off troopers they had killed.

Like the leader's horse, their ponies were painted and adorned with feathers and skins.

They moved into the boulder field below Petre, fading from tree shadow to rock shadow. Only his vantage point allowed him to see them fanning out among the boulders, bays and buckskins and paints carrying blue-skinned, war-painted riders.

Petre eased back down the rock, cautious not to make a sound, relieved that for the moment the Blueskins were not hunting him and Is. At the same time, he dreaded telling Is that her worst fear was coming true. People were about to fight and die because of what she had done, when she had only meant to save the stallion's life and escape the oppression of her existence.

Petre found Is leaning against a tree, resting her back from the hours of riding. She lifted her chin toward Petre as he approached, dark hair falling back from her too-pale face. Gaunt, hollow-cheeked strain had replaced the easy, unconscious beauty Petre had always found in her face before. He hated to tell her what he'd seen.

"Blueskins," he kept his voice to a whisper. "War party. They're setting an ambush."

"For us?" she asked.

"No." At least so far the Blueskins were unaware that the woman for whom they were about to fight was only a few hundred yards above them.

"They're concerned about something behind them," he told her. "My guess is they've tricked some of the Alliance troopers into chasing them."

"So they'll draw them into the ambush, and . . . kill them?" Her voice dropped.

Petre let out his breath and nodded. He did not like what was happening any better than she did, but if the Blueskins would keep the troopers busy he and Is might slip by them.

For the first time in the days they'd been riding together Petre saw the strength and stubbornness that had been so much a part of Is return to her. She moved toward the stallion.

"What are you going to do?" Petre whispered, suddenly worried.

"Stop them."

"Is, wait!" Petre whispered urgently, catching her arm because he knew she wasn't going to listen to him. She threw his hand off as she spun to face him. He caught a glimpse of her eyes, wild and angry, and in that instant he knew she was beyond listening to rational argument. Then his attention was forced to the stallion. Lark moved toward Petre, drawn up to his full impressive height, ears pinned back, massive neck arched, muscles tight as he stepped forward on pillar-like legs and hooves that could crush and kill. Petre had never seen Lark display any aggression before. He fell back a step in surprise. Lark faltered. His ears came forward. For a moment he looked confused, as though he didn't remember what he had been doing. Then he lowered his huge head and sniffed gently at Is's hand. His soft brown nostrils fluttered as he let out his breath. Only kindness and intelligence shone from his eyes.

Is's hand trembled as she reached out to him.

"He's changing, isn't he?" Petre asked softly. He saw the back of her head nod and she buried her hand in the horse's mane to hide its shaking. Petre's heart fell. Is didn't need to face this right now, but he had to know how quickly the shift was likely to happen. They might still have a chance to make it to Amil's.

"How much longer will you be able to control him?"

"Three days," she said, her voice without expression. "No more."

Petre let out a long breath. There was no way to stop what would happen to Lark unless there were some answers at Amil's.

"Does this mean his rider is coming nearer?" he asked. Although Is trained the stallions, each horse was connected by a microchip in its brain to a special warrior, a berserker, who would ride him into battle.

"Yes. If the troopers have Lark's berserker with them that would be the easiest way for them to find Lark and to control him once they take him." The words were dead of hope.

"We have to go on," Petre said. "We might make it to Amil's in two days." He knew Is didn't care. She didn't believe they could save his people or her stallion. Still she nodded. She had agreed to try because that's what John would have wanted and she would hold to that bargain no matter how painful or hopeless it was. Petre felt a little rush of pride for her.

He swung onto Celeste and watched Is mount Lark.

"We're going to just . . ." She gestured back to where the Blueskins would lure the troopers into the boulders and kill them, " . . . leave them?

"We can't stop them. Even if you gave Lark to the troopers now, the Blueskins would try to take him back. They'd still kill each other. Is, you're not responsible for the Blueskins or the troopers. You didn't ask them to fight each other. They made their own decisions. You can only allow them the freedom to do so."

He watched the stubborn set of her jaw as she refused to meet his eyes. She had no love for either Blueskins or troopers. Though she'd been mishandled by both, Is did not want to be the cause of a war between them. He was proud of her for that. She had every right to hate both sides and wish they would wipe each other out.

"It would be wrong for you to let them force you into an action you don't want to make. Then they are taking *your* freedom away," he said more gently.

Hluit society was based on accepting the responsibility of freedom and allowing others to do the same. But Is had not been part of the Hluit long enough to know how to deal with the really hard decisions sometimes demanded by that philosophy.

Into her hesitation, Petre said, "C'mon, let's get out of here." He sent Celeste past Lark and when he looked back the stallion was following. For the first time, Petre was certain that his decision to ride John's mare instead of his own horse was a good one. Lark was attached to this mare almost as much as he was to Is. Maybe between the two of them they could hold Lark against his urge to go to his berserker. Maybe they could keep the great amiable horse he was now from changing into a crazed war horse that would attack anyone except his own berserker.

They made a wide detour around where the Blueskins were setting their ambush. Petre wanted to get another ridge between them and the Blueskins before they stopped for the night. They let the horses drink at a little stream at the bottom of the drainage before setting off to climb the next ridge. With winter so near, darkness would come early, even earlier under the enormous branches that reached far above their heads.

Petre could feel Celeste tiring with the steep climb. He could imagine how much more work it was for the massive war horse to climb this slope. He could hear Lark's labored breathing and on a particularly steep place he heard the great horse slip, sending a small avalanche of mud and rocks ricocheting into the trees below. He twisted around in time to see Lark make a mighty lunge, Is crouched over the stallion's withers, encouraging him with her voice until he regained his footing.

Lark stood blowing, head lowered, and a muscle in his flank quivering. Petre took a moment to assess the situation. All four of them were exhausted, but Is would not ask for rest and the war horse had not been bred to quit. Hardening his heart, Petre sent Celeste onward. Their path was so steep now that they had to traverse the slope in switchbacks gaining only a little elevation at a time.

It was growing darker by the moment but finally Petre caught a glimpse of lighter sky in a break between the trees above them. "We're almost to the top," he told Is. "We'll rest there."

Her silence was consent. Now they urged their horses directly up the bank. Its slope was too steep for walking and the horses took it in a series of powerful lunges.

Finally at the top, they stopped to rest. They hadn't noticed the wind lower on the slope with the protection of the trees, but here on the exposed ridge it struck them head on. The horses sent clouds of steaming breath into the wind where it whipped away and disappeared. Steam rose from their long winter coats now damp with sweat, and it too streamed away. It was too cold to let them stand for long.

The sky was shaded toward indigo as Is and Petre turned their horses down the long decline. Stars were becoming visible until branches once again closing overhead blocked them from sight. Under the dense canopy, it was already twilight but at least the wind was gone. There would be nowhere to rest the horses until they reached the bottom of the drainage, they had to trust to their horses' night vision to find the way in the deepening darkness.

Going down was no easier work for the horses than going up had been. Again the more massive stallion was at a disadvantage. Petre heard Lark sliding behind him as mud and dislodged stones came down between Celeste's legs.

"Better let me go first," Is said, her voice tight.

Petre was glad to oblige. Better to have Lark in front so he could not send Celeste careening down with him if he lost his footing. As they broke out of the trees for a stretch, Petre could see Lark almost sitting on his massive hindquarters as he half-walked half-slid down the mountain. His tail dragged the ground. His hooves cut long furrows through the dirt. A mudslide preceded him, rocks and leaves rattled down the slope. Once again Petre was impressed with Lark's strength and courage, not to mention Is's.

Celeste picked her way daintily. She did not like to slide but where it was too steep to walk she sat back in her hindquarters, walking with her front legs and skiing on her hind hooves. Despite the treacherous terrain, she seemed controlled and balanced. Petre felt well taken care of and safe on her back, and he understood why John had loved this mare so much.

The ride seemed to go on forever. Petre imagined how tired the horses must be but there was no way to rest them on this steep slope. As the ground gradually became less steep, they heard the welcome sound of water. A few moments later they came to a little creek.

The riders dismounted gratefully and both horses immediately dropped their heads to eat the grass along the water's edge. They loosened the horses' saddles and Is unbridled Lark. It would be another cold camp, no fire, no tents. It was just as well. They were too exhausted to do more than unroll their sleeping bags and munch the cold meat nuts, and dried fruit the tribe had sent with them.

Petre ached from tension and lack of sleep.

"I'll watch," Is said. "I can't sleep anyway."

Petre was too tired to resist. "Promise you'll wake me when that bright star goes behind that mountain," he said, pointing. That would be approximately half the night. He fell asleep waiting to hear her promise.

He woke to a feeling of dread and emptiness so profound it was as though Is was already gone and all his people were dead at the hands of the Alliance. Unable to fight this forlorn feeling lying down, he sat up. The star was almost lost behind the trees of the next ridge. He could make out Is sitting wrapped in her sleeping bag, her head down. He thought maybe she had dozed off until she spoke.

"Waking up's the worst," she said as though she knew exactly what he had experienced.

Petre could only agree. In sleep there was the relief of oblivion. Fully awake he could submerge his grief in the need to survive. But at the moment of waking all his defenses against grief and fear were down. He arranged himself, wrapped in his sleeping bag, sitting against a tree next to Is so she could see that he was on watch, and could sleep if she would.

After a very long time, during which Petre thought she might have dozed off, Is spoke. "I shouldn't have let him go back into the Mirror." She was speaking of John, blaming herself for his death.

A harsh little sound came from Petre's throat. "You couldn't have stopped him." He knew John.

"I could have ridden away," she said harshly. "He had already made the Mirror repair what the Alliance had done to him. He could talk. If I had not stayed, he wouldn't have taken the risk of going back in there. If I hadn't been there, he would have had to go back to Ondre's camp himself to tell them what he'd learned. He would still be alive."

Petre didn't know what to say to that. He didn't know the circumstances of John's death but he knew better than to try to ease Is with some empty platitude about how it wasn't her fault. In his heart he felt sure she had done what seemed best at the time but she would not accept those words from him, not with her harsh sense of honesty and self-criticism.

This was the first time Is had seemed willing to talk about John's death. Petre was afraid to say anything for fear he would say the wrong thing. Is was here, doing this because John would have wanted her to try to save his people, to save her horse, and herself. The truce she had made with John's memory, with Petre, and with death was too fragile. All Petre could do was wait in silence for her to continue, if she would.

"You don't know what it was like," Is said. "To be connected like that with John. I couldn't understand how he got the Mirror to do it, but he must have used something like the technology the Alliance uses to connect a stallion to his berserker. Only the connection was between John and me...." Her voice trailed away and Petre knew it must have been beyond description.

"Not only could John speak," she said. "I could hear him think. I could feel what he felt. It was like . . . it was like . . . he loved his people so much, they were all inside him. You and Ondre, of course, but, everyone else too, all of them."

Petre was struck by the realization of how that experience must have affected Is. From an early age, after Blueskins had killed her parents, she had been a ward of the Alliance, raised in a boarding school. Not only was she not loved, there was no one there to defend her. Petre knew enough about those schools to know that Is had needed defending from the predatory older boys, from the cruelty of children raised without kindness, and even from the teachers in a system that preyed on its citizens. Then to find herself not only loved by one man but also included – enveloped – in that man's love for all his people . . . Petre could imagine how strong that must have been for Is.

His heart reached out to her. He ached to say something to let her know how much he too loved her, but he feared there were no words she would accept from him. He held himself still and let Is continue.

"John should have gone back to Ondre's camp and told them everything he had learned, but that wasn't good enough for him. He wanted to learn more. No one had ever gotten inside the Mirror like that before. If he could learn all about its powers he could bring that back to his people."

Petre could well imagine. John was never one to stop at enough. He always wanted to do more, give more. It was so easy to get caught up in his intensity. John had a way of making you feel more magnanimous and more courageous than you really were. It was easy to believe how John would have made Is feel that they should not stop with having repaired his ability to speak. But Is was not done.

"I could have made him go back to Ondre's camp if I had just ridden away. The only reason I didn't was because I wanted to feel more of what he was making me feel. I wanted to stay there forever with him, connected like that. I didn't want to go back. I didn't care about how important his message was to everyone. I didn't care about anything except how I felt."

Her confession twisted in Petre's heart.

"I could have made him go back and I didn't," she said harshly.

Petre could not let that stand.

"Is," he said, "I loved John, he was my brother-of-the-heart." Petre referred to a Hluit custom where a person would have their brother-by-blood, or brother-by-marriage, but also the brother they really wanted, a brother-of-the-heart. It was a custom that held true for sisters, fathers, and mothers so that any Hluit could have family members of his or her choosing as well as his own biological family. "Even though he was my brother, I was never connected to him as you were. Not only were you lovers, but then you were connected by Alliance technology that broke down all separation as if you were inside his mind, his heart. John and I were only brothers, yet I was often carried away by his enthusiasm. I could not resist him even when I knew he was leading us into trouble. You were connected so much more deeply than that; of course you could not resist doing what he wanted."

He heard her take a shaky breath.

"I didn't know anything could hurt this much. I didn't know how much it would hurt, not only me but everyone," she said, her voice cracking.

She had known much pain, beginning with her parents' deaths at the hands of the Blueskins, then her upbringing in the Alliance school, and later the loss of one after another of her beloved stallions. But the grief she felt now was far worse.

"I wish I had never brought Lark to your people. Now they're all going to be killed too. Petre, I can't stand it," her voice had gone hoarse. "I can't . . ."

But he heard the anger as well as the pain. She would not cry. She would not quit. He gave her the only kind of help she would accept from him – honesty.

"My people have always known the day would come when the Alliance wouldn't tolerate our existence anymore," Petre answered. "We are prepared."

Is shook her head. "They will *kill* your people, Petre. You know they will."

Petre knew from firsthand experience what the Alliance troopers were capable of doing. He was afraid for his people too. But to Is he said.

"We are prepared. It is one of the reasons every one of us must study our martial art. We know how to fight. We know the land. We can run and hide and fight . . ."

He heard her let out her breath in a low sigh and heard the catch in it. She had agreed to this, right or wrong. He let the subject drop. Eventually Is spoke.

"I didn't know there was anything special about Lark when I took him. I just couldn't stand to lose another of my stallions. You don't know what that was like."

Petre did not refute her. As a Hluit he had been raised in a loving environment surrounded by friends and extended family, deeply connected to the land and the horses. It was no wonder to Petre that Is had stolen a stallion and fled. It was more of a wonder that she had stayed as long she had, watching one horse after another be taken from her to be ridden into a battle from which no one ever returned.

But Is had been raised on Alliance propaganda and it was hard to break free of it. It was not until she met the Hluit that she had learned that everything the Alliance had taught her was false. The berserkers did not fight the Blueskins. In fact the Alliance had created the Blueskins for the express purpose of attacking outlying farms. The Alliance had no qualms that a few innocent farmers were killed from time to time. The attacks were designed to keep Alliance citizens fearful and controlled, and to keep them out of the Boundary where the Alliance was running top secret experiments.

For generations the Hluit had watched the berserkers and their magnificent horses come onto their land only to die there. The warriors would engage in a battle with something the Hluit could not see. They would fight until exhaustion drove them to their deaths. Though none of this made sense to the Hluit, they had learned not to interfere. The berserkers were single-mindedly set on their own destruction and they would fight the Hluit as fiercely as they fought their mysterious unseen adversary. The Hluit had named that adversary the Mirror. To them it was as invisible as glass, yet the berserkers and their stallions must have seen a formidable foe in the clear air that surrounded them.

The Hluit could not understand why the Alliance created such magnificent horses, not to mention the men who rode them, only to send them to such bizarre deaths.

John had discovered that the Alliance was trying to create some sort of life after death. The Mirror was really a computer program that took the essence of man and horse apart as it killed them and tried to recreate them in some living form inside itself. But the Alliance didn't know the Mirror was keeping its best attempts secret and John thought his people might be able to use that knowledge as leverage to negotiation for their own freedom from the Alliance. The Alliance considered the Hluit to be an experiment too, and the Hluit needed some way to keep the Alliance from deciding to terminate their experiment.

For all the answers that John had given them there were still questions, especially about Lark. John had not learned anything about a stallion like Lark who could apparently move across time as easily as he moved across the land.

The silence had grown long between Petre and Is so that he hoped she was finally asleep. A sliver of moon had climbed up over the ridge, found its way through the fringe of trees there, and now hung like a curl of ice above them. Even without a full moon the night was so clear, the stars so numerous and bright, that Petre could easily see Is propped against her tree, her head hanging down.

In the distance an owl called and was answered by another on the ridge behind them. For a while Petre listened to the owls talking back and forth as they moved closer together. If the owls were courting, all was well in this valley, no large troops on the move. He listened to Is's breathing grow deep and regular. She had fallen asleep sitting up, her head now cast to the side. She looked uncomfortable but at least she was asleep and he dared not do anything that might wake her.

Cold found its way into Petre's sleeping bag, boring steadily into his back where it was exposed. He ignored it, not wanting to risk waking Is if he moved. Instead he imagined the beauty of the night seeping into him so that instead of cold misery he felt the joy of oneness with the land. A million stars were flung across the sky, some bright and hard as diamonds shimmering in the crystalline air, some so far away they formed a distant soft mist. Others seemed to have fallen into the trees where they flickered between the branches as if caught there.

The horses had finally stopped eating and were standing side-by-side, heads hanging low. The stream ran behind them, a little rill of silver stars fallen into the grass.

The owls had moved on. A profound stillness settled into Petre, calming his fears, blanketing his mourning heart with tranquility.

Chapter Two

Night lightened gradually toward dawn. Neither of them had slept much. They packed up the horses and set out, munching trail rations as they rode. For the first hour or so, the trail wandered up hill, then it began to dip and rise, each rise higher than the last until they passed over the shoulder.

Clouds were moving in, marching across the sky in a billowing gray front sinking down to meet them as they climbed. The weather would be warmer for the next day or two, warm enough to rain instead of snow, Petre thought, and was glad. Snow would make their tracks too easy to find. Rain could be used to their advantage.

As they descended into a little bowl high up on the ridge, Celeste suddenly threw her head up and stopped, ears pointed, nostrils flaring at some sound or scent Petre couldn't catch. Any moment she could whinny, giving them away. Petre slid from her back and cupped his hands over her muzzle, willing her to silence, realizing again that she was not his horse and may not obey him.

The blast of the stallion's neigh practically in Petre's ear was deafening. Instantly horses appeared in the woods below them as though they had materialized on the spot. Blueskins! Too late now.

The Blueskins deployed in a ragged line, every rider, every horse watching them. Dressed for battle, the warriors had been sneaking quietly through the trees.

But now this group of war-ready Blueskins had seen the horse and woman for whom they had been about to fight. It seemed unlikely that they would let them pass, not when more honor could be gained by capturing them.

When Is had traveled through this land with John, the Blueskins had accepted his "ownership" of her because John had fought and defeated one of their best warriors. Petre doubted they would extend that ownership to him but he had to try.

He stepped forward, away from his horse and assumed a proud stance, hands on hips, chest thrown out. Secretly he suspected the Blueskins didn't see a great warrior in front of them. His round face was not meant for staring down fierce warriors and his body refused to show its fitness in the classical hard-muscled way.

For long heartbeats the Blueskins assessed him from behind their frozen faces. Then one rider moved his horse forward. When he was fifteen meters away he slipped from its back and advanced on foot.

Petre's heart sank. He and Is would not be allowed to pass until Petre had proven that he was tougher, more courageous and a better fighter than any man who cared to challenge him. Great honor would be bestowed on each man who tried to take Is and Lark from him, even if that man failed. But if one of them beat Petre, that Blueskin would win Is and Lark and even greater honor. Under these conditions every man present was likely to challenge him.

Petre resisted the urge to glance behind him. There was no way out except to fight. He had to focus on that. He dropped into the ready stance his people used – a stance that looked so deceptively unready – weight in his center, knees slightly bent, muscles and mind in a relaxed state. The last was the hardest, but also the most important, and he didn't quite make it work.

Though all the Hluit practiced a martial art, Petre had never been in a fight where death was a likely outcome. In fact, he had never been in a fight where anything much was at stake except that he would lose and be kidded for it. Although his people trained in self-defense, they didn't stage matches or recognize winners, but in their own unofficial ways the young men constantly tested each other. Petre was accustomed to losing those contests when he couldn't avoid them altogether.

But to lose here meant death. It also meant that the Blueskins would take Is and the stallion and all hope would be lost for his people

Petre focused on the man in front of him. A good eight inches taller than Petre, the man outweighed Petre considerably and all his weight was solid well-coordinated muscle. He would have reach on Petre and a greater strength that didn't even bear thinking about.

Petre would have to rely on speed and cunning to make up the difference, but he didn't feel very cunning. He was uphill of the Blueskin but Petre couldn't think how to use this to his advantage. The footing, slick pine needles on a slope, would interfere with his speed and balance more than it would with the Blueskin's strength. Meanwhile the other Blueskins were dismounting and forming a half circle to watch. No help there. Is's voice cut into Petre's wildly yammering mind.

"I'm traveling with *him*," she announced, glaring at the Blueskins. "I won't go with you."

Not an eye flickered to her. It didn't matter what she wanted. Even though she was a legend, almost a god to them, she was still a woman. Like any other woman in the Blueskins' eyes, listening to her would be a loss of stature. They might in-a-sense worship her but they would not obey her.

The Blueskin sensed Petre's distraction and feinted. Not yet an attack - he was wary of the power Petre must have, for how else had he captured Is and Lark – so he was only testing. Petre held his ground.

The man began to circle, moving lightly on the balls of his feet, showing grace and coordination to match his size and strength.

Petre knew a dozen ways to overcome a larger, stronger opponent but now his mind went blank. Then stillness came over him. This moment, this man became Petre's entire universe. There was no room for thought. The man closed with him as sure as death. Death, the great focuser. It came when it would, irony or no irony, and a person's need to continue living not withstanding.

Petre was aware of every detail as though all of his senses had doubled in intensity. He could hear the man breathing, see the sheen of sweat over his rippling muscles as he feinted again. Everything had become – of all odd things – beautiful. The orange and black slashes of paint across the warrior's blue tinted face and arms, the play of light and shadow over his skin, even the fierceness of his expression seemed perfect somehow. There was no fear in Petre now, only awe at the incredible beauty and intricacy of life. He felt his connection to all of it and understood that he was about to die.

There was no fear or grief in him, but improbably, joy. Everything was so perfect, so right. The whole world and everything in it was connected . . . in love with itself. There were no words for it, only a certainty he felt through his whole being. It was as though for each movement the man made there could be only one conclusion. If the man stepped with his right foot his whole body would have to move just so, and then Petre would step with his left foot, not forward, but to the side. There seemed no other option for the man, no other option for Petre. The Blueskin would move just so . . . and Petre would move just so.

Petre felt the exact moment at which the man started the swing. So slow it seemed, so easy to avoid the fist that should have doubled Petre over. Easy to move just enough to the side. Effortless to turn, match velocity with that fist as it went by and lead it forward and down just a bit further than the Blueskin had intended. Even the way the Blueskin's feet left the ground and somersaulted clear over his shaven head, which might have been surprising, wasn't. Petre's mind was caught in the cartwheeling of the man's limbs flashing through sun and shadow, the orange streaks of paint leaving trails through the air. The second warrior, who picked that moment to charge from behind intending to grab and choke Petre, was part of it all. It would have been impossible not to match his forward movement and duck properly to lead that man's momentum.

He went flying over Petre's back, drawing his own airy spirals of blue and orange. And then he collided with the first man just as he was regaining his feet. Something ungraceful, disharmonious and angry happened between the two men, jarring Petre out of his trance. He thought wildly, *I'm doing it! I'm really doing it.* And in that instant his foot slid on the pine needles. As he twisted to regain his balance his other foot went out from under him too.

He felt two things as he fell: astonishing joy that he had at least been able to experience those moments of transcendence, and profound disappointment for having lost it. He ended ignominiously on his backside on the ground. The third Blueskin was on him already. One hand closed on Petre's shoulder, the other on his throat. He was struck by the realization that this was how he would die. This was how he would leave Is.

The Blueskin had inadvertently caused Petre to twist around so Petre was able to get his knees under him. Ignoring the choking hand, he grabbed the hand on his shoulder and pushed off with a foot, spinning on one knee as he ducked under the man's arm. The Blueskin ended up with his arms crossed. Using the momentum the Blueskin had given him and adding his own force, Petre twisted the man's wrist hard enough that his other hand was forced to let go of Petre's throat. Petre rose to his feet as he completed the turn and cranked the man's wrist with enough force to cause the man to fall backward.

The fourth Blueskin was already coming but Petre was back in that special place where time was slow and everything followed its predestined path. The man's grabbing hands missed Petre's shoulder by an inch as he spun back in the other direction. For an instant the blue-tinted hands were right in front of Petre's face. It was easy to grab one and twist the wrist back on itself, changing the man's direction faster than his body could follow. The wrist made a small arch, turning back the way the man had just come. The body made a bigger, slower arch, legs flying over the warrior's head. When the man was fully committed to the somersault Petre let go.

The next Blueskin came charging from the line and suddenly froze. His eyes went wide, staring past Petre. Petre turned to see Lark trot forward, great hooves lifting high with suppressed power, flat yellow teeth bared, ears pinned against his neck, nostrils pulled into angry slits. Petre caught only that frozen glimpse before everything shifted to the quick time in which it was really happening. The stallion lunged, his front feet striking out in quick succession, quicker than any human could move - connecting twice. The Blueskin's head snapped back just before his body was flung through the air like a boneless rag.

Petre's moment of calm shattered with that man's bones. He spun desperately around; all the Blueskins were backing slowly away, their eyes riveted on the war horse. Lark, shaking his head and stomping his front feet, advanced on the nearest man. There was no doubt the stallion would rear again, strike and kill, but that man could not break and run. Pride would make him stand and be killed.

Is was on the stallion's back, but she had no control of him now. Petre saw no way to stop Lark. The fight was over. Lark did not need to kill anyone else, but Petre didn't know what to do. The war horse was as likely to kill him as any Blueskin if he got in the way.

At that moment Celeste came past Petre at a trot, making a deep base-rumbling sound that was surprising from a mare who was usually so feminine. Petre had heard that sound only a few times before, and only when a mare had a desperate need to quiet a young colt. It held reassurance but also command. It was the sound of an older wiser horse speaking, a mother to a colt.

The stallion stopped in his tracks. For a moment more he held himself in an aggressive posture. Then Celeste reached him. Her nostrils fluttered as the rumbling sound she made took on a gentler note. Towering over the smaller mare, Lark lowered his huge head and touched noses with her. Though his head alone was nearly twice the size of hers, he would never harm her. His nostrils whuffled softly as the tension left his posture.

Petre took a slow breath and stepped toward Celeste with confidence he didn't feel. He kept his movements slow and non-threatening, and kept her between him and the stallion. The moment of truth came as he mounted, exposing himself to Lark's teeth and hooves. To his relief, Is turned the stallion and set off, so he didn't have to go in front of those massive, deadly hooves. He did not know if he would be safe from them even though he was riding Lark's beloved mare.

Petre didn't have to look back to know there were no Blueskins following. Reaction set in and he began to shake. He could have died. Is could have been taken, the whole mission ended as suddenly as that. He reached out and caught a handful of Celeste's black mane, steadying himself.

It didn't matter to him where they went as long as it was away from the Blueskins. But when they came to a little open meadow, Is slipped from Lark's back and slid his bridle off in one practiced motion. Without a glance at Petre she sat down on the grass and wrapped her arms around her knees.

Petre had no choice but to dismount too. He could see there was no pushing Is. He settled himself beside her, not too near, and waited. Her hair hung about her face, tangled and unbrushed. Her lips, which Petre had once thought so sensual, were drawn into a tight line. He looked away before she could catch him watching her.

"Is he dead?" she finally asked. "Did Lark kill him?"

Petre visualized the way the Blueskin's head had snapped back, heard the terrible sound of Lark's hooves striking his chest, and saw again the distance the man had been thrown through the air and the boneless way he had landed.

"Yes," he said softly. "Lark killed him."

They were silent a while, both dealing with the suddenness of a man's death.

Is gestured to Lark grazing contentedly beside the mare. "The stallions don't ever do that," she informed Petre. "Once they start getting aggressive, they don't ever calm down. They get more and more dangerous. It takes them three days. Then, even though I've trained them all their lives, I can't handle them any more. No one can, except the berserker they're keyed to."

Her voice was filled with the pain of the horses she had lost that way, gentle, kind animals she'd trained and loved who had turned unmanageably dangerous. "But look at him," she said of Lark. "I could walk up to him right now and he wouldn't harm me. You could. It shouldn't be that way."

"Maybe, he's not going to change . . ."

"No, you don't understand," Is cut him off. "I never taught him to rear and strike. He did that himself. I just . . . when you went down, I thought they'd kill you. I couldn't just sit there. I sent him forward. I don't know what I expected, but I couldn't do nothing. I just wanted him to push the man back, or something. I didn't mean for him to kill that man." She stopped herself. "Or maybe I did. I was furious. But not really at them, they were just being men."

She ran down, leaving Petre wondering at the men she must have known in the Alliance. The Blueskins had intended to kill him and rape her, and she said they were 'just being men.'

"Maybe Lark isn't like the other stallions," Petre suggested gently.

"No." Her voice was angry. "He has the scar under his forelock. He has the implant, just like all the others. When his berserker gets close enough it will make him impossible to manage. The only person who will be able to control him then will be his berserker." She had seen it happen too many times to doubt it.

"But maybe," Petre said. "If we were at Amil's cabin we'd be too . . . too far away. Maybe it won't activate across all that time."

Is turned away from him and Petre could see that she had already resigned herself to Lark's loss, just as she had lost all the other horses she had ever loved. He could think of nothing to say.

"You've never seen them change." Is's voice was dry of any emotion. "They would bring the colts to me as one or two-year-olds." In spite of herself, pain caught in her throat and Petre could imagine how appealing a horse like Lark would have been as a colt. All legs, with great knobby knees that he would grow into one day. He could imagine Lark's inquisitive eyes in his long serious face topped off by a little fuzz of a mane standing straight up.

"I usually had five or six horses of different ages and different levels of training. It was just them and me at the border station. I would have years to train them," Is said, her voice flat again. She wouldn't say, "and years to love them."

Instead she said, "I'd train them to accept a rider, and I'd ride them in the mountains until they were fit and sure footed. And then I'd train them to be . . . " Her voice shut down again. Is had involved herself deeply with each horse, and they had trusted her and given themselves to her completely.

"Then their berserkers would come." Is looked away from him, staring at something he couldn't see, but he heard the anger in her voice. "And the horses would go mad. I couldn't believe it at first. I almost got myself killed before I finally accepted it. Lark will be the same way. He'll try to kill anyone who gets near him. Me. You. Anyone."

"But if you keep him far enough away from his berserker, it might not happen," Petre pleaded.

"That may be impossible."

"But weren't you thinking of doing that when you took him?"

"No. I didn't think about it at all. I just had to get out of the Alliance. I couldn't stand it anymore. I didn't know if I'd make it. It seemed more likely that I'd be killed before I had to worry about Lark changing."

Petre was suddenly overcome with fear that Is had already given up too much. She was still moving inexorably toward her own death and he could not stop her.

"I saw John take on a whole band of outlaws once," Is said, "I guess I should have known you could handle the Blueskins like that. I could have kept Lark out of it but I didn't know you didn't need help."

"I didn't know either," Petre admitted. His hands made a small blunt gesture of defeat. "I thought they'd kill me, and take you . . . and . . . I desperately didn't want that, but you've seen. I'm not very good at our martial art. I skip practice a lot. Is, I don't even like to fight. Then . . . everything slowed down. I could see everything before it happened. It was almost . . . easy." He finished, still in awe of the experience. He could feel Is looking at him, but he couldn't meet her eyes.

"Ondre would say that your attitude is good," she told him. "The whole purpose of your art is to *not* fight."

"I know. I just didn't know it would work like it did. When I really thought I would die everything changed."

"That's part of your teachings too," she reminded him. "Removing all ego from an encounter. Not fearing to win or lose, or to die. Just embracing the moment."

"Yes, but I didn't know *I* could do that."

"Sometimes it's like that," Is said pensively.

Petre was reminded that she must have done many things she had not known she could do. Stealing the stallion, fleeing alone into the wilderness, facing the Blueskins and facing the Mirror - all were brave acts. But coming to trust John enough to love him after all the Alliance had done to her might have been the bravest thing of all. Petre dared to think that if she could do that once – if she could heal herself that much once – might she not be able to do it again? He pushed the thought away roughly and stood.

"Let's move on," he said more gruffly than he had intended.

Is rose obediently and went to Lark.

"I don't even understand why the Blueskins want me," she said as they mounted.

It was not an easy question to answer. The Blueskins were a tough tribe of warriors. They often went in small war parties to raid the outlying Alliance farms. They sometimes took women back to their camps and kept them as sort of slave/wives. But no one had ever known them to organize into big war parties like they were doing now. It was unlike them to take on the better-armed and better-mounted troopers. They liked one-on-one conflicts where courage could be displayed and honor won.

Blueskins didn't care anything about Alliance policy. They wouldn't change their ways for political or moral reasons.

"They have a legend about you, Is," Petre said, "or at least about a woman with hair the color of shadow on a huge horse the color of the ground. According to that legend the woman and her horse will appear sometimes, out of nowhere, and disappear again just as suddenly. They believe the horse comes out of the ground and the woman out of the shadows and then they go back into them. They think it is magic and they want that magic, that strength, for themselves. If one of them can capture you, that magic will become his."

"But Ondre told me that the legend existed before I ever came here, before I was even born," Is objected.

"We think that when you were alone in the Boundary, running away from Blueskins and troopers, Lark may have taken you back in time, so that sometimes the Blueskins you saw were years in the past. When they saw you appear and disappear, they told their people about you and the story was passed down the generations." *Such a sensible explanation,* Petre thought, *so simple. And so impossible.* He could understand why Is was having difficulty accepting it.

It was hard for Is to think of how people, maybe hundreds of years ago, could have seen her and told others the story before she was born. From her perspective, life seemed to be going along, one day following the next in order. The idea that she might have influenced things in the past so that she was already known was hard to accept.

They climbed out of the bowl and from there it was a straight shot to the top of the ridge. To their right the world dropped away, ridge after ridge fading from dark green to distant violet. To their left a shoulder made a gradual descent into the forest below.

"That's the way we have to go," Petre told Is. "At the bottom of that shoulder, off to its left side, where we can't see from here, that's where Amil's cabin is."

Is looked where he was pointing but said nothing.

"Maybe you should lead," Petre suggested.

They descended the shoulder, avoiding the crest and staying a little lower down on its side so they would be more difficult to spot if anyone were looking. This hid them but, unfortunately, it also hid what was happening on the other side of the shoulder. So it was that when Is decided it was time to cross over the crest she almost rode straight into two Alliance troopers. The troopers were as surprised as Is. The one nearest her recovered first, forced his horse to surge forward and made a grab for Lark's rein. Lark reared from the unexpected pain in his mouth, dragging the trooper off his smaller horse. Is kicked the man in the head making him let go of the rein. The second trooper saw his buddy go down, drew his weapon and fired. Is screamed in pain. The sound panicked Lark. His great hooves dug into the ground as he took off at a gallop. The trooper took aim for a second shot; Petre shouted and drove his heels into Celeste's side. The mare lunged forward and plowed into the trooper's horse with such force that the horse was thrown to its knees and the trooper pitched over its head.

Petre didn't look back. If the man recovered fast enough to shoot, it would do no good to have seen it coming. This side of the shoulder was open with few trees for cover. It would have been smarter to turn back the way he had come but Is was going this way. The only thing Petre could think to do was to put himself between her and the trooper with the weapon.

Celeste flew over the ground. Petre crouched low on her withers. The next shot went wide of them to their right. It was like nothing Petre had ever seen before. A chartreuse streak stained the air. An evergreen ahead and to their right burst into flame. The horses shied, veering left.

"No, Is!" Petre screamed. "Don't turn. They're trying to turn us. There might be more troopers in that direction." He saw Is trying to pull the panicked stallion back on course.

Celeste, lighter and quicker than the great war horse, was closing the distance between them when, suddenly, she stumbled. Her outstretched neck disappeared from in front of Petre as her front hooves missed their stride almost as though the ground had been pulled out from under her. Petre had just time to kick his feet loose from the stirrups as they fell. At the speed they were traveling he would probably be thrown clear of the horse as she somersaulted. They might both roll and get up again not that much worse for it. If she didn't roll over him! The ground rushed at him with incredible speed and he was out of time.

Just as Petre expected to feel the impact, Celeste's front feet found solid ground and she flung her head up trying to recover. For an instant he couldn't believe the gallant little mare could do it. Then he was fighting to throw his own weight back against the momentum that was carrying them both forward and down. For another few strides the mare staggered, then as suddenly as she had lost her balance she recovered it. She stretched out her neck and ran as hard as she could. Petre's feet automatically found the stirrups and he regained his position over her neck before he thought to look back. He expected to see the trooper closing on them – a bad stumble like that should have cost them ground – but instead there was only an empty field stretching away to the crest of the hill. No troopers anywhere!

Petre whipped his head around to face forward again. The hair crawled on the back of his neck. Two horses and two men couldn't just vanish.

Then he understood. It wasn't any ordinary rock or hole that had tripped Celeste. Between one galloping stride and the next they had crossed into a different time, a time when there weren't any troopers to pursue them.

As Celeste pulled alongside the stallion, Petre saw the unnatural way Is was clinging to Lark's mane. The gray color of her face sent fear though him that overshadowed everything else.

"You're hurt!" He expected her to pull up.

Instead she stared straight ahead, jaw set, and kept going although she slowed to a walk.

"Is please . . . let me see how bad it is." But she kept going.

"Is, we have to stop."

"No," she growled through clenched teeth.

Petre saw blood spreading in a dark stain down the side of her jacket, down the thigh of her pants. He watched as it ran along the skirt of the saddle and dripped to the ground in bright red splatters on the grass. He couldn't stand it.

"Is, we have to stop. You're bleeding too much."

"No."

"If you pass out we'll never find Amil's."

"If we stop now, we'll never find it." With her words the great stallion turned sharply left into a steep descent.

Petre dropped back and let Celeste follow. He had no idea how to stop Is anyway. He dared not grab the stallion's rein or place himself across the horse's path.

They were descending into thickening forest. Branches reached over them, blotting out what was left of the afternoon. Petre was acutely aware that it was later here than it had been just a few moments ago when they had run into the troopers. Though he could barely make out the dark form of the stallion and his hunched rider in front of him now, Celeste never hesitated, sure and confident with her superior night vision. Petre was reduced to listening to the stallion's footsteps, listening for the sounds Is would make if she fell from his back. Listening . . . to the calling of an owl.

They rode for what seemed like hours. Petre's heart veered crazily between hope that Is knew what she was doing and fear that he was letting her push herself too hard. Finally they broke out of the forest. Afternoon had turned to night. An almost full moon rode high in a sky bleached by its light. Only a few of the very brightest stars were visible. A glimmer of water caught Petre's eye. Running along the valley floor a stream sparkled under the moon's light. Dry grass swished as the horses walked into the open. With a start Petre recognized where they were. He twisted around to look where the ruins of Amil's cabin should be, but there was only a dark, impenetrable shadow. Ruin? Or house? An owl hooted again, a soft, almost welcoming note. A moment later Petre saw the flash of white feathers catch the moonlight as the bird swooped from the trees.

The horses turned toward the cabin site and for a brief moment moonlight glinted off a roof. Relief flooded Petre. The cabin was whole! They *had* found it. *Be here*, he prayed silently. *Be here, Amil, please.*

As they approached, the wooden planks of the porch creaked and a man walked out into the moonlight. His white hair caught the light and gleamed like the wings of the owl had gleamed. Petre breathed relief. The old man stepped down from the porch. His glance took in the war horse and his wounded rider. He turned to say something to Petre and stopped suddenly. For a moment he stood motionless, as wary as a hunted rabbit. *He is afraid of me*, Petre thought. *But that's ridiculous. He was just expecting John, not me.*

Amil was the first to recover. "Bring her inside."

Petre slipped from Celeste's back and reached up to help Is from her saddle. She started to dismount but collapsed into his arms. "We're here," he whispered. "You got us here." But she was already unconscious. Gently he touched his lips to the top of her head, letting himself breathe the scent that was hers alone and willing his strength into her. When he looked up, the old man was watching him with eyes that held the intense keenness of a night predator.

Petre hesitated, unsure of this man. Amil turned and went back into the cabin without a word, leaving Petre to make up his own mind. Petre became aware of a warm slippery wetness soaking his arm where it crossed Is's side. The blood made his mind up, he carried Is to the door, then paused. There was something familiar about this place. Something . . . maybe only Is's description of it. The only light inside was a dim red glow from a wood stove. Then Amil opened the stove and sparks exploded in a shower as he tossed a chunk of wood onto the coals. Something familiar? Then it was gone. Flames leaped up. Light blazed across the bookshelves floor-to-ceiling along two walls just as Is had described it.

Petre carried Is in and laid her on the floor near the stove because he didn't see a better place. The cabin had only a small table with three chairs, a sleeping palette in a far corner, and walls of books.

In the light from the fire Petre could see that Is's whole side was sodden with blood. There was a tear through her jacket as though it had been cut with a knife. He wondered how any weapon could have done this to her from a distance. When he undid her jacket he saw how the slice had gone through her flesh as well. Blood had soaked everything and was still coming. Petre felt sick in his stomach. This was a bad wound. If internal organs were injured, there might be little he could do. Steeling himself, he started to work the jacket off her shoulder. Lifting her arm made blood flow in a sudden spurt.

Amil knelt by them. "Sit her up a little. Support her head. I'll get this off."

They soon had the wound exposed. A horrible gash started under her left shoulder blade and traveled around her ribcage in a downward spiral. The flesh and muscle of her side hung open exposing what looked to be ribs when she breathed.

"Lay her on her side," Amil directed. The wound gapped wide as they repositioned her. A thick clotty blood welled out.

Amil stood abruptly. "I need water." And a moment later, moving about his kitchen area, he said. "Good, good. I have freemoss.

Petre knelt on the floor cradling Is's head on his thigh. Freemoss grew abundantly in this area, forming a thick soft mat over rocks and fallen trees. It could be used almost like a sponge or it could be eaten. Either way, its medicinal properties were probably better than anything Petre had in his pack.

Is's skin was pale even in the orange light. One of her eyes came open a slit revealing nothing but white behind it. There was too much blood, old black clotted stuff, and new cherry red. Petre hesitantly lifted the flap of torn flesh and closed it so the edges of the cut touched. Holding it together with his thick blunt fingers he again willed his life into her.

Amil returned with a bowl of water and several clumps of freemoss and began to sponge the wound. The water was only slightly warmer than frozen as it ran over Petre's fingers. Blood sloughed from the cut and ran in rivulets down Is's stomach and back. Goose bumps rose on her skin and her nipples contracted. Petre eased the edges of the wound apart, letting Amil run the cold water over the bloody exposed flesh. As quickly as the blood was washed away more came, but in those quick glimpses they could see that the wound had not gone deeper than her ribs and had not cut into her internal organs. Relief eased from Petre with his breath.

"Not deep," Amil agreed. "Just loss of blood, and shock. Close it now."

Petre carefully replaced the flap of skin so the edges aligned. Blood still seeped out. Amil sopped it up with the freemoss.

"What happened?" he asked.

"Troopers shot her."

Amil's hands hesitated. One white eyebrow arched in surprise. Then he continued to sponge the new blood away.

"Shot her? With what?"

"I don't know. Some sort of projectile." Petre didn't want to explain that the troopers were from a different time and the weapons were different from anything Amil would have known. This one could slice like a very sharp knife without touching the person with anything more substantial than light.

Amil continued to wipe the new blood away. His hands were gentle, competent, even loving. Petre watched with an odd mixture of emotions he was too exhausted to explore or even name.

"That's probably all we can do with this," Amil said. He took the bowl of bloody water and freemoss away and came back with a towel. They dried Is and applied pressure to the cut but it continued to bleed.

"It should be stitched," Amil said.

"I have clips in my pack that will hold it together," Petre said.

"Good enough. Here, let me hold her while you get them." Amil moved in close as though to replace Petre and from some deep place, the mistrust Petre had felt earlier resurfaced. He hesitated, not wanting to leave Is. The moment stretched awkwardly.

"Well?" Amil finally asked. It was a question, not a challenge and it opened the door for any response.

Chiding himself, Petre eased Is into Amil's hold and went out to the horses. The moon made the night nearly as light as day and he could see Lark trying to graze with his bit in his mouth, trailing his reins on the ground. Petre took a moment to slip off Lark's bridle. The great stallion let Petre interrupt his grazing without the slightest show of aggression. Petre undid both saddles, speaking gentle praise to the horses as he worked. He found the first aid kit in his pack and brought it along with Is's pack into the cabin.

Warmth from the cook stove had noticeably permeated the room. Petre had to trust that their pursuers would not be able to see *this* light. Amil was as Petre had left him, supporting Is and applying pressure to the cut to keep it from bleeding. Now it seemed foolish to have mistrusted the old man. Petre knew he was overtired from their days on the road, exhausted from worrying about Is, and wound tight from their last narrow escape.

He took an antiseptic cream from his kit and smeared a little along the lips of the cut. Then as Amil held it together with his fingers, Petre pressed one end of a clip into Is's skin on one side of the cut, spanned the torn flesh and pressed the other end of the clip into the good flesh on the other side. Is murmured at the new pain and Petre hesitated. His fingers rested lightly on the next clip, reluctant to push it into her flesh and cause her more pain. He was aware of Amil watching him and of what he revealed about himself but he didn't care. When Is didn't wake, Petre finished with the clips. They would hold the cut together while it healed. By the time they were no longer needed the small teeth that were now imbedded in her flesh would have dissolved. Petre placed a pad of freemoss over the clips and taped it down. Alliance technology could have cleaned and sealed the wound with light, but the Hluit had only more traditional methods.

Is had begun to shiver from the cold water and loss of blood even though the stove was blasting out so much heat Petre was sweating.

"We have to get her cleaned up and into something dry," Amil said.

Petre lifted Is into a sitting position and they worked her bloody shirt and jacket off her other shoulder. Her leather riding pants were a sticky mess and Petre imagined that Is would be embarrassed, and possibly furious with him, as he helped Amil get them over her hips and off her legs. Blood covered her thigh. Amil brought him some clean water and freemoss.

Petre was glad when Amil went away again, leaving Is some privacy. Blood was all down her side and her leg. Petre cleaned her up the best he could. He could not help but appreciate her beautiful form and the softness of her skin in the warm firelight. She had stopped shivering and seemed to be in a deep, peaceful sleep. The grief of the last few days was gone from her face and she was beautiful to Petre in a way that made his heart hurt.

When he had Is clean and dry he put one of Amil's shirts on her and together the two men got her into her sleeping bag. Petre folded his wool vest for her pillow, making her as comfortable as possible. As he smoothed the hair back from her face, a deep sadness stole into his heart. She would never accept this kind of care from him if she were awake.

Amil had stayed in the background but Petre felt the old man watching him. He knew he had revealed too much to this stranger – how he loved this woman who had loved John and did not love him – but it was true and he could not have acted in any other way. When he confronted Amil with his own gaze Amil looked away.

"You look like someone I met once," Amil said lamely. "But that was a long time ago. It couldn't be you, I suppose?"

"No," Petre said. "I never met you before." But he wondered at the feeling of familiarity the whole place held for him and decided it must just be from the way Is had described the place to him.

"I'll wash her clothes in the stream," Petre said, feeling the need to do something concrete and familiar.

"You should not go that far. She does not hold you like she did John," Amil said in a rush.

The hair stood up along Petre's back. "You . . . you know? We didn't just ride in here. We…" he let it trail off, unable to say those impossible words.

"Yes," Amil said gruffly, "I know you're from the future. What happened to John?"

"He is dead."

"Huh." It was a sound of denial.

"It's a long story," Petre equivocated.

"All I have is time," Amil replied, and Petre was aware of the layers of meaning in the old man's words. His mistrust resurfaced stronger than ever.

"Come on boy," Amil snapped. "If you will not tell me what's going on, how can I be of help? You have come to me for help, no?"

Exhaustion clouded Petre's mind like a drug. He had no good reason to distrust this man so.

Amil turned away from him, removing the challenge and the pressure of his impatience. "We'll have tea," he said more civilly, "wine, if you prefer, and talk. I do not often get visitors here. You will excuse me my roughness?"

"Yes, I understand." Petre accepted the apology, such as it was. "I am also not at my best tonight. We will make allowances for each other, and I will drink tea. Wine would knock me out right now."

Amil gave a good-natured sounding chuckle. "No doubt you will be easier to converse with than John was," he said. As he began preparing the tea he told of how John and Is had appeared at his doorstep. A girl riding what could only be a stolen war horse, and a man riding bridleless on a mare of such beauty and refinement she could only have come from the breeding program of great horsemen. But the man could not speak at all.

"When he tried to say anything he would start to laugh hysterically, or maybe cry. I couldn't tell which. But he was desperate to get a message across." Amil gave a shake of his shaggy head, remembering. "And her," he cocked his head toward where Is slept, "she was like a wild cat ready to defend him." He paused and looked at Petre speculatively. "Much as you are ready to defend her, I would say."

Petre met Amil's eyes. Let him see the truth there.

Amil nodded a little to himself and turned away. Petre watched him setting out teacups and kettle, putting pinches of leaves into his little homemade strainer. His movements were precise and unhurried, nothing wasted. The beautiful porcelain cups were at odds with the rustic cabin.

"You will find you do not need to protect her from me," Amil said over his shoulder. "I am interested only in the truth. It is why I took the books," he gestured at the walls of bookshelves. "They contain the true history of our world. They are the record of the beginning of many experiments, the chronicles of many lines of research that fell out of favor or needed to be covered up for one reason or another. They were to be burned. It was in the best interest of the leaders of 'our Great Alliance' that certain things be forgotten."

He brought the teacups to the table and met Petre's eyes. "Although I rescued this information from the certain destruction of fire, it will just molder away here and be lost. Nothing would please me more than if something that I saved in my day could be used by your people who are so far in the future."

Amil's simple words touched a chord in Petre's heart. Truth and honesty were highly prized in Hluit society. Because of their nomadic existence, their history was handed down orally, and it was extremely important not to let inaccuracies, let alone deliberate lies, slip in.

"My people also desire true answers," Petre said, "not the Alliance lies."

"So we will trade our stories, eh? And see what truth we can make of them?"

"Fair enough," Petre agreed.

Amil brought a pot of hot water from the wood stove and poured it into the kettle to steep. The pungent steam rising through the tea leaves carried the promise of relief from fatigue and made Petre realize how tired he was.

"For me," Amil said, "John's visit raised more questions than it answered. I had never heard of his people or their horses. Before I stole the books, I had spent many years as a Librarian at the Research Center at Court South where all records are kept. I felt I should have known about any horse breeding programs and any people who were not the usual Alliance citizens. But . . ." Amil opened his hands as though showing he had nothing.

"We are nomadic horse-herders," Petre said. "We live in the Boundary. We have lived this way for many generations now. We are descendents of a small group of people who were so disaffected with the Alliance that they were allowed to go live behind the Boundary. The Alliance looks on us as an experiment in utopian living. They expect us to fail."

"No doubt you see yourselves quite differently," Amil suggested.

"We would like them to recognize us as a free and sovereign people."

Amil gave a little grunt of understanding.

"I will tell you our history if you want," Petre volunteered, "but first tell me about John."

"Yes, John. He was desperate to get his message across. We finally settled on a system where he pointed to words in a book and I wrote them down. Unfortunately, whatever the Alliance had done to him to keep him from talking, affected his ability to communicate in any fashion. He didn't seem able to read anything except one of the ancient texts. It was written in the root language from which our present day speech arose, but it is long since dead. No one speaks it, and only a few can read it well." He sighed. "I am not one of those few. When I had finished writing the words he pointed to I could barely make sense of them. I hope your people did better."

"Your translation was quite good," Petre told him. "It was just that you could not possibly have understood some of the references John made."

Amil leaned back in his chair. "I understood that he was a spy for his people and I was able to ascertain that he had been at Court Center. From that I knew that he had been spying in the highest and most secret research center of the Alliance. I could only guess that his mysterious 'people' had the education and background to have been able to prepare him to pass as an Alliance citizen of the Scholar class."

"Yes," Petre said. "Although we live a simple life without the technology the Alliance has, we are not uneducated. It has always been our practice to keep spies in the Alliance. It keeps us informed as to their intentions toward us, but it is also good for each generation of our people to have firsthand knowledge of the Alliance people."

"Know thine enemy," Amil said.

The overly simplistic statement stopped Petre short.

"They are not necessarily our enemy," he said dryly.

"Oh?" Amil was surprised. "Then you have not come here to find some information that might help you overthrow their government?"

"No, we only seek information that may give us the leverage we need to ensure our own future."

Amil snorted. "Your people are naive."

"There are a few hundred of us, there are hundreds of thousands of them," Petre responded in his people's defense. "We are nomads living with the land. They have great technology and vast cities. We have no desire to overthrow, or to rule. We only want to be left in peace."

Amil turned away and Petre had the uneasy feeling that Amil did not believe him.

Amil drew the strainer full of leaves out of the water and poured the dark steaming tea into their cups and the moment passed.

"I seem to remember that John's message was littered with words for urgency and extreme danger," Amil kept a conversational tone.

"Yes," Petre admitted. It had not been a well-ordered and concise message. It reflected the disarrayed thought patterns caused by the damage the Alliance had done to John's mind. But the warning had come through clearly.

"He seemed to be trying to convey that he had found a 'key' to something," Amil remembered. "I could only translate that thing as a 'mirror/non-mirror.' What in the world is that?"

"It's a computer really. But we only learned that recently, from John. For generations we have called it the Mirror. It didn't seem to have an exact physical location but it was capable of killing people. We couldn't find it if we went looking for it, but then it would kill someone we didn't think was anywhere near it. But John was somehow able to find its physical location and get inside the actual computer part of it. He was able to use one of its programs to fix what the Alliance had done to him. He could talk before he died."

"So what was this 'Mirror' intended to do?

"To overcome death. To keep the essence of a person alive after his body dies."

"Ahhh," the sound expressed Amil's fascination. "But of course, that would be a project worthy of the attention of the highest Alliance officials."

"Yes. They engineered an entire line of men, berserkers, and created the war stallions like Lark, whose sole purpose is to be killed by the Mirror." This was still hard for Petre to accept. For the Alliance to create such magnificent animals as the war stallions – and the riders in their own way and to train them until they were superb athletes – just to have them destroy themselves was beyond his comprehension.

"The Mirror takes the men apart as it kills them," he told Amil. "Not physically, but psychically. It was supposed to learn some way to absorb them and keep them alive after it kills their physical bodies. I guess their deaths had to be slow. . . like they had to give up their lives, their life forces themselves, or something, not actually be killed." His voice reflected the horror he felt at the whole idea, but Amil made a satisfied sound, understanding the plan.

"Ahh. Life after death, such a goal would explain the grandiose scale of the whole berserker mythos. In my day, we did not yet have the Mirror. But we had our own berserkers, ones with a bluish cast to their skins. Their purpose was to patrol the edge of the Alliance and drive wild beasts back into the Boundary so the outlying farms would be safe

"We still have the Blueskins," Petre told him. "Only now they live in the Boundary, and their purpose is to prey *on* outlying farms."

"Kill the Alliance's own citizens?" Amil said thoughtfully.

"Yes. And then the people are told that the purpose of our present day berserkers is to hunt the Blueskins and keep the farmers safe. Alliance citizens don't even know the Mirror exists. They don't know anything about the life-after-death experiments. It isn't going to be for them, only for the highest officials."

"I see," Amil said slowly. "So the Alliance still controls its people with fear and lies, just as it always has. The Blueskins are a great way to keep prying eyes out of the Boundary, eh? It's nothing to them if a few citizens are sacrificed to maintain their lies."

"Exactly," Petre agreed. "You should know, Is's parents were killed by Blueskins."

"Ahhh," it was a sound of dawning understanding. "So she became the perfect tool for the Alliance to use for training its war stallions. She would be willing to see those stallions sacrificed because she believed they fought the Blueskin?

"Yes." The word came out heavy with the pain and treachery Petre knew Is had suffered. "But she reached the point where she couldn't stand to see her horses taken away to their deaths. So she took Lark and fled into the Boundary, even though she knew the Blueskins lived there, and she knew her own government would hunt her down and kill her if they caught her."

"Umm," Amil looked at Is speculatively and Petre thought he saw admiration in the old man's eyes. "She is a woman of immense courage."

Petre didn't refute him. His own esteem for Is was great.

"She told me of finding John, dying, after the Alliance had let him escape with poisoned rations," Amil said.

"Yes, it was supposed to be a death sentence and perhaps a warning to our people if we found his body. Is saved his life."

"So John took her to his people . . . to your people?"

"Yes, but John couldn't leave it at that. He and Is went on and faced the Mirror together. Using the Mirror's technology John was able to forge some sort of link directly to Is's mind, like the link between a berserker and his horse. Then Is waited outside while John went in and searched for all the knowledge he could. This seems to have gone on for days before the Mirror noticed and killed him."

"I see," Amil said slowly. "And does the Alliance know what John did?"

"We don't think so. They probably believe that John died from their poison. They keep track of the Mirror's progress through special transmissions that are sent by the berserkers as they die. John thought that those transmissions were somehow powered by the stallions' deaths, at least partly. Since John wasn't a berserker and there was no war-horse involved, the Alliance would not have automatically received a transmission. They would not know about it unless the Mirror told them.

But John thought that the Mirror was hiding a lot from the Alliance. It hadn't told them about other people it had killed, so we suspect it didn't tell them about killing John either."

"So has this Mirror succeeded?" Amil asked. "Has it created life after death?"

"In a sense. It has every berserker and every horse it has ever killed stored inside it in holographic and digital form . . ." Petre caught himself, wondering if Amil would understand those words. "That is, it has pictures, three dimensional pictures that move and look as real as life."

"But that isn't what the Alliance wants," Amil said thoughtfully. "They want the essence of the person, not just stored but alive and doing the things that living people do – learning, changing."

"Yes," Petre agreed.

"So, it has failed?"

"John believed it has completed its program but it has not let the Alliance know."

"'A ghost of great power,'" Amil quoted. "John had me write that for him. 'I have information concerning a man of great power, a beast of great power, and a ghost of great power.' The berserkers, their horses, and . . . the true completion of the Mirror's program. It creates ghosts?"

"Yes. We call them Dark Bodies. They are frightening and disorienting in the same way as the illusions the Mirror creates. They have been known to kill people, but we do not understand the mechanics of how they do it. Is told of John communing with them even before he went to the Mirror, and Is heard them speaking although she couldn't understand them."

"So what is this 'great power' they have? Just to frighten and kill?"

"We do not know. It is one of the things we hope to find out."

"You may search my records," Amil said. "But the Mirror was so far after my time I don't know what help you'll find."

In spite of himself Petre felt a shiver go through him at the reminder that he wasn't sitting in an ordinary cabin on an ordinary night having a conversation with an ordinary man. In Petre's lifetime this cabin was a burned out ruin with only a few chimney stones to mark where the wood stove he was staring at had stood. The man who sat across from him was long dead. But somehow, Is and Lark had brought him to a time when Amil was alive, and their pursuers couldn't see them.

Petre took a big swallow of tea that burned his throat. Porcelain rattled as he returned the cup to its saucer.

"Also stolen," Amil said, noticing. "The Alliance's finest. While I was at it, stealing the books, you know, I took a few other things that pleased me. Although I suppose these cups must seem to you a rudimentary technique with clay and heat."

"No," Petre managed to say. "They are beautiful. And the making of porcelain has not changed that much."

Amil smiled. "Take care, then, not to break them and tell me about these Dark Bodies."

Petre laughed and managed to take another sip without rattling the cup. The old man watched him with a sparkle in his eyes perhaps understanding the challenge Petre had set himself.

"So does the Alliance know about these Dark Bodies, these ghosts?"

"No, John thought the Mirror was hiding them, perhaps because it thinks the Alliance will turn it off when it has completed its program."

"Um," Amil made a sound of disagreement. "Or perhaps it has its own plans for these Dark Bodies, eh?"

"What plans?"

"I don't know. But it must perceive the Alliance as a threat to it."

"Or the Dark Bodies may only be its hands and eyes," Petre countered. "Maybe it's just trying to study people in some way other than the one it was programmed to use which always kills them."

"But why would it hide that from the Alliance?"

"I don't know."

"And to what end would it study people that way?"

"It was programmed to be self-teaching."

"And also to have no morals against killing," Amil reminded, "and so why would it seek another way to 'study' without killing?"

Petre had no answer for that.

"No wonder John was trying so hard to warn you."

Petre leaned back in his chair, seeing where Amil was leading. "The Alliance has lost control of what the Mirror learns," he acknowledged. "It was only supposed to kill the berserkers who are simple minded, know no fear of death, and don't understand anything about what the Alliance is up to. When it killed Hluit scouts it learned to distrust the Alliance. It has also killed Blueskins and occasionally other outlaws who pass through our lands looking for a place to hide. Who knows what the Mirror has learned from them."

"Exactly," Amil agreed, and sipped from his cup. Petre thought about taking another sip but changed his mind, knowing his hand would shake.

"And then there is the problem of the horse." Amil added. "A horse who can cross the years as well as the miles." His voice had grown wistful. He leaned back in his chair, tipping his head up to stare at the ceiling. Petre fell quiet feeling that the old man must need a moment to digest it all. His gaze followed Amil's. Hand-hewn timbers supported the peaked roof. Several of the dark crossbeams were streaked with white stains. Everything else was unpainted dark wood.

"Do you think he is the only horse they have that is able to do this?" Amil asked. "Because if they have others they may be able to follow you here."

"We think he is the only one because of the way they are so desperate to get him back, but truthfully we don't know," Petre admitted. "I'm sorry that we may have placed you in danger. We had nowhere else to turn."

"Danger is no stranger to me, boy. And I believe your people are in much worse danger than I."

"They are," Petre agreed. "The Alliance intends to kill all of us if we don't turn Is and the stallion over to them."

Amil gave him a keen look. "That seems excessive even for them."

"It seems that way to us too," Petre said dryly and Amil gave a little chuckle at his tone.

Amil stood abruptly and went to put more wood in the stove. His sudden display of agitation seemed odd to Petre.

Petre glanced over at Is. Her face had regained a little color and she seemed to be deeply asleep.

"Is doesn't know this, but while she and John were at the Mirror I went on scout duty and I ran into some troopers." He had gone mostly to put some distance between him and Is. She was in love with John, his best friend, and Petre had never meant to do more than befriend her. She had needed help to adjust to Hluit society because John was in no condition to do it.

"The troopers caught me," he said bluntly. "They had come further into our land than they'd ever come before, so I was following them. I didn't know there was another contingent behind me. Anyway, they caught me and roughed me up enough to let me know they would have been glad to beat me to death, or any other Hluit they caught. Then they let me go with a warning: Give them Isadora and the stallion or they will find and exterminate all of us." His blood ran cold with the retelling of it and he heard the drop in his voice.

"I took the message, as they knew I would. Of course they tried to follow me but Des, my horse, and I lost them. My people will not give them Is. We will withstand them the best we can."

The words were so easy to say; the actual experience had been terrifying.

He had been riding along a stream bed when he had first seen their tracks. Shod horses. The Hluit and the Blueskins rode their horses unshod. He started to track them, staying well back, taking advantage of every cover, watching out for their scouts.

It was some time before he realized he had gotten himself caught between two contingents, the one he was tracking and another one coming up behind him. He stayed with them using every bit of his skill to remain unseen until he was sure they were headed through Bent Pass. Then he began working his way off to the side, hoping to slip out of the trap he was in as the troops narrowed to get through the pass. Instead, unknown to him, one group broke off from the main body and turned in his direction. Just when he thought he was safe, he found himself surrounded again. This time by troopers who were scouring the woods with the best heat-seeking equipment the Alliance had.

Petre realized his mistake and headed for a nearby gully but it was too late. In his memory he heard the unmistakable click of a metal-shod hoof striking a rock ahead of him. He froze and Des stopped motionless. To their left, a bit jingled. To the right, Petre heard the soft giving squeak of leather as someone shifted his weight in a saddle.

It was too late to make the ravine. They had only trees and shadows to break up their outlines, only luck to hide them. Suddenly horses were visible below them, a line of riders sweeping the forest as though looking for something. Every third man held a small device in his hand, swinging it slowly back and forth in front of him.

Petre held his breath, willing his heart to quiet. Alliance technology could find a person by the heat of his body, or by no more than the sound of a racing heart. With Des sweaty from climbing there was no hope the troopers would miss them.

The closest man spun in his saddle and pointed his device directly at Des. Instantly others turned toward her. For a moment they didn't seem to see the motionless horse. Then one of their horses whinnied a loud welcome and Des moved. But Petre was no longer with her.

"What is it?" one of the troopers asked. "Hluit or Blueskin?"

"No bridle," someone answered. "Hluit."

"Silence," the commander snapped. And then loudly, "Hluit, come out or I'll shoot your horse."

Petre, watching from the low branches of a pine saw more horses coming up behind the first line, and more.

The commander leveled something at Des that had a short barrel and some sort of dial at the nether end of it. "Hluit," he said again, loudly. "I'll start by crippling her."

"That won't be necessary," Petre said as calmingly as he could manage.

Weapons snapped up to point at him in the tree. He eased slowly around the trunk, trying to show that he was unarmed. With so many weapons trained on him, it was hard to let himself drop to the ground.

"Bring him," the commander said, and started his own horse forward.

Two men came toward Petre. "Walk."

He glanced toward Des but a rider moved between them and tossed a loop of rope over Des's neck. She followed that man obediently as he rode away and Petre had no choice but to walk.

They kept him marching until dusk. When they finally stopped, the spot they chose had many large boulders for cover. Men deployed among the trees and rocks with their weapons ready.

Petre wondered at that. Surely thirty-some highly armed Alliance troopers were not expecting to be attacked? Certainly not by unarmed Hluit. Hluit who practiced a code of peaceful co-existence with each other, the land and all living things. Hluit whose main means of defense was a martial art rooted in non-contention and non-aggression.

And surely this number of troopers didn't fear attack by Blueskins. The bands of warriors were ferocious fighters, but they had never been known to take on this many armed and forewarned troopers. The Blueskins' idea of a good fight was hand-to-hand combat in which courage could be displayed and honor won or lost.

A trooper searched Petre, removing two knives, and missing the one in his boot. Then they led him to stand in front of their commander.

He was a tough looking square-shouldered man who spoke with an impatient angry edge to his words.

"Why were you following us," he demanded without preamble.

"I wasn't . . . " Petre started and something slammed across the back of his knees, hard. He went down, one leg doubled under him and the other shooting out helplessly so that he landed on his back. It was so fast that even his trained reflexes couldn't break his fall.

As he tried to roll to his feet, his calf muscles knotted in more pain than he could ignore. He twisted onto his hands and knees and heard someone snicker cruelly.

"Hluit, do you know why we are here?" the commander demanded.

"No." Petre replied, wondering if they would hit him again for the lie.

"We're here to retrieve government property," the commander said. His hard eyes assessed Petre.

The cramp in Petre's leg was easing but he stayed down. It could be useful if they thought he was more hurt than he really was.

"We're looking for a woman," the commander said. "Isadora Drey, an Alliance citizen. She is a traitor who took one of our war horses. She is nothing to your people. She is Alliance property and so is the stallion she took." He gave a jerk of his head and two men came forward and lifted Petre to his feet.

Petre let himself be heavy on their arms, standing on one leg as though the other was too badly hurt even while he wondered at himself. He couldn't fight this many armed men. He couldn't escape, and he could not hope to prevent them from doing anything they chose to do. But the anger that was always slow to rise in him began to rise, bathing him in heat and recklessness.

The commander drew nearer to Petre.

"Isadora Drey is trash," he said, almost spitting the word in Petre's face. "She is not worth anyone dying for her."

Petre met the man's eyes. He knew he should act intimidated and deny ever having seen Is or the stallion. But anger formed a hard knot in his guts. These men would deliver Is for the kind of punishment that had left John unable to speak just as if barbarians had cut out his tongue. In his mind's eye Petre saw John, his mouth working to form a word, his anger and helplessness building. And then he heard the sound his friend had made. Not a word, but laughter, helpless hysterical laughter. He saw John falling to the ground, beating the earth with his fists until no one could tell whether the sound he was making was laughing or crying.

Petre met the commander's eyes and knew that man saw his anger and defiance. Distantly a part of his mind was yammering that he would do no one any good this way. But he could not stand the thought of the Alliance getting Is back to do something equally awful to her. If these troopers even took her back to the Alliance. They might just exact their own punishment, beat her and rape her and kill her.

A blow from behind caught him across the side of his head and threw him to the ground. For a moment there was no pain. Then it came roaring into his head, loud as Great Falls, threatening his vision with black edges. For a time it took all his strength and all his anger just to stay conscious.

Finally the sound receded and Petre caught snatches of conversation around him. "He don't know nothing. He ain't gonna come 'round anyhow. Paul hit him too hard."

A forest of bootlegs surrounded him. Petre tried to get to his feet. Blackness whirled around the edges of his vision threatening to cover him completely. He had to make himself still again to make the world be still.

"Hey, look it," someone said. "Little woman try'n to git up."

Petre was appalled at their viciousness and surprised by their uneducated speech. The Hluit, for all their nomadic lifestyle valued education and free thought, but the Alliance kept all its citizens in ignorance, never allowing them to learn more than the vocation that had been picked for them. For Is that vocation had been training the great stallions for war. For these men it had meant training them to be tough and angry and giving them an enemy outside of the Alliance to hate. Usually that enemy was the Blueskins, but right now this Hluit captive would do. These men would never be allowed to learn to read, so that they might educate themselves. They would not be taught to do simple math, for they would never have need of that either. They would not be able to get anything the Alliance didn't give them. They would never use their minds for anything except anger and viciousness and fear. And they would not even understand enough to hate the people who had done this to them.

Someone nudged Petre with a foot. "Git up, you."

Petre got to his knees. The world swam about him. Faces leered at him.

"C'mon, girlie, git up," someone chided him. Others laughed.

Petre climbed slowly to his feet, willing the trees to stand still around him. Dizziness made his stomach churn. Someone prodded him in the ribs and he took a step so not to fall. His stomach heaved. It took all his control not to go to his knees and vomit like a dog in front of these men. They prodded him again and he took another step and another. His vision began to clear. They had set up camp among the rocks and were taking him toward a headquarters of sorts. The commander who had questioned him before sat under a tarp stretched between several boulders. In front of him was a table and on it lay various implements that Petre recognized as sophisticated tools of Alliance technology. They let him take a good look.

"Do you know what you are seeing, Hluit?" the commander asked.

"All this to find a stolen horse?" Petre sneered, awed by his own audacity because he did not want to be hit again.

The commander gave a nasty chuckle "We have a better way to find the stallion. This is to find your people. All of them. No matter how they run or hide."

The blood drained from Petre's head so fast that his legs gave way. He staggered and nearly fell as the world swooped around him.

Several people laughed, but the commander just watched him with cold, penetrating eyes.

"We can find every person, every child, every woman, and every horse." He paused to let his words sink in.

"If your people do not turn the traitor, Isadora Drey, over to us we will kill them all."

Again he paused, then continued casually. "To find the stallion, we have brought his berserker. When we are close enough the stallion will sense his proper rider and he will become unmanageable by anyone else. And if the horse does not come to us, we will go to him. His berserker will guide us for he and the horse are connected by a chip in each of their brains. All of our war-horses are connected to their berserkers that way. Isadora Drey knew that. She should have known she couldn't get away with taking him. She should not have placed your people in jeopardy over such a horse."

He took a step toward Petre. "Your people should not try to protect her. She is a coward and a traitor. She has betrayed your people by not telling you the truth of what would happen, just as she has betrayed her own people. Surely she is not worth anyone's life."

He was watching Petre keenly and Petre tried to show no emotion. The woman he knew as Isadora was no coward and no betrayer.

"We have a job for you, Hluit," the commander continued. "We are going to let you go and we want you to tell your people what you have seen here. Tell them we will find and kill every last one of them. Tell them *how it will really be.*" He gave a quick nod to one of the men and that man came forward to stand facing Petre.

Petre looked at the hulking man and the others gathered around menacingly. But he thought the commander's words meant they were going to turn him loose, so he wasn't ready for what happened next.

The man reached out and slammed the flat of his hand against Petre's shoulder. Petre reeled back, staggering. His head exploded in white pain. Searing brightness filled his vision. He didn't even know he was falling until he hit the ground.

Over the roaring in his ears he heard laughter. Then someone kicked him in the ribs and he could neither see nor breathe. He sucked frantically at air that refused to be drawn into his lungs and heard the harsh howling of his empty throat as his lungs refused to fill. Blackness threatened the edges of his vision as the light flickered and began to fade. He fought the darkness as though he was fighting his own death.

Air came seeping back into his lungs. But so slowly, too slowly to relieve the screaming need of his body and the howling panic in his mind. Then they kicked him again. And again. While he fought only to breathe.

"Enough."

Petre heard the word through the roaring in his head and the wheezing of his own breathing and he understood that they were going to let him live.

"Let him up."

He made it to his knees. The pain in his ribs kept him from being able to take a full breath. Fear that he would suffocate tried to take over his mind. He forced himself to get control of his breathing, bringing each breath slowly, if shallowly, into his abdomen.

"Look at me, Hluit."

He raised his eyes to the commander's and knew the man saw his fear. The commander nodded with satisfaction.

"Go back to your people, Hluit. Tell them how it will *really* be. Tell them to bring the traitor to us, Hluit, and none of them needs to die." None of them needs to die anyway, Petre had thought through his own anguish.

"It didn't make sense," he told Amil. "The Alliance so overpowers the Hluit, surely they could just walk in and take Is. Undoubtedly with all their equipment they could find her. And they had just told me how the stallion's special berserker could call him. We could make things more difficult for them, but certainly the Alliance did not really *need* our cooperation. That's when I realized that for all their weapons and equipment they really didn't think they could find Is and Lark without our help. So here we are, hiding where they probably can't find us, but my people are back there. . ." he made a vague gesture. He didn't know if any of them were still alive or maybe fighting for their lives even now.

"We didn't come here just to hide," he continued. "Is would never have agreed to that. We came to see if we could find something in your records that will help us understand the stallion or the Mirror. The Alliance has lost control of both of them. If we could gain that control for ourselves . . ."

"You could annihilate them," Amil concluded.

"No, I doubt that," Petre said surprised and appalled. "We would not do that if we could. We only want enough leverage to make them leave us in peace."

Amil studied him for a long moment, and then shook his head. "They cannot be trusted, no matter what sort of deal they make."

"We have to try."

"Nothing would please me more than if I could help you," Amil conceded. "But you must understand that all the research that led to the Mirror, and the eternal life experiment it represents, happened long after my time. I doubt that you will find anything in my records to help you there. But the horse? When Is and John left, I made it my business to find out all I could about John's people and their horses. I came across certain references that might help you but I will need time to find them again, and you need rest."

Petre could not deny that. He sighed, releasing the last of his energy. He was exhausted. Except for occasional catnaps, he had barely slept in days, not trusting Is to take the watch in her defeated and apathetic condition. The constant worry for her, the constant wariness, and the hoping had all taken their toll.

"I'll wash her clothes," Amil said. "You rest. Then we will see what we can find."

Chapter Three

The two Hluit scouts sat quietly at their small fire. They had been in the Boundary for a month watching the comings and goings of Alliance troops. Yesterday their relief had arrived and the two men were now headed home. The fire was a small luxury they had not allowed themselves the whole time of their scout duty.

They sat listening to the coals hissing, watching an occasional blue-white flame lick into existence and disappear. The silence between them was the companionable non- need for communication that had developed from long service together.

Neither man was expecting trouble. Then from the darkness behind them Dhave's horse snorted in sudden fear. Both men spun to look in the direction of the horses but their eyes were night-blind from having stared into the fire. Dhave's horse snorted again, this time giving the loud blast of extreme warning. The sound reverberated off the mountains around them and almost hid the short frightened nicker of San's younger horse. Both men were in motion by then, San kicking out the fire as Dhave slipped into the darkness in the direction of the horses. A mountain lion or a bear could frighten them. They were above the altitude where the great lizards were a problem, too cold for them here. Blueskins or even Alliance troopers could be trying to sneak up on them, he supposed, but the horses would not have been afraid. Dhave's stolen Alliance weapon was already in his hand. His index finger stroked its blunt barrel, setting it for a bright wide discharge that would scare any wild animal away.

He spoke calmly to the horses he could not yet see. "Dawn, Sil. Ho Girls." Dawn was an experienced scout horse. She did not panic easily and both horses should quiet at his voice. Trained for scout duty, they would stand silently, not responding to the passage of other horses so their riders could remain undetected. They would come, stay, and move off on hand signal, or voice command. They could even be made to lie down to hide their bulk in open meadowland where cover was scarce. They had complete confidence in their riders and gave them complete obedience.

It was Sil, Quicksilver, who broke first. She gave one scream of pure terror and Dhave heard her pounding away in an all-out gallop. A second later, Dawn's hoof beats joined hers in uncontrollable panic. No simple mountain lion or bear would do that to these horses. Thoroughly alarmed now, Dhave circled back toward the fire site. He remembered a rock outcropping just east of it, which would supply cover and allow him to hear whoever came. San would have heard the horses bolt. He might have headed into the rocks too. While Dhave was moving toward the rocks as silently as his skill allowed, he recognized the futility of his strategy. No band of riders, be they Blueskins or Alliance, would spook Sil and Dawn. Dark Bodies and herd fogs frightened horses the way those two had been frightened, but they were a long way from where those things were usually seen.

He stopped dead in his tracks at the sound of San's voice   "John?" First questioning and wondering. Then with more conviction, "John, it *is* you. We all thought you were dead. It's good to . . ." and then a soft sort of wordless sound " . . . ugh?" A statement of disbelief.

That was enough for Dhave. He sprinted directly toward the voices, his finger triggered the blazer. Dark shattered into brilliant light as he reached the clearing only to be met by a strobe-instant of complete stillness – San on the ground, his throat red. A man at the edge of the light, twisted in mid stride to look back in surprise. In one hand he held a knife, in the other San's pack. Just that one heartbeat to see and remember every detail. Then the man was gone and Dhave ran to San, dropped to his knees, touched the wound at his neck. It was only a small nick, an inexpertly done slash that had only gotten through because San had not expected it. But it had cut the artery. Such a small thing to kill a man, to take his friend, to change the rest of his own life. Blood welled out, paused, welled. Dhave shoved his thumb against it, pressing, crying out to his friend and knowing it was no use.

For a time he was frantic, shouting, fighting for his friend's life, denying this tiny cut could kill him, denying there was nothing he could do about it. Then he became still, his hands covered with blood, his friend cold and lifeless and one image burned into his retinas. He could look at it now without haste. The man at the edge of the clearing – his face turned toward the unexpected light, his eyes wide with surprise – was John, a knife in his hand. The pack took longer to register – San's pack. John had been stealing food, clothes (?) from a man who would have given him those things and more! Across the scene, across the questions Dhave was beginning to ask, ran the thunder of the hooves of panicked horses.

Chapter Four

Is stirred in her sleep and whimpered, a faint, helpless frightened sound that she would never allow herself to make if she were awake. Sitting beside her Petre came awake, heart racing, trying to remember where he was, what was wrong, what he should do. He fought his eyes open to the warm glow of morning sun streaming through the door. . . and remembered. Amil's cabin, they were safe here, for the moment.

He had fallen asleep propped against a wall, a book open on his lap. Lying beside him Is stirred again twisting her head as though avoiding a blow. A little blood had seeped through her bandage staining Amil's white shirt with a streak of bright red. Worried, Petre reached out and touched her forehead. No fever. No infection. Just a dream. The fear eased from him with his breath. His hand lingered a moment letting his love flow to her through that simple contact until she was quiet again.

He stood and felt the leaden weight of his tired muscles. A few hours of sleep sitting up had hardly been enough, but it was all he would allow himself. How much time had passed for his people? Had the troopers found them yet? Had the killing begun? Or was it already over back there, in that other time where all his friends and family lived?

Petre forced his mind away from such dire thoughts and went out on the porch. A beautiful clear crisp morning greeted him. The horses grazed just a few yards away and the snow-capped giants of the range dominated the end of the valley. So calm, so tranquil.

Celeste raised her head as he approached, her delicate ears pointed. The sun lit her bay coat with ruby highlights and warmed Lark's liver chestnut color to the richness of chocolate. Petre ran his hand along Celeste's neck and found the place on her withers where she loved to be scratched. She leaned into his fingers and in a moment her eyes glazed over and her nose twitched in a comical way that was most uncharacteristic of her usually refined and delicate manner.

Petre laughed softly. It was good to reach this horse.

Lark came and drooped his enormous head over Petre's shoulder. "You just have to see what I'm doing, don't you?" Petre chided him. He was delighted that Lark showed no aggressiveness this morning and he dared to hope that maybe the stallion's berserker was too far away for Lark to feel him. He reached up and rubbed behind Lark's ear where the bridle had left a swath of dried sweat. The enormous war horse tipped his ear into the rubbing and his head got heavier and heavier on Petre's shoulder. He was like an oversized kid's pony this morning. *Stay this way*, Petre begged silently. *Is can't take losing you right now.*

He felt another presence and looked up to find a great white owl perched in a tree not far from them. For a moment its eyes seemed to hold Petre's gaze with depth and wisdom. But it was only an owl.

Petre heard the boards of the porch squeak and turned to see Amil had come out of the cabin to call him. He went back to find Is awake, sitting up in her sleeping bag and Amil busy at the stove.

"Gruel?" Amil said instead of a greeting.

"Thanks," Petre responded. He glanced at Is. She looked pale and tired with dark circles under her eyes.

"How're you feeling?"

"Fine."

The lie served him right for the stupidity of his question.

"Then how 'bout a foot race?" he teased.

She glared at him, but Amil laughed. He seemed nothing but a harmless old man this morning and Petre was ready to put aside the suspicion and unease he had felt the night before. He had been overtired then and extremely worried about Is. It was not Amil who was doing anything odd by being here, he simply lived here. It was Is and the stallion and Petre himself who were out of place. Amil brought Is a steaming cup.

"To restore your blood," he said handing it to her. The familiar scent of healing herbs wafted on the air, and for the moment Petre felt almost content. He sat at the table and watched Amil dishing out the gruel. His shaggy white hair hung down his back in uneven lengths as though it had never seen scissors and rarely a brush. Petre, half-dozing in what to him was an overheated room, saw the feathers down the back of a great white owl, one overlying another shift as the owl moved. Startled, he blinked himself awake and found Amil standing over him, steam rising from the bowl of gruel, mixed with his white beard, his white hair. One shaggy eyebrow arched upward in a question. Belatedly Petre took the bowl.

As soon as breakfast was over they started on the books. Finding the information Petre needed would have been an overwhelming task, but fortunately Amil knew his books. He gave Petre a stack and instructed him what to look for in the indexes, then got busy himself. The silence was broken only by the rustling of pages, and Petre was glad to see that Is had dozed off.

"Here! I knew it was here someplace." Amil's triumphant voice startled Petre and woke Is. Amil pushed a book across the table in Petre's direction. "That may be the first reference to the experiments that led to the creation of a horse like Lark." He gestured at the book.

Petre began to read at the place Amil indicated. "The ultimate degree to which this link between a fine horse and a sensitive rider can be taken has never been fully explored. Evidence exists of certain trainers and certain horses developing a communication beyond what can readily be explained by conventional, or even extremely talented training…"

The text went on to cite examples ranging from ancient anecdotes to the author's own eyewitness accounts. Then it led into the author's attempts to isolate and study the phenomena.

"What is this document?" Petre flipped to the front page. "*A Proposal for the Scientific Development of the Ethereal Connection Between Equine and Human.*" The date predated the beginnings of the development of the berserkers' horses. These pages should have been crumbling under his fingers if not already turned to dust. Instead, the binding was still supple. The pages, though yellowed with age, showed no sign of the sort of degradation they would have shown by the time Petre lived. His hands trembled, rustling the pages as he turned them.

"So this is the beginning of the research that led the Alliance to eventually develop the computer chip they implant in the war horses' brains," he said more steadily than he felt.

"No," Amil said. "Read further. This research not only predates that, it takes an entirely different direction. You'll see. I'll show you later documents where the split becomes more apparent. The research begun by this man, don Bocher, steered away from the mechanical enhancements that became typical of the berserkers and their horses in your time. The people who followed in the line of don Bocher's research limited themselves to genetics. They bred for the qualities that make some horses so sensitive they seem to be able to read their riders' wishes before the riders themselves are aware of thinking them."

Petre knew exactly what Amil meant. His own horse, Des, was like that. He could begin to think something and Des would do it. All the Hluit horses were like that to some degree, but some went beyond others. Hluit lore held that there would be one horse in every person's life with which they would have that special once-in-a-lifetime bond. Petre suspected Celeste had been that horse for John and Lark was that horse for Is.

"You're saying they bred horses that had the same kind of link to their riders that the war horses have to their berserkers. Only, instead of computer technology it was done genetically?"

"Yes."

"But it must not have been as good, or reliable, or something, because what they use today are the computer augmented horses."

"Perhaps." Amil drew the word out. It didn't sound like agreement. "It would seem that the computer chip would be more certain to work every time and easier to mass produce, less variable. But there could have been other reasons for their decision to go with the computer-augmented horses too. You'll read for yourself, but I am beginning to believe the horses don Bocher's research created might have had other abilities that weren't realized at the time."

"You mean he made horses that could travel through time, like Lark?" Is's voice was tight.

"I don't have anything that exact," Amil told her. "The research I stole comes from long before Lark was created. But there were some incidences recorded. Horses from the Bocher Stud sometimes disappeared mysteriously. There are records of the orders to triple the guards at the Stud. Records of searches that swept nearly the entire continent looking for the stolen horses, but no records of arrests or executions. There's an account of a trainer who went insane. They say he ran away with one of the research horses. When they found him, he told a crazy story about taking the horse for its usual exercise only to return and find the Stud no longer there, all the horses and people gone. They must have at least half believed something unusual had happened because they didn't try him for the treason charges such behavior would have usually demanded."

Is tried to get up and froze, grimacing, as pain gripped her side. Petre went and helped her to the table. Neither man said anything about their concern for her. The will to live was more important than the proper care of her cut. It would heal. It was only a physical wound.

Is looked at the document she couldn't read and Petre thought, *I could teach you to read*. But he didn't say it. Instead, to keep the conversation going, "What happened to the horses they bred?"

He expected an easy answer. Instead Amil gave him a strangely speculative look. "I am not yet certain. But I would like you to read something." He rummaged through the bookshelf and returned with another volume. "Here," he said after a bit of paging.

"The horses of the Bocher line tend to a certain physical type," Petre read out loud for Is, "fine of bone, extremely refined heads, small ears and large intelligent eyes. They exhibit fine hair coats and small dense hooves. Skeletally they have one less rib than other breeds and frequently one less vertebra. Their coloring is predominately bay, with the associated black manes, tails and lower legs. Sorrels do occur. White markings are unknown . . ." Petre skimmed down the page unable to read aloud as fast as he had to know. "Their size ranges between fourteen hands and fifteen hands, two inches . . . willing, kind and gentle in attitude . . . extremely intelligent . . . "

"They sound like Hluit horses," Is said.

"Are they?" Petre pinned Amil with his stare. Suddenly every vague suspicion of the night before seemed sharp and deserved again. Amil looked away.

"I don't know." His voice and his movement were casual, as though he was unaware of Petre's suspicions. "But I take it all your people's horses are similar in type to the one I've seen, and bridles are not necessary for training them."

"Yes. So you think my people stole those missing horses?"

"No. The Hluit didn't yet exist."

"Right." It was hard to remember the time differences. "Maybe the horses were given to us after the Alliance dropped this line of research. We would have taken them so they wouldn't be destroyed?"

"Or perhaps they were given to you so the experiment would continue," Amil suggested. "It fits the Alliance pattern of dumping experiments into the Boundary to complete themselves."

"But how could we complete an experiment we know nothing about?"

Amil shrugged. "Perhaps your herd just serves as a genetic repository should the Alliance ever want to continue that line of research."

That made some sense. Cut off from outside genetic influences the way they were they had little choice but to keep the herd "pure." They weren't tempted to interbreed their horses with the Blueskins' inferior animals. But they would have bred some mares to Lark. A chill swept over Petre. Was that part of the reason the Alliance was so desperate to get him back, so that the Hluit would not get any of his offspring?

"My people should know about this," Petre said suddenly. "We keep some written records but mostly we rely on a verbal history. It says nothing about this." Petre stood and paced around the small room strangely upset by the depth of his reaction. "It is important to us to know the truth and not forget. It is one of the ways we resist slipping into uneducated savagery. But this, if it is true, has been forgotten."

"Or was never known," Amil put in.

"How would we not know?"

"If you were not told . . . "

"Why?" Petre demanded. "That doesn't make sense even for the genetic repository theory. We might have bred to the Blueskins' horses to improve their animals. We might have brought in other Alliance horses to breed."

"A little out crossing is good," Amil said. "And your people could be trusted to choose carefully."

"Or maybe they have given up on it," Is said. "It must have been a dead end." Her voice was dead of hope now. She had wanted for there to be some clue for how to save Lark in all this. She leaned on her elbows on the table causing her side to bend too much. Fresh blood seeped into the stain on Amil's borrowed shirt. Petre restrained himself from saying anything to her about it and found Amil watching him. There was something about the old man's gaze, feral and wise with an ancient sort of wisdom, like the patience of a predator. Petre was reminded of the white owl watching everything, waiting.

"It's all done with the chip in his brain," Is said about Lark. "It can't be removed. It can't be stopped. He'll go berserk like the other stallions. We won't be able to stop it." Her voice was dry of any emotion. This was something she had accepted before they came to Amil's.

Petre cast about desperately for something to bring hope back. Several times he had caught her staring at the books she couldn't read. Within the Alliance only people in the privileged Scholar class were allowed to learn to read. In fact it had been against the law for Is to even touch a book or be in the same room with someone who was reading.

"You shouldn't give up," Petre told her. "We haven't read enough yet." As nonchalantly as he could he slid a book over to her and went back to his own reading. But he was watching when she reached out, a little hesitantly, and touched the cover with such gentleness and all consuming attention that Petre could nearly feel the slide of the soft leather beneath the flesh of his own hands.

It was not just the book, it was the freedom to learn that had been so denied to Is. The Alliance government controlled access to the tools by which its citizens could help themselves. That was the real atrocity they perpetrated against their people. For Is to even look at a book, let alone touch one, was a crime that would have been severely punished. But now, in Amil's cabin, Is let her fingers explore the lacings that bound the cover and she closed her eyes. When she opened the book her eyes were still closed. Her fingers stroked down the page, feeling the slight roughness the letters made on the paper, feeling the weight and texture of the page as she turned it, hearing the rustle, capturing Petre in her sensations.

When she finally opened her eyes, he saw tears glistening there. Slowly he realized that Is was saying goodbye to something long withheld from her and now, when she could no longer accept it, within her reach. She was memorizing the feel, sound, texture and scent for she would never hold a book again. Never learn to read.

In that moment Petre understood her intention. As soon as they were done here, she would return to the Mirror and get it to kill her the same way it had killed John.

The pain that swept through Petre felt as though it would stop his heart. He could not let this be an ending. He sought desperately to turn it around.

"I could teach you to read." His voice was too loud, abrasive in the sanctity of the moment Is had created. She would not know that he had understood her feelings.

She shook her head, not looking at him. She did not want to learn anything new. She wanted to be done. To die.

Petre couldn't find the words that would give her hope. He glanced around as though for help and found Amil watching him and knew that Amil had understood the exchange.

Petre turned back to the book in front of him. His only chance to save Is was to find something here to save Lark, not to mention that he also had to find something to save his people. For a moment it seemed impossible. Despair threatened to overwhelm him. He forced himself to think.

"If Lark was bred from horses like the ones we have, shouldn't our horses have some of the same ability to travel through time?"

He looked up to find Amil watching him closely and again he was reminded of some sort of predator, waiting. But for what? He pushed the thought away as fanciful imagining.

"But surely we would know about our own horses," Petre said, anger coloring his tone. "Even if no one told us, surely we would have discovered for ourselves if they had some sort of ability to cross time."

"Maybe not," Amil said quietly. "After all, you would not have believed such a thing was possible. If there ever was an incident of time travel you would have found some other way to explain it."

"There have been incidents of very bizarre things," Petre admitted. "We attributed them to the Mirror and the herd fogs, and Dark Bodies – all things that have to do with the Mirror. You're saying the horses could have . . . but the horses seem terrified of all such phenomena."

"Tell me about these herd fogs," Amil said. "You have not mentioned them before."

"They seem like a dense fog, only they come all of a sudden. A person will find himself surrounded by fog, disoriented and much more afraid than the situation warrants. People have been known to wander off their routes and be gone for days or weeks, and when they come back they think they were gone no more than an hour. They seem confused and muddled and some have stayed that way for a long time, or even the rest of their lives. Some have never come back. Sometimes we find their bodies miles from where they should have been. That's why we call them herd fogs, they seem to be able to lead people away."

Petre paused, gauging Amil's reaction before telling him more. Amil sat still, waiting patiently for Petre to continue.

"We have always thought the herd fogs were associated with the Mirror because the Mirror seems to affect people in a similar way. It muddles them up and makes them see things no one else can see."

"And you said the horses are terrified of these phenomena?" Amil questioned.

"Yes, I don't see how the horses could have anything to do with causing them," Petre said. "I was caught in a herd fog once. It seemed unrelated to the horses, or the land. It was more mechanical than organic. When it surrounded me I tried to get out by walking right through it. When I touched it, there was a tingling sensation, not like damp foggy air, more like the electricity before a lightning strike. Light and sound got all mixed up in my head," he said slowly, remembering. "It was like I could hear light, and taste sound. It was like there was all this information around me that I could have learned, but I couldn't get it. I was completely overloaded and then I started coming back into myself."

Aware that both Amil and Is were watching him keenly, he tried to explain more clearly, remembering that Is had once been caught in a herd fog.

"As I came back into myself, instead of sensing too much information, I could feel only one thing at a time. I think my ability to process sensations had been taken apart and each sense separated out so that I couldn't process more than one thing at a time. First I was aware of weight, of gravity. Something we always just take for granted seemed unusually important. Then I became aware of temperature the same way. And finally, sound. Each sensation separate. There were even some senses I'd never had before, but I couldn't hang onto them. I have no names for them, no words to describe them," he said helplessly. "Since then, I've often thought that what I experienced could be similar to the way the Mirror takes the berserkers apart while it's killing them. The fog might be part of the Mirror, like a hand is part of a person. I think the fog coalesced to try to hold me, to examine me the way a person might hold some small creature in the palm of his hand to look at it. It didn't seem alive, organic, like a horse."

Knowing he had not explained half of what he had felt, Petre wound down. Amil was studying him intently but not with disbelief.

"How did you get away?" Amil asked.

"A breeze came, only it wasn't just a breeze. I think it was Dark Bodies. It had a purpose . . . and life. I don't know how to explain the difference between it and the herd fog except that it was organic and the herd fog was not. I don't know why Dark Bodies rescued me, or even *if* they rescued me. They might have just been passing through and the fog was in their way. The breeze shredded the fog and as the fog was dissipating – you know how a real fog has little droplets of water in it – well this fog had little droplets of illusion. I could see how all these little pieces had been forming around me and now they were being disassembled into free-floating information that formed no meaningful picture. It was being blown apart, its information scattered into random particles just like the droplets of water in an ordinary fog."

"And the Dark Bodies? What could you sense of them?" Amil asked.

"Very little," Petre said. "I heard a whispering like trees blowing in the wind or leaves rattling across barren winter ground. I remember being very cold, but I didn't feel wind."

"You're sure it wasn't just an ordinary breeze?" Is asked.

"Oh yes, I'm very sure."

"You were afraid," Amil said. "More afraid than you have ever been in your life."

Something about his tone brought Petre up short. "You've met them," he said.

Amil seemed to give himself a shake. "No, of course not. The Mirror hasn't been created yet, remember."

With those words, Petre felt as though he had been jerked sideways out of one nightmare and into another. "Right," he said, trying to get centered. It was all right, it was normal, he told himself, to be in the cabin a hundred years in the past talking to a man who was long dead.

"But you weren't afraid in the herd fog?" Is asked.

Petre remembered that Is had also been rescued by a wind when she had been trapped by a herd fog while she was traveling with John. *Coincidence,* Petre wondered.

"I probably would have been afraid of the herd fog except I was so busy trying to cope," he answered truthfully. "There was way too much information coming in, mostly through all the wrong sorts of sensations – like tasting sound and hearing light – and some of it was meant for senses I don't even have."

"It was like that with the Mirror," Is said pensively. "When John was doing whatever he did to fix the link between us, there was bright sound and loud light. Then all of a sudden everything was back in order, but much more so. Everything was so intense. I don't know how to explain it." With her words Petre came a step closer to understanding the intensity with which she had been linked to John. He also understood how John had repaired the damage the Alliance had done to him. He had made the Mirror take him apart and reassemble him so he could speak again. So simple to think those words, yet so impossible to comprehend them.

Then for a blinding moment Petre thought, if John could do that, use the Mirror's ability to strip out and put back together his own senses, maybe even mixing them with Is's senses when he did so, could John have made the Mirror give him eternal life? Was John now a Dark Body?

But Is had felt him die. She should know about death. She had seen her parents die. She had been with horses when they died. And she had sat with a dying berserker and felt him change into a Dark Body. Surely she would know the difference, if anyone would. She had been positive John was dead. Ondre had asked her specifically, "Are you sure John is dead," and she had answered without doubt. Petre could not bring himself to ask her again, especially when it was probably just his own desire to not believe John was dead that was making him have these thoughts.

John is dead, he told himself savagely, a*ccept that.*

Still, if John had gotten that much control of the Mirror even for a few days, there might be some way for another Hluit to get control of it. If they could regain the control that the Alliance had lost, they may be able to bargain with the Alliance for their own peace and freedom. They might be able to make the Alliance recognize them as a sovereign people not just some experiment that the Alliance was running and could terminate at any time.

But Petre had no idea how to replicate what John had done. No one did. And even as clever as John had been, in the end the Mirror had killed him. If there were some sort of help for the Hluit in all this, Petre knew he was not the one who could find it. He knew horses, he knew the land. He did not know anything about computers and Alliance technology.

Amil seemed to have read his mind. "The answer must be in the horses. Your people have to experiment with your horses. This time traveling ability may have been more or less in plain view all the time. Since no one believed it, and you didn't know how to ask your horses to do it, you never noticed it. But it should be there, in your horses. If you can get control of it you could use it against the Alliance. You could . . ."

Petre felt an immediate and very strong resistance to the idea. "I don't know," he interrupted. "It seems there could be incredible unthought-of ramifications from fooling around with past things."

"Yet you came here," Amil pointed out. "Yes, in desperation to hide Is and Lark."

"And to look for possibilities," Amil reminded him. "Well, you may have found those possibilities. Your people do not have the luxury of the kind of time it takes to weigh all the possibilities against the dangers."

True, Petre thought. My friends, my family may already be dead, or fighting for their lives at this very moment.

"This might be the opportunity you need."

"What opportunity? The Alliance is about to try to wipe us out."

"Your people are warned and mobilized. The Blueskins are already at war with the Troopers. You can use that to your advantage. And you may have a secret weapon in your horses, if you learn to use it."

Petre started to object, feeling resistance deep in his soul against using the horses for war, for killing people, for *taking over*. The Hluit had always honored their horses – not worshipped them and certainly not enslaved them. Nor had they demeaned their horses by treating them like spoiled children. The horses had been recognized as part of the world, part of the whole that made the people whole.

"What else would you do," Amil demanded, overriding Petre's objection. "Will you wait until your people are decimated and enslaved and your horses are taken from you? What opportunity will you have then? This may turn out to be the thing you're looking for. The way to overthrow the Alliance government . . ."

"Whoa, we are not looking to overthrown the Alliance, we are looking for a way to live separately but at peace with them."

"You will have to overthrow them, boy."

"No, that is not what we are trying to do, and even if we wanted to, I don't see how we could. We're a few hundred herdsmen against a few hundred thousand with huge city fortresses and weapons," he said, shaking his head at the thought of the weapons the Alliance had that his people didn't even understand.

"Not with open war," Amil said, exasperated. "Use Lark, or use your own horses, go into the past, insert a few people into their government, change a few key things."

"But surely that would change the present in ways we couldn't predict."

"Yes, change it for the better."

"I'm not sure we have the wisdom to do that."

"Maybe not. But think of all the suffering the Alliance has caused. Surely you can do better than that."

"I don't know," Petre objected. His people did not want to rule or overthrow or put themselves above anyone else. They trained from birth to harmonize with the land, the horses and each other. Even in their martial art there were no winners and losers. A person's standing was not judged by putting himself above others. Everyone was only as strong as they could help the weakest ones to be strong.

"Anyway," Petre said, "Is can barely control Lark." *And we may lose him to his berserker at any moment*, he thought. "There's a big difference between finding your cabin and doing the kind of thing you're talking about."

"I know," Amil said. "But you have to try. Otherwise the Alliance will wipe out your people and never give it a second thought. You have to learn to use your horses."

Again, Petre felt a great resistance drag at his soul as though he had walked off a path and brambles had snagged him and brought him to a stop. "No," he said, "we only want peace."

"Peace," Amil spat, "in a false freedom? Like you have now? The Alliance thinks it owns you and can do anything it wants to with you. They think you are an experiment they can terminate at any time. You have no more freedom than the Mirror. You have been programmed with a certain mindset, certain beliefs, and turned loose to complete their experiment. Can't you see that?"

Petre was suddenly on alert. "What do you know about it when we are so far in your future?"

Amil stood abruptly. "I'm not sure what I know. I'll let you decide for yourself." He turned toward the bookshelf. "It's not just the horses, your people . . ."

The rumble started in the floor, inaudible and almost below the threshold of sensation but all three felt it. Petre's eyes locked on Amil's and he saw fear there.

Outside, the stallion trumpeted. Is leaped up, heedless of her side, and charged out the door.

Petre went after her just in time to see Lark rearing up on his hind legs, pawing the air, his ears flattened against the huge crest of his neck. He was a terrifying sight. Is skidded to a stop and Petre nearly crashed into her. Amil was a stride behind them.

"You can hold him," Amil said to Is, low and urgent. "You *have* to hold him."

"How? He's changing. The chip has been activated. No one can . . . "

"Use the mare. Call her to us."

Is started forward. Petre moved to stop her. Amil caught his arm. Petre flung him off.

"He'll kill her."

"No. Watch."

Is stopped halfway to the horses. The stallion reared again, teeth bared, threatening her. His huge hooves slashing the air above her head could kill her with one strike. Is ignored him, her eyes fixed on Celeste. The stallion landed, snorted, and struck the ground with one gigantic front hoof. At any second he would lunge forward and strike Is the way he had killed the Blueskin. Is kept her attention on the mare. Something seemed to build between her and Celeste, connecting them and holding Petre frozen in his place. Celeste started walking slowly toward Is as though drawn by an invisible rope. Is turned and began to walk toward the cabin. The mare followed. The stallion snorted again, tossing his head, making his mane fly, then he began to follow too. With each stride he seemed to settle until he stood at the steps of the porch and lowered his head to graze.

Petre breathed out relief. "How did you know?" he asked Amil very quietly.

Amil looked at him a long moment. "Can't you see it?" he finally said. "I thought *you* could see."

Petre shook his head, confused and distrustful of whatever Amil was implying.

At that moment the tremor started again. This time it was strong enough to shake the ground under their feet. Behind them objects crashed off shelves in the cabin.

"Earthquake," Amil said.

Petre had never experienced an earthquake but he knew earthquakes had created the whole chain of mountains that formed the Boundary.

The horses threw up their heads and began to mill around each other. Lark tossed his head and snorted with a hollow echoing sound, white rimmed his eyes. Celeste pranced in place, head high, tail high. They both looked as though they couldn't decide which way to run. Is was already in among them before Petre realized she had left his side. The stallion seemed especially bothered, not aggressive now but frightened, and a horse of his size and strength could be as dangerous in fear as in rage.

"Is!" Petre started toward her. The horses picked that moment to wheel around, forcing Petre to move quickly aside. Now Lark was between Is and Petre, and as Petre tried to go around Lark, the stallion turned to go in the other direction. Petre had to leap out of the way as Lark's massive hindquarters came about, moving him farther from Is.

The horses were so terrified that at any second Petre expected them to bolt away in a mad gallop. Instead they began to circle Is as if held to her by invisible lunge lines. Petre had to move back as the horses gained speed until they were running as fast and as hard as panicked horses could run in a small circle. Petre was forced even farther from Is and from the cabin. He heard Amil shout.

"She's holding them!"

Then vertigo struck Petre. Instead of the horses wheeling around, the mountains seemed to be in motion, wheeling around him. He gasped and staggered. What was wrong with him? He could not get his balance. Had one of the horses struck him in passing? If he fell here he would be trampled. The ground shook. Thunder roared in his ears. He couldn't tell if the sound was from the galloping horses or another earthquake. In an instant it was over. Everything was silent and still. He lay face down on the ground – the still, solid, quiet earth. He raised his head and saw the remnants of a chimney. He was on his feet in an instant, taking a step toward the rubble in disbelief.

"Is?"

He had lost her! And the cabin and Amil and both horses. Grief and something like terror assailed him.

"Is!"

His voice rang across the empty valley, reverberating with despair.

He stood staring at the tumbled rocks of the chimney and could not believe it. Is, Lark, Celeste gone! He had moved only a few feet from her, pushed back by the running horses. It was not fair. It was not possible.

He walked around the ruin. He called frantically "Is, Lark, Celeste!" Walking turned into running, his voice became a wordless scream. He made himself stop, stand still, take a few deep breaths. He closed his eyes. With all his might he willed himself to be standing in the middle of the room he knew was here. When he opened his eyes the fireplace would be whole, the wood stove would be in front of him, the table behind him, the bookshelves surrounding him. He waited until the image was complete. He could feel the warmth from the fire, hear the rustle of a page being turned, smell the sweet rosin rising from the burning pine. He opened his eyes . . . to crumbled stone. A cold wind blew across his sweaty skin and soaked shirt. He had run out of the cabin without his coat.

The reality of his situation penetrated. He was alone without proper clothing, without tent or sleeping bag in the mountains with winter coming. He had the knife he wore strapped to his thigh and a smaller one in its hiding place inside his boot. He knew how to survive and that was all he knew. He did not know if he had been returned to the right time. He may have lost not only Is but all of his people, or he may be losing them now even as he stood here.

He turned toward the mountain's shoulder where he and Is had come into this valley (just yesterday?) He knew where to look for Hluit scouts in the passes, if they were still alive. The cry of a hunting owl sounded somewhere ahead and he began to walk.

Chapter Five

"Ondre. Ondre," a low voice insisted urgently.

Ondre opened his eyes to the dimness of predawn light inside his tent. At his side his wife Ellie stiffened, also awakened, sensing foreboding.

"Ondre."

"Yes. Give a moment." He slid from the sleeping bag and started to tuck it back around his wife but she was already rising. He pulled on pants and slipped out into the chill air of winter's early hours. Ellie was a moment behind him, wrapped in a fur robe, extending one to him.

The young man who had awakened them moved restlessly. His breath clouded the air as he spoke. "My father has come in from scout duty on the far side of the Boundary. He saw something. He wants to tell you."

The boy's nervous manner, the early hour, and the request to tell Ondre personally all meant bad news.

"Is?" Ondre asked. "Petre?"

"No," the boy said, hesitating. "John."

"John!" Ondre's heart did something crazy that left him out of breath and weak. His brother was dead. Is had felt him die.

"My father saw him," the boy affirmed. "Come. Let him tell you. It isn't good."

Before any hope could rise, Ondre broke into a run, dashing through the camp he knew by heart, heading for Dhave's tent.

The tent's door flap was loose, inviting entry. Inside, Dhave sat hunched by the fire, having just come in. A fur robe had been thrown over his back but frost was still melting on his hair and it showed in glistening droplets in his moustache as he turned. His dark eyes met Ondre's, haunted with pain and loss.

Ondre's demeanor changed from haste to timelessness. He settled himself by the fire. Someone, maybe Dhave's son had set water to heat. Ondre poured three cups. Ellie came in behind him, read everyone's body language and settled herself beside her husband. She was his other hand, his other half, half his soul. Of course she would be with him now.

Dhave started to say something, cleared his throat and began again.

"San is dead." His voice was like gravel shifting in the bottom of a river. "John killed him."

Ondre had been expecting many things but not that. His brother would never kill San. San had been his friend. And John was dead. Ondre put his disbelief into a question.

"You saw him? You're certain? John?"

"Yes. I am positive. It was him, and I heard San speak his name before John killed him. It was John."

"Why? John wouldn't . . ."

"He killed San to take his pack." Dhave's voice was dark as rage. "For food, for clothing, I don't know."

San would have given John those things and anything else he needed. The thought that John was capable of killing his friend was too unbelievable. Dhave began to tell the story.

"The wound was just a nick," he finished. "Just the tiniest nick, but it cut his carotid artery."

"It could have been a mistake. Some sort of accident," Ellie said. "Maybe John couldn't recognize you, or San. Maybe the Mirror messed up his mind worse than ever. Maybe he just meant to warn San back and when he saw what he'd done he panicked and ran."

"I've thought about that." Dhave's voice was slow and deep. "I've also thought, if you wanted to kill a man with the absolute most efficiency with a knife you couldn't do better than that one tiny cut."

The silence stretched until Ondre broke it. "Is that what you believe?"

"I don't know. I am trying not to believe anything. I loved your brother; but San is dead."

"The horses wouldn't run from John," Ellie said, her voice the sound of calm reason.

Neither man spoke for a long time. Finally Ondre said, "One of the Mirror's illusions would scare the horses, but it couldn't cut a man."

"It wasn't an illusion," Dhave said. "It was a real man and it was John."

Nobody refuted him. After a bit he continued. "We have to tell people what happened. We have to warn them, if they see John they must be on alert for their lives."

His eyes suddenly raked Ondre's. What he was saying was that people must be told to be prepared to defend themselves against John, to kill him if it came to that.

Ondre met Dhave's penetrating gaze. "I understand. I am glad you came to me first. I will back your decision."

Dhave folded forward and put his hands over his face, muffling his voice. "I'm sorry." His hands scrubbed at a vision he would like to erase. "I saw his eyes. He wasn't sane."

Chapter Six

Petre watched the vultures wheeling in slow spirals in the azure sky. The land stretched away below him in forest clad slopes. Beyond them snow covered peaks hung above the clouds as though unattached to the earth. If he took the few steps needed to cross the ridge and looked back the way he had come, he would see the mountains receding into foothills and possibly catch a glimpse of purple-hazed distant plains. Alliance land.

Both Sides Ridge was famous for its views, but Petre wasn't there for the scenery. He was looking for Hluit scouts. He'd been tracking a party of three horses until he'd lost their imprints on the rocky ground at the start of Both Sides Pass. So he'd come up to the top of the ridge. He didn't even know if the three horsemen were Hluit or Blueskins. It seemed unlikely they'd be troopers with unshod horses and just three of them.

There were now four vultures where there had been three a moment ago. He watched them circling and tried to read the land, wanting to avoid the places from which the scent on those thermals would be rising. His experience of the last three days told him the vultures meant dead troopers, maybe a dead Blueskin or two in with them.

Yesterday he'd come on the first carnage from upwind, moving so quietly the vulture hadn't heard him. Suddenly confronted by the big black shape, Petre had jumped back, heart yammering, as the huge bird launched itself heavily into the air, its enormous wings thrashing to lift its overfed body from the carcass of a half eaten horse. The horse stared at Petre from eyeless sockets. For a moment Petre had remained frozen by the sight of violent, needless death. The rider lay a few feet away, his neck nearly severed, probably by his own sword, which was missing. The Blueskins had taken it along with the rider's boots and the horse's saddle.

A crow cackled its disapproval at Petre's interruption of its meal. Another joined in, and another until Petre had moved away. There was nothing for him to do there and he had been afraid the racket would attract someone. For the first time Petre had been glad that Is wasn't with him.

He gave himself a mental shake trying to forget the too-vivid images of death and looked out over the vista before him. The sun was low in the sky, casting long violet-tinged shadows between the ridges. Failure weighed down his heart. He had wanted to prevent war. If he was lucky perhaps it had not yet touched his people, but it would. He had not found anything at Amil's they could use, a hint that their horses might have some special ability, a hint that there might be something more. Something about his people themselves, but what?

He should not have been so careless as to get too far from Is when she was busy holding the horses. But at least he knew she could do that – she could hold them there. That gave his heart some relief. Maybe the berserker had called Lark and Is had held him. If so, it might mean that she could not only keep Lark there, she could keep him from changing. She would never have to come back. Lark's berserker would never ride him to the Mirror and his death. Is could stay at Amil's for the rest of her life. Petre's heart twisted painfully in his chest at the thought of never seeing her again. He tried to tell himself it was for the best.

Is had expressed trust and liking for the old man. Perhaps Amil would teach her to read. Perhaps something more would develop from that. Maybe she would come to accept from Amil something that she could not accept from Petre. If that happened he should be happy for her. It was inappropriate to feel jealous, but he was not sure that was what he felt. There was a huge emptiness within him, and fear. He had to let go of Is. He should concentrate on his people, even now they may be in a desperate struggle for their lives.

He should have found Hluit scouts by now. Both Sides was a natural place for them. He started down. Maybe whomever he was following would stop to water their horses at the spring halfway down the pass. He'd go there and look for tracks. He went slowly, watching for signs, watching for ambush. He might be tracking Blueskins. He found where they'd watered their horses but they had not camped. He kept going, searching the shadows for shapes.

Even with all his care he didn't see the horse until it moved. Its head jerked up, ears pinpointing some slight sound he'd made. Immediately two other horses raised their heads. Hluit horses. Petre breathed again. They had been napping, heads hung, hind legs cocked, tired from crossing the pass. Otherwise he wouldn't have gotten this close.

He spoke to them soothingly, soundlessly. He saw one horse suddenly look beyond him. He started to turn, saying, "Hello, I am haa . . ."

The blow caught him across the side of his head. The day flashed bright as a strobe of lightning, then black. The roaring in his head deafened him. He could hardly breathe. The smell of leaf mold filled his nostrils. Slowly he realized he was lying face down in the stuff. He tried to turn his head. It was hard to lift his head, too hard. He just wanted to give up but a sense of urgency gradually crept in. By the time he succeeded in moving, turning his head was not enough. He had to get on his feet. He made it to his knees.

"Stay there."

The voice was fierce with anger. The accent was Hluit. Petre decided to take the man's advice mostly because he couldn't get to his feet anyway. On his hands and knees he could see the man's boots and the bottoms of his leather leggings.

The strangeness of his reception began to penetrate. The authoritative voice had been covering fear. Why would Hluit scouts fear him? They could see he wasn't a Blueskin or a trooper. Blackness flickered around the edges of his vision. He took a breath against it. Maybe if he sat . . .

As he moved a second blow caught him across his shoulder, flattening him. His head exploded in pain. Nearby there was whimpering like a hurt animal. He heard a woman say, "Wait. Look at the horses. They aren't afraid of him."

He couldn't understand why horses should be afraid of him. He carried that thought down into darkness.

Much later he opened his eyes to predawn grayness. The trees were indistinct shapes, gray on gray. Another campsite . . . time to get going . . . the ache in his body was the familiar pain of having lost Is. He had failed in his mission. He couldn't immediately remember where he was, but it didn't really matter. He just had to keep going. Find his people. He turned his head seeking clues to jog his memory. Pain lanced through his neck and shoulder snatching his breath away. For a moment he was helpless before its onslaught. Then training took over. Forcing his awareness into his lower abdomen, he concentrated on breathing slowly and deeply. With each exhalation he let go of the tension in his knotted muscles. He heard the rustle of leaves and a man knelt by him and spoke to him but Petre was locked in his own struggle just then.

Gradually, the pain receded and he became aware of the taste of vomit in his mouth. Then he began to remember. He wanted to say something reassuring so the man wouldn't hit him again. He wanted to ask why they had hit him in the first place. Why did they think the horses should be afraid of him?

Instead, the man offered Petre a cup of water and all coherent thought fled before the pure need imposed by thirst. The water ran down his throat and he could have been immersed in it for the intensity of the sensation entering his body. Its cold clearness washed through his brain.

He straightened up slowly and looked around. There were two men and a woman. All three had the slight fine-boned build that was typical of his people.

"I'm sorry I hit you," one man said. "I thought you were John."

All of Petre's hard won sense and cohesion vanished instantly. "John?" he asked stupidly. John was dead. They meant some other John. Why would they want to hit any John? "Ondre's brother?"

So they told him and the more they talked the more Petre wished that it didn't make sense.

"He's killed twice and been seen a few other times," the young man who had hit Petre concluded. "He seems to be heading back to the Alliance, but . . . I'm sorry I hit you . . . but no one expected you here, on foot, without Is."

So they knew who he was and he was beginning to recognize them. The one who had hit him was named Tonn. Petre had practiced with him in the martial art class and remembered him as not yet knowing his own strength and still trying to prove himself. The other two were not much older. He had practiced with them too but he didn't know them well. He told them what he'd learned at Amil's cabin and why he was on foot trying to get home.

"You can take my horse," Tonn offered immediately.

"No." Petre had changed his mind. "I want you to take my message to Ondre and the council."

"Where are you going?" the older boy asked.

"To the Alliance. To Center."

"Why?"

"Because that's where John's going."

"How do you know?"

"Center is where John lived as a spy."

He watched the look the three of them exchanged. It was the girl, Phran, who spoke. "It's also where he was caught and tortured," she said with the reasonable tone young people use to humor their elders when they think those elders have finally proven to be completely crazy. "Why would he want to go back there?"

"He may not want to," Petre said, feeling his way. "The Mirror may want him to."

"You mean you think it's controlling him?"

"I don't know." Put that way it seemed too fantastic. But to some extent the Mirror had already shown that it had the ability to take over a person's mind using fear and illusion and its herd fogs. But taking over the kind of control it must have of John's body was an order of magnitude more difficult. And what could be its purpose? It was easier just to believe John was insane and killing randomly without purpose.

"Even if the Mirror could make John do something like that, why would it want him to go to Center?" Phran asked.

"It's the headquarters of the Alliance government."

He watched them exchange another look and he couldn't blame them. He had nothing at all to go on but a gut feeling.

"You can't just walk into Center . . . " Phran tried a different tack to dissuade him.

"I'll contact Benson," Petre told her. "He'll be able to get the right papers for me. I'll have a cover. I'm not crazy." The three exchanged a glance again. "I've gone there before, I know what I'm doing," he assured them.

This time the older boy spoke. "I don't think you understand about John," he said in a respectful, reserved way. "It's not really him. He wouldn't kill like that. Even Ondre backs the decision to treat it like it isn't John."

Ondre's love for John was well known and the risk and pain John had put himself through for his people was legendary. No, John would not kill like that.

"You can't reason with him," Tonn added. "The second man tried that."

"I understand," Petre said to reassure them, knowing that he really didn't understand. The killer they described wasn't John. Is was sure John had died. She had felt him die. It was easier just to believe that.

Petre didn't want to go to Center. He didn't want to face John's living body wondering if any part of John was alive inside it. If he survived that encounter he didn't want to face Ondre and tell him he had killed his brother. He didn't want anything to do with any of this. But he had to go. If there was any slight chance of rescue for John, Petre could not live with himself if he didn't try. Somehow it was for Is. She wouldn't abandon John.

Chapter Seven

Petre paused at the edge of the meadow feeling reluctant to leave the protection the trees offered. It had been raining all morning, starting as an icy drizzle that found its way into his borrowed raincoat and all the way into his bones. Now the drizzle had become a steady downpour. The horse he had borrowed from Tonn held his back humped and his tail clamped down tight against the cold. He did not want to leave the protection of the canopy either and he stood with his head low and ears to the side, his winter coat was slicked down with water, rivulets ran from his mane and dripped miserably from his ears.

The wind picked up, blowing curtains of rain across the open meadowland in front of them. It looked cold and totally uninviting out there. Petre sat a moment mustering the heart to push the two of them onward.

Suddenly the horse threw its head up. Two horses burst from the trees at the lower end of the meadow – horses Petre knew only too well. The riderless mare, streaking low to the ground, swept like a sheet of rain in front of the ponderous war horse thundering his heart out to keep up.

Lark! Celest! Is!

Petre had only an instant to recognize them and then the whole meadow erupted into pandemonium. Troopers burst from the trees on either side, shouting. The mare veered sharply, turning up hill toward Petre. She was panicked now, eyes wide, tail high and no longer moving with the ease and efficiency she had shown a moment ago.

The stallion tried to turn, lost his footing on the slippery grass and somersaulted into the advancing line of troopers. Horses reared and swerved trying to stop or turn too fast on wet grass and went down colliding with each other in a tangle of flailing legs and thrown riders. Simultaneously, horses burst from the trees behind Is and added to the confusion as they tried to stop in time.

Petre lost track of Is and the stallion as the mare charged past him and his own mount spun to go with her. Caught stunned, Petre was nearly thrown. The next few moments of his life were completely consumed with the reflexive desire not to fall as his horse took off after Celeste. Any idea of going to Is's aid was lost as slapping branches made him duck low on his horse's neck. In that position it was impossible to stop or turn his running horse.

The incline finally slowed both animals. By then it seemed to Petre as though he should collect Celeste before he went back. With that many troopers in the meadow there was no chance he could charge in and rescue Is. Any attempt would require some planning and a lot of luck. He'd have to follow them and watch for an opportunity, he could only hope that neither Is nor Lark had been hurt.

He rode Celeste when he went back to look for the troopers. Tonn's gelding followed behind. Riding Celeste as tired as she must be was not the most logical move, but Petre was past limiting himself to logical actions.

He had to be very careful. The troopers would have scouts ahead and guards behind watching for trouble from Blueskins or Hluit. Petre thought about trying to enlist the Blueskins' help to free Is, but then she would be their prisoner and that did not seem like an improvement. Besides, Petre shared Is's desire to avoid having other people killed.

He was reduced to riding a great distance behind, following the troopers' tracks and being wary of being picked off by Blueskins himself. A couple times he got a glimpse of Is mounted on a trooper's horse, hands tied to the pommel. He occasionally picked Lark's massive hoof prints out of the confusion of prints left behind. His heart was in turmoil. He had never thought to see Is again, he had made himself hope to never see her again. Now here she was, a prisoner of the Alliance, and they had Lark.

By the third day it was obvious they were going through Castle Pass and Petre swung wide to get to a vantage point ahead of them. As the soldiers passed below he made a rough count of forty-some. Finally he got a good look at Is and he could see she was not injured and he was relieved. But he saw how her hands were tied to the saddle, she was blindfolded and her horse was being led by riders on each side of her. They were taking no chances that she could somehow disappear even without her stallion. That gave him pause. Did the Alliance truly believe she could?

Even at this distance he could pick out Lark among the other horses. It was easy to see that the person riding him was a large man who must be Lark's berserker. The depth of the feeling of loss that stabbed Petre's heart caught him by surprise, as though the horse had finally been taken from him in some permanent and irretrievable way. He had not realized how much the great war horse had come to mean to him and he was amazed at how sad he felt that Lark's fate was now sealed. He could imagine how much worse it must be for Is.

Petre found the Hluit scouts who were watching this pass. He left Tonn's horse with the scouts while he rode ahead on Celeste to try to reach Center before Is was brought in.

Once Petre reached land that belonged to the Alliance he could no longer ride. In the Alliance no one was allowed to own or ride horses except the berserkers, the trainers and the Guard. Petre could not pass for any of them. He left Celeste with the last group of his people's scouts and went on foot joining the farmers and artisans who were always coming and going on the road to Center.

Days later, Petre reached the outer gate to Center and stopped there at one of the inns. It was full of people and noise and the smell of food and drink.

Moving through the diners, Petre caught the owner's eye. He raised his hands and spread them as though smoothing something between them, and then he found a seat in a back corner. The owner came to him as soon as he could.

"I need work," Petre told him while his hands ran through another series of movements and he watched the innkeeper, Benson, taking in the double meaning.

"You may speak freely," Benson said.

"I am Marcine's son," Petre said low. "Phil Donter is my father. I have news of Ondre's brother John and news of Isadora. I have need of help."

"What sort of help?"

"To get into Center."

"Why?"

"That's where John is headed. That's where they're taking Is."

When Petre left in the morning he was wearing the simple robes of a Minister and carrying papers that would get him not only through the outer gate but into the heart of Center itself.

Chapter Eight

The place wasn't quite a dungeon but it was close. The massive stone walls radiated cold and a sense of age. Petre was well aware of how much weight was supported above his head as he walked along the corridor between the underground rooms. Above him towered eight stories of stone and metal, a manmade mountain. Though it was not the tallest building at Center, it was the most massive and foreboding. To Petre it felt as though these thick walls would cut him off forever from air and light, trees and wind, crushing his soul with their weight. But Is had been imprisoned here, so he had come here also.

He wore the robes and carried the identity of a Minister. While the Alliance government discouraged religion, it recognized that at times people needed some form of hope beyond this life. The Ministers were government approved nonsectarian "ministers to the people." The government ignored the religions that flourished among the poor and in the outlying lands, but if a person was dying, or had somehow come afoul of the law in any of the big centers, they were assigned a government Minister.

Posing as a Minister was one of the easiest disguises for Hluit spies to assume, yet it had very limited value as the Ministers were not privileged to any high level research or politics. For Petre it was a perfect disguise because Ministers often visited prisoners.

For all its faults the Alliance usually kept prisoners in more humane conditions than this. Of course they didn't usually keep prisoners very long. Whatever "treatment" was deemed appropriate was meted out before turning them loose to suffer their own consequences. In effect prisoners were used as test subjects for some very sophisticated tampering with brain and neural pathways. Thus a man who needed his hands to make a living might find himself without the use of his hands or in great pain any time he tried to use them in a certain way. A person who needed to communicate would find himself without that ability, as John had.

Is had been moved down to this dark and unsanitary basement where guards were not necessary because the guards who had been posted to watch her kept dropping dead.

Center was alive with rumors about those deaths. Most said there was no mark on the men. They appeared to have gone to sleep and never awakened. People said Is was a witch, that that was the only way she could have survived in the Boundary. They said she'd bewitched the stallion and she could kill with a glance. The government was trying to keep everything quiet but the rumors were rampant.

Petre suspected that the only reason they hadn't killed Is was that they were keeping her in reserve in case they needed her to control Lark.

He had seen Lark only once as two men were trying to move the stallion from an exercise paddock back to his stall. Lark had seemed docile enough but the men were taking no chances. They led him between them on lines attached to his halter. Suddenly Lark had stopped, thrown his head high in the air and whinnied. The men pulled on his leads trying to get him into the barn, but Lark ignored their puny human efforts trumpeting another loud blast. The men jerked on the ropes desperately. Lark's ears flattened against his neck as he reared, raking the air with his great hooves and dragging the men this way and that. But he did not attack them.

From his vantage point Petre had overheard the men.

"He's supposed to have bonded with his berserker. They shouldn't have us trying to handle him. He should have been gone from here already. What are they waiting for?"

"They've got something special planned for him," the other man answered. "It's because of that woman. She's some kind of witch."

That seemed to be what everyone believed. So the whole basement was deserted and delivering food to her had fallen to a lowly expendable Minister.

Even for Petre, who knew Is, it took a great deal more courage than he had expected to walk to her cell at the end of that corridor. The underground closed-in space made him feel trapped. His footsteps echoed and the swish of his robes was magnified making it sound as though someone was following him. Once he stopped suddenly trying to catch the sound of continuing footsteps, but it was no good in the confusion of echoes. Then he was mad at himself for being so spooked.

He stopped at the designated door and knocked lightly before using his key to open it. As it swung slowly inward, he stayed back, just in case . . . just in case . . . he didn't know what.

"Is, it's me," he called softly. The impromptu cell had been a storage room. It was without windows, without light, and from the smell, without a toilet. Unable to see Is in the dim light from the corridor, Petre held the tray in one hand and felt along the wall for a switch. He was suddenly furious that they would treat her, or anyone, this way.

"Is, I'm going to get you out of here."

He had no idea how he was going to do that but he was too furious to notice.

Yellow light flared as he found the switch. No furnishings. The only thing in the room was a pile of something with a coat thrown over it in the farthest corner. It took Petre a moment to realize it was Is. She didn't move or acknowledge him.

"Is . . ." The lump that rose suddenly in Petre's throat shut off his voice. He set the tray down and crossed the room to her. A stride from her he stopped. She hadn't moved. He could see now that she was sitting cross-legged, slumped down, with the coat pulled over her. Her eyes were open staring at the floor. She could probably see his feet. He dropped to his knee in front of her.

"Is?" He wanted to touch her. He needed to hold her to reassure himself as much as her and to strengthen both of them but he found he couldn't violate the distance she had placed around herself.

He sat back on his heels so he would be at her level and looked around. There was nothing for warmth except the coat Is huddled under. There was no bed. There were three trays of untouched food near the door, including the one he'd left there. Three trays, three days. It had taken him that long to get assigned to bringing food to her. She obviously intended to starve herself to death.

Petre began to talk, telling her the truth about everything. He told her about John. He told her about seeing Lark but he had not been able to get close enough to tell if the stallion would still let him approach. He told her that winter had finally come, the passes were all closed and the Hluit were safe until spring. Then he told her one thing that might not be the truth, he told her he could get her out.

For a long time she didn't move but her eyes had changed. She wasn't staring into the distance waiting for death, she was thinking. Petre fell silent and let Is take her time. No one was going to be in a big hurry to come looking for him if he didn't return.

"It's not John," she said finally, a flat positive statement. Then she raised her head. The misery had left her eyes and they were filled with anger. "If you get me out of here, I am going to take Lark again or die trying."

He understood her. She was telling him she would not slip away and hide. If he got her free, she would likely get herself killed. He understood and for the first time he agreed. A fighting death in the open air was so much better than this. To choose a better death was the only thing Is had left. He met her gaze and nodded.

She accepted his covenant.

"When?"

"Tomorrow." While he was promising impossible things, why not.

Chapter Nine

For Petre it was even worse in the underground corridors at night. No one had bothered to light them. He didn't dare risk attracting attention so he used the dimmest setting on his glowtube. It made just enough light for him to see the wall on his left side if he stayed close to it. The other wall, the ceiling, even the floor a few steps ahead could have vanished except that the closed-in feeling was so strong. It was different from the darkest night in the Boundary and the closeness had a different feel than even the densest forest, foreboding and cold.

Petre was trying to ignore such feelings, telling himself it was just a different sort of dark. But the reason he could walk up to Is's cell with no one to challenge him was because she had no guards, and she had no guards because they kept dropping dead. His nerves tingled with warning.

Relieved to reach her door, he reached out with the key and was suddenly overcome with such weakness he had to lean against the doorframe. For a moment he couldn't believe this was happening to him. The light fell from his hand and dimmed even further. Shadows leaped at him. A breeze whispered across his skin causing the hair on his arms to stand up. Then adrenaline surged into his system and he began to fight. His hand shook uncontrollably as he tried to get the key into the lock. Everything seemed to recede. His legs gave way and he slid down the door. He just managed to turn the key as he slipped. His weight flung the door inward and he crashed into Is's cell on his hands and knees. The door hit the wall and bounced back into him, knocking his support out from under him. He fell heavily on his face. Trays of uneaten food clattered into each other. The noise racketed through his skull like cymbals struck too close to his ears. He rolled in pain, trying to escape the sound and in the pale light of the glowtube he'd dropped he saw something rush toward him. An enormous white owl hurtled out of the dark on soundless wings. As it swooped at him, he curled into himself knowing it was no owl. There could be no owl here. It was his own image of death rushing for him. He held his breath, prepared for some sort of pain, and then it just passed over him and through the doorway tipping its wings to clear the doorspan.

"Don't kill him. You can talk to me now without that. If you kill him, I swear I'll never speak to you again. No matter how many people you kill, I'll never talk to you . . ." Is's voice carried Petre into unconsciousness.

Something rattled him about as though he were on a bucking horse. He pulled away from hands on his shoulders, becoming aware of Is's voice. "Wake up. You've got to wake up."

He took another breath before he opened his eyes to the cell, the greenish glowtube light, the memories.

"It was a real owl," he said which was probably not the smartest thing to say to someone trying to determine if you are rational enough to help her escape a castle full of armed guards.

No answer. But then it hadn't quite been a question.

"Can you move?"

That was a good place to start. Leave all those pesky questions about who she had stopped from killing him and owls which didn't belong here. He got himself into a sitting position. All body parts seemed to work. There was some sort of pain but he couldn't pinpoint it and decided it was better not to look at it too closely right now anyway. He got to his feet and found he was a little shaky. There seemed to be a time lag between telling his body to take a step and realizing that it had done so. Nothing he couldn't handle as long as he didn't have to do something too dexterous, like run fast, scale high walls, or jump from rooftop to rooftop. Fortunately his plan didn't call for any of those things.

Without a word Petre peeled off his outer cloak and handed it to Is. She put the cloak on as he unwound his scarf and handed it to her. When she was done tying it around her head and neck Petre could no longer tell that she was a woman. He hoped they would pass as two Ministers on some late business of their own. Most people wouldn't give them more than a cursory glance. If anyone stopped them he'd do the talking and Is would act cold and impatient to get going. It might not get them through the wall, but with luck it would get them to the stables.

Petre locked the door behind them. Nobody would be checking on Is until he brought her food in the morning.

The first part of the plan, walking out of the building, was the most dangerous. Once they were outside they'd have every excuse to be bundled up and hurrying as it was raining and freezing out there.

Petre went up the stairs in front of Is. The climbing helped his coordination and he began to feel more normal again. The stairwell opened into an enormous chamber on the ground floor, wide open with a high ceiling and stone floor with only a few columns to keep them from feeling totally exposed. Unlike the basement, this first floor was well lit and relatively well traveled even at this time of night. Petre motioned Is to stay behind while he had a look around.

For the moment no one was in sight and they began to walk hurriedly as though they had somewhere to go. Petre's heart raced. A man came out of a side corridor and passed them with hardly a glance. Two other people walked across the floor intersecting their path, talking and taking no notice of two Ministers. Others came and went across the floor moving about on their own errands. They'd made it halfway to the door when a voice challenged them.

"Say, wait a minute Brothers."

Although the tone was friendly enough, Petre's heart froze.

He glanced back and saw a fellow Minister hastening toward them. For an instant he just wanted to bolt. There was no way Is could fool another Minister in this brightly-lit hall.

Petre leaned to her and whispered urgently, "Keep walking like you're in a hurry, but don't run. I'll stop and talk to him."

There was no time for more than that. The other man was too close. Petre raised his voice and said, "Sure, sure I understand," in a slightly sarcastic voice followed by a suggestive laugh. "I'll see you at the meeting tomorrow, then."

He turned and walked back to the other Minister. With a sly grin, a shrug of his shoulders and a little shake of his head, Petre said, "He always has some woman waiting."

With any luck the other man would assume he knew whom Petre was talking about. There was one Minister in particular, Lore Elsa, who was infamous for taking advantage of his position with women at every opportunity. He was also about the same height as Is.

Still smiling Petre went on, "What can I do for you, Brother Shaw?"

Minister Shaw glanced after Is, but Petre's question recaptured his attention. There was something he wanted from Petre. "Well," Shaw said in an expansive, overly friendly voice. "Some of us have been worried about you, you know, having to take the food down to that woman."

He gestured toward the stairwell that Petre and Is had left only minutes ago and laid his arm across Petre's shoulders as though they were the best of friends.

With a sinking heart Petre realized he would be detained. Shaw wanted grist for the gossip mill. He wanted to know what it was like to go down that corridor, to open Is's door, to be near the woman who had killed two sets of guards without touching them.

Petre tried to put him off. "There's not really anything to tell. I just open the door enough to put the food in and lock it up again."

But Shaw was having none of it. "You were down there such a long time this morning. We were beginning to get worried."

So it had been noticed. Guards had stood at the stairwell, afraid to venture any closer, but ready to shoot Is if she came up instead of Petre. He wondered if they had seen a large owl. Surely he would have heard.

Petre looked down and scuffed his foot on the floor, pretending to be embarrassed. "Well . . . you know . . . it took me a little time to . . . well to open the door," intimating that it had taken him a while to get up his courage.

Shaw seemed to be buying it. "I guess it would," he said in a friendly way. "Any one of us would be a little bit nervous down there."

The truth was that they were all so scared that they had pawned the job off on a visiting Minister who had no seniority and no clout. That suited Petre's purposes just fine. But Shaw wanted more. "Did you see her? Didn't you even take a peek? Weren't you curious?"

Shaw was obviously more interested in having a story to tell than hearing the truth. Petre only wanted to get away from him as quickly as possible. He didn't know where Is would go on her own, if she would wait for him or try for the stables alone. He mentally kicked himself for not having foreseen that they could be separated. They should have discussed a plan.

"No, I just put the food in there and left," he told Shaw.

"But how do you know she was even in there? Maybe she escaped?"

"She was there," Petre said quickly. He couldn't let Shaw decide to check for himself. Then he had to make something up. "I could hear her. She was walking around in there and when I unlocked the door she stopped."

"Did she say anything?" Shaw was intense.

Petre wanted to just say no and get going. But Shaw wanted something he could spread around. If Petre didn't give it to him, Shaw would likely make it up. When Petre heard it again Is would have two heads and the teeth of a great lizard. She would have attacked him, or bewitched him. Now there was a thought to worry about. While Petre believed Shaw was only trying to get gossip, Shaw could turn into an informer if he thought anything was suspicious. Petre could not afford to antagonize Shaw.

"Well," he drew the word out. It didn't matter if Shaw thought he was embellishing. "She did say something."

Feeling Shaw's intensity, he let the moment stretch. "She said, 'Food? You call that food?"

Shaw laughed and Petre joined him. The food Petre had taken down was the same as what was fed to the guards, the Ministers, all the staff. It was bland, awful mass-produced mush and everyone complained about it.

True or not, it was a good joke that would make good retelling. Shaw should now be in a hurry to go find an audience for his new joke but etiquette required that he not reveal his purpose. So they stood and chatted for a time while Is got further away and Petre grew ever more frantic inside. Finally Shaw released him.

Petre walked out the door Is had taken and hesitated on the porch. It was cold. Wind blew a drizzle of freezing rain slantwise under the roof wetting the marble slab he stood on. By morning everything would be coated in ice. Petre had been sweating talking to Shaw, but now the wind found its way into his coat chilling him. He'd given his shawl to Is and he didn't dare put on a hat for fear that Is would not recognize him.

He walked out from under the portico and down the steps feeling the freezing rain wetting his head and working its way down his neck and into his clothes. Ice was already forming on the walkway.

When he got near the stable Petre left the walkway, skirting the light that escaped from the second floor windows. Grooms and trainers lived above the stable. It would not do for someone to see him prowling about out here. He decided to enter through the door to the indoor arena, assuming no one would guard that at night. Ignoring the huge wooden doors that could admit six horses abreast, he slipped in through a smaller door.

Though the arena wasn't heated, it provided relief from the cold rain. For a moment Petre just stood near the door. If Is were in here she would have heard the door open and close. Petre risked calling her name very softly. No answer. There was no sound except the wind and rain blowing against the door.

He edged around the arena. No point in leaving footprints across the well-raked loamy soil they used for riding. The stables adjoined the arena, separated only by another wooden door. Normally there would be no guards at that door, but any noise – horses whickering a hello, a startled snort – would bring someone immediately. Every sound could be heard from the rooms above the stalls and an apprentice would be sent down to check the horses.

The door into the stable was set on rollers. Petre held his breath as he pushed it slowly back, but it slid soundlessly on well-oiled runners and he thought, of course, some apprentice would be shot if the door operated in a less than perfect fashion. The stable glowed in a ghoulish red light designed to not disturb the horses' nocturnal vision while making it possible for people to check on them without having to switch on the lights. Petre walked slowly down the aisle willing the horses to be silent. Mostly they were dozing, heads down, hips cocked aslant as they rested one hind leg or the other. Straw rustled as some of them turned to watch him. He had to go all the way to the end of the aisle to the one extra-reinforced stall where they had put Lark. He could see already that the door wasn't latched but he had to go anyway, to be sure. He had to stand and look through the bars and see that there was no horse inside – and no Is.

Petre's emotions were in chaos. Hope, fear and even a touch of betrayal ran through him. Is had taken the horse and gotten out without setting off an alarm. That meant Lark still knew her and still obeyed her. That created the hope. She was with her stallion and she was free.

She hadn't needed him and she hadn't waited for him. Of course. And yet the sense of loss and betrayal was there. Is hadn't meant it that way. If she were caught, Petre would be safer if he wasn't with her. He might even convince everyone that he had had nothing to do with her escape. They believed she was a witch and no one had seen anything suspicious, except Shaw. Petre knew he could probably bluff his way through that, yet he had no intention of trying. If they tortured him, he could give away information that would endanger the other spies the Hluit always had within the Alliance. Although Petre didn't know the specifics of who they were or where they were, he knew about the spy network in general.

For the first time Petre considered how rash his actions had been. He had acted in passion to free Is from that horrible, stinking underground cell. He had thought he would have time to try to talk her out of her own rash desire to take Lark; or if he could not, then he would have joined her. He had not considered others he might endanger.

Now that Is had the stallion, her best hope was to head for the front gate and try to get out. There would be no way to hide Lark's disappearance. At best they had until morning when the apprentices came down to feed the horses, but someone could come down to check on the horses at any time. The alarm would go out and then they would discover that Is was gone too. The whole place would become an armed fortress. Her only chance to get out was tonight. Now. Fast. And it wasn't much of a chance.

Petre left the barn the same way he had come in but a lot quicker. He wasn't cold now, he was too desperately afraid for Is to feel anything else. He hadn't gotten around to being afraid for himself yet, trapped as he was in this walled stronghold that would momentarily go on high alert.

He hurried as fast as he could go on the icy ground, straining his ears to hear the first sounds of the alarm being given – a guard challenging Is at the gate, a stallion's scream of rage as he attacked, Is's scream of pain, anything. He began to run, slipping and sliding on the ice.

Is should have reached the gate by now. It should be over. He should be too late to be any help. But if she hadn't charged in blindly, there might be some way he could help her. Create a diversion. Distract the guards. *Please wait!* His heart pounded. *Please.*

When he came within sight of the gate he tried to stop too fast and slid on the icy ground, nearly falling. No Is. No stallion. No ruckus.

He faded into deeper shadows and tried to think. He could see two guards inside the gatehouse in the light and warmth. Why shouldn't they stay inside and be dry, the gate was closed. No trouble was expected and in any case no one was going to get through, or over, that gate without setting off all sorts of alarms.

Petre stood gulping the frigid air into a chest that wanted to constrict against the cold and lungs that ached for oxygen not ice. He didn't hear the movement behind him until Is spoke his name.

Petre spun around, his heart about to explode; he realized his mistake too late. The stallion would attack quick movement. But Is wasn't mounted on the stallion. "Where's Lark."

Is paused a long moment. Petre couldn't see her expression well, but he had the impression that she thought he had asked her something very stupid.

"You couldn't hear them?" she finally asked. And when he kept staring uncomprehending, she added. "In the cell. You couldn't hear them?"

Petre vaguely remembered having heard Is tell someone not to kill him, but he'd been befuddled by the drain on his energy. Then the urgency of escaping had kept him busy. Now he felt like his mind was stripping gears.

"The Dark Bodies," she said with the exaggerated patience of someone talking to an idiot. "You couldn't hear them talking?"

"No." So it was Dark Bodies that had killed her guards and drained his energy.

"I couldn't hear them," he told her. "What did they say?"

"Lark's gone, his berserker took him. They're trying to get through the pass."

"They can't Is, it's already winter there." Petre regretted his words the moment he said them but he'd been too upset to think first. Is didn't need him to point out how hazardous the trip would be this time of year.

"A whole guard went."

That made more sense. They would carry their own supplies and they'd have a whole string of horses to take turns breaking the trail. They wouldn't have to watch out for Blueskins. The Blueskins wouldn't expect this. But those answers only raised more questions.

"Come on," he said. "We have to get out of the rain. We need to talk." He wasn't sure if Is would follow him. "Take my hand," he said and when she did, her hand was like ice in his.

He led her to a deserted warehouse where they huddled under the protection of a doorway arch in near total blackness. Is told him about the Dark Bodies as he held both her hands and couldn't see her at all. Her voice came out of the dark, expressionless and as cold as her fingers, a monotone of horror.

"The Dark Bodies say the Mirror has gone crazy. It's going to 'preserve' everyone at Center who might know how to turn it off. It's going to take over the Alliance's computer network. It doesn't want anyone left who can control it. It's . . ."

"Wait," Petre pleaded, desperately trying to catch up. "What do you mean 'preserve?' It's going to kill everyone who knows about it and 'preserve' them as holograms? As Dark Bodies? What?"

"Holograms. It has enough Dark Bodies to do its killing now. They've already started. They can go anywhere. They . . ."

Petre gave her hands a shake to bring her back to his questions. "Is, wait, the Dark Bodies killed your guards? Were they working for the Mirror? Does that mean the Mirror wants you loose?"

"I don't know. It can't control the Dark Bodies completely. *They* wanted to talk to me. So they killed the guards, to take their energy, so they could make me hear them."

"So the Dark Bodies, themselves, wanted you to know about the Mirror? Why? What's all this to them?" They were dead berserkers, some of them long dead.

"I don't know." Is hadn't thought about it. She was too absorbed in her own grief and her own need to escape. Petre felt the small bones in her hands move in some unconscious desire to be gone from here, gone from him. He tried to engulf them in his own larger hands, tried to will his warmth into them. She was nothing but bones – starving three days in her cell, probably longer than that if she had started when they first caught her.

"What else did they tell you?"

"John. John's going to . . . ." Her voice stopped coming and except for her lifeless hands in his, she might have vanished altogether.

"What is John going to do?" Petre hated himself for pushing her. She didn't answer.

"What is John?" He tried another tack.

"John's dead." Her voice was more of a plea than a certainty. She began to shake. He had to grip her hands to keep from losing them.

"Please tell me."

"He's . . . It re-animated his body. He's carrying the Mirror's . . . brain . . . to Center, to here, to . . . infect the Alliance computer net." She was shaking so hard she couldn't finish.

Petre pulled her against him and held her, trying to stop her shaking by the force of his own strength. A million questions flooded his mind. One he had asked himself thousands of times as he followed John across the Boundary, could the Mirror take over a body that was completely dead? Or did something of John still exist?

He tried to pull himself together and think what to do.

"We've got the get you out of the city."

"How?"

Petre didn't have a plan, but he couldn't tell Is that. "There are people I can contact, they'll help us. It may take a little time. We have to hide you first."

He realized now that he had gone about things entirely in the wrong order. He should have gotten help before he got Is out of the cell. Yet his decision to rescue her had seemed right at the time – seeing her crouching in her own filth trying to starve herself to death.

The anger that came with that memory made him more than a little crazy. He took her by the hand and started walking, trying to think of a safe place to hide her.

"Petre," she said, "I should try to get out tonight. They don't know I'm missing yet. We don't know when they might decide to send someone to my cell to get me. Once they know I've escaped it will be impossible to get through the gates. I need to go tonight."

Petre hesitated in his stride. She was right.

She misread his hesitation. "You don't need to be involved. You've already done more than enough . . .

"No," he said, "I can help." He set off again and she followed him. "The North Gate is used by a lot of farmers. We might be able to stow you away in an outgoing wagon. Like you said, they don't know you're not in your cell. If I go back and take your breakfast down tomorrow just like you're still there the guards at the gate won't have any reason to do more than a cursory search of the wagons."

He might buy her a day, two days, more. He would send Is out alone and stay behind. It was the hardest decision he'd ever made in his life. But it was her best chance.

"Petre," she started to object, "when they find out I'm gone you'll be in danger. I can't . . ."

"There is no better way," he told her firmly.

He took her to the North Gate. They paused in the shadows near one of the Inns frequented by the farmers who came and went through this gate. Light streamed from the windows of the Inn illuminating the rain in silver streaks, the shine of water on the ground and the dark bulk of three wagons parked in the yard. Their teams would be stabled in the barn, the door closed against the cold and wet.

They sneaked up to the wagons and found that two were empty and ready to leave, while one was full and still inbound to the city. Both empty wagons had large tarps, folded neatly behind the driver's bench.

Petre let Is choose which wagon. Let it be her luck.

The tarp must have weighed a hundred pounds. Together they were able to unfold and refold it in such a way that Is could hide under it without having too much weight on her.

In a whisper Petre told Is of the places she could try to reach in the Boundary where Hluit scouts would find her. If the wagon took her north and west she should try for Steep Pass. He described the rock that looked like a horse's head that marked the entrance to that pass. Hluit scouts would be watching Steep Pass. If she found them, they would take care of her. If the wagon took her more east, she should try for Lone Rock. He described that to her and several other places she might find herself near. But as he talked he felt how hopeless it was. If the wagon made it through the gate that was only the beginning. The drivers might discover her. They might try to turn her in for a reward or for fear of punishment if they helped her. If she avoided that, she could freeze or starve. If she made it into the Boundary she was as likely to get picked up by an Alliance patrol as by Hluit scouts. It was even possible there would be some Blueskins about. Petre may well be sending her to her death. His voice faltered.

Is found his hand and squeezed it. "Petre," her voice sounded gentler than he'd heard from her in a long time. "Don't worry. It doesn't matter what happens to me."

Once again she reminded him that death was what she wanted. He couldn't think of anything to say. He squeezed her hand and then, quickly, before she could object he brought it up to his face and touched his lips to her fingers. Then he turned, vaulted over the little side railing of the wagon and dropped to the ground. She called after him, just a soft whisper, maybe not even intending him to hear.

"Thank you."

Chapter Ten

Petre carried the tray in front of him and walked past the guards and down the stairs. He had gotten back just as the earliest cooks and tenders were beginning to stir. No one had taken undue notice of him. It wasn't unusual for a Minister to be out late or early seeing to some ill or dying person.

Feeling even more fearful now than he had when Is had been in the cell, he waited from heartbeat to heartbeat for the sound of an alarm. The wagons would just be hitching now. The heavy slow oxen being prodded into position by livery boys while the farmers lingered over the last hot meal they would enjoy at a table for days, or weeks for the ones who had furthest to go.

Petre wondered how Is felt, cold and fearful, or not caring? It must have been a long night for her. Still it had to have been better than this cell. He opened the door and looked around the empty unfurnished room and thought of the owl.

A white streak on the wall caught his attention. His gaze followed it upward. At the very top was a recess where a little pale light showed through. He thought it must be a vent that opened just above ground level. It was too small for a person to wiggle through and far too high for someone without aid to climb to anyway . . . but an owl?

He examined the wall and found more white streaks. A bird had sat on that ledge and stained the wall with its droppings. A large bird could have pushed aside the grating that had probably covered that vent, but it would be a most peculiar thing for an owl to do. He tried to slow his racing heart.

Owls were opportunistic hunters. One could have learned to come and go that way to hunt the rodents that lived down here. It wasn't likely, but it wasn't impossible. There was no reason to be so spooked by an owl. He turned the light off, locked the door behind him and headed back the way he'd come.

The morning passed without an alarm. The wagon *must* have left by now. By the end of the daily Minister's meeting Petre was sure Is was free. It might not last long. It might not end well. But she was free of that freezing stinking cell. She was outside the walls and on her own. That knowledge gave him a sense of inner triumph he had not expected to feel.

Petre found time between a couple of his scheduled visits to make an unscheduled one to a Hluit man whose Alliance name was Don Field. He coordinated the Hluit spies at Center and Petre should have come to him first, before helping Is escape. Now he had much explaining to do.

They walked in one of the fruit tree groves, originally intended to make Center proof against siege, so they could not be overheard. Petre told Field about Is's escape and what she had told him about the Dark Bodies, the Mirror and John.

The lines in Field's craggy face grew deeper as Petre talked. "We have to get you out of here. Fast," he said when Petre was finished.

"And the information?"

"That's the easy part. Couriers will have it home before you."

Petre couldn't stop himself from asking what he already knew would be done. "You'll tell everyone to watch for Is?"

"Of course." They walked on in silence for a bit while Field worked on the problem.

"You'll get new papers," he told Petre. "They will ask for your return to your village. They'll say your father is ill, maybe dying. When you get the papers, take them to the Head Minister's office. He should approve them. They'll look authentic. Use real names. No reason he should check."

But if he does? Petre stopped himself from asking. He could end up mutilated like John. No one would be able to help him. Field would be in charge of trying to protect all the rest of the spies so that no matter what Petre told the Alliance he wouldn't bring the whole network down with him.

Field hesitated in his stride and met Petre's eyes. "Once they realize that Is is gone, all hell is going to break loose. If that happens before you get your papers, try to get out on your own. If they catch you . . ."

He paused, reaching into his coat to fish out a locket on a chain. He opened the locket and there was a small pill inside.

For the first time, Petre realized the enormity of what he'd done. Field closed the locket, took it off his own neck and handed it to Petre.

"Wear it," he said. "If necessary you can bite right through the locket."

Petre met Field's eyes and found within himself the certainty that he could do this and would do it if he had to. The older man nodded once, a quick ducking of his head, accepting Petre's covenant without words.

Petre put the chain around his neck and tucked the locket down inside his shirt. He didn't trust his voice, but felt he had to defend his actions. As they began walking again, he finally spoke. "The information is important though."

"Yes," Field agreed. "It is very important. And *it* will get out."

He paused before continuing. "You might like to know that Ondre is coming here."

"Because of John? Is John here then?" Petre's heart knotted, Ondre here hunting the brother he loved so much!

"Partly because of John," Field acknowledged. "No one knows if John's here yet, but the scouts who picked you up told Ondre you were certain John was coming here. Now, from what Is told you, I'm even more certain of it. But the main reason Ondre and a few others are coming, is to try to negotiate for peace. After all, the Alliance has the stallion now. What you have told me may give them more negotiating leverage."

That made Petre feel a little better. But now it would be even worse if he were caught. He had to leave the city, he couldn't help Ondre. Petre's duty, as it seemed it had always been, was to try to help Is.

Field glanced over at him. "I couldn't have left Is in that cell either. I just wish you'd asked for my help first."

That evening as Petre carried Is's tray down to her empty cell there was still no alarm. Without the owl, rats had found the food and cleaned the plates. Petre carried the empty dishes back up with him. When they did discover that Is was gone, it would be better if they couldn't tell how long she'd been gone. There was still no sign of the papers Field had promised. Every instinct told Petre to run, get outside these walls before it was too late.

Two harrowing days passed before Petre came back up from "feeding" Is and found the papers waiting for him. The Head Minister was out of his office so Petre left the orders with the secretary and went about his daily schedule.

In the afternoon, as he walked back from a deathbed visit, he heard the sound of many feet jogging in unison, overtaking him from behind. He knew the castle guard sometimes exercised on the grounds, so the sound of jogging was not immediate cause for alarm. Still, Petre turned off the walkway without letting them see his face and pretended to have business in another direction. As the guard ran on by, intent on their own orders, Petre tried to calm his racing heart. He had nearly talked himself out of his worry when he saw a second patrol jogging toward the castle. That was all he needed.

He pulled his collar up and his hat down and turned away. He didn't dare try to contact Don Field now. He had to get himself out.

Petre had formed a backup plan for himself the day he'd talked to Field. But he needed rope, a grappling hook, and lots of luck.

He altered his course toward one of the inns that clustered around the nearest gate. A rope shouldn't be hard to find. Many farmers used ropes to tie their loads, and some used steel hooks to help them load bulky objects like bales of hay.

Petre waited in a concealed spot until it was late and the sounds of dining had died down at the inn. Lights were going out in the bedroom windows before he approached the stable. Most stables had livery and livery apprentices whose job it was to watch out for the comfort of the draft animals. It wasn't unusual for apprentices to live in the stables.

Knowing it was unlikely he could slip in, get what he needed and get out without being seen, Petre walked in boldly. If he were lucky and only a junior apprentice was awake, he might bluff his way through.

The massive winter door didn't roll as easily or as quietly as the door at the stable where they'd kept Lark. Petre left it open, letting the cold air blow in, hoping to apply pressure to hurry the proceedings. He marched down the aisle with quick impatient steps. On his left, draft animals were tethered to rings in the wall. Most were oxen but there were two mules, heads hanging in slumber, large ears at half-mast. Farmers were not allowed to own horses and even mules were unusual.

On Petre's right were pens for pigs, goats, sheep and chickens that had been brought in for sale. The barn smelled richly of their combined odors but the picket area was clean and well bedded in straw. Many of the animals were lying down. A few stirred at his intrusion. He barely glanced at them, marching down the aisle like a man of authority. A sleepy-eyed apprentice scrambled off a hay bale at the far end of the aisle and came hesitantly toward him. Petre didn't give him a chance to collect himself.

"Ah, there *you* are," he said as though speaking to something slightly lower than any of the other animals in the barn. "My Master wants his rope inside with us tonight. He wants to be sure it will be easy to work with in the morning." For all Petre knew, it might not be an unusual request with the freezing nights.

The boy didn't question him. With his words Petre had placed himself as an apprentice but undoubtedly a senior one and of a trade much more prestigious than livery. He marched right on past the poor boy, heading for where he could see harnesses and other equipment hanging neatly on hooks. He had to spot "his Master's" rope and take it before the apprentice offered to get it for him so it would not become apparent that he didn't know his Master's name.

There were several ropes but no grappling hook hanging with any of them. Petre's heart sank but he couldn't let it show. He stalked up to one harness with a neatly coiled rope hanging with it and hefted the rope as though he owned it. He paused a moment inspecting the harness then gave a disapproving sounding grunt as though the livery apprentice hadn't cleaned and oiled it well enough to suit him. Then he looked around as though missing something and spun on the boy. "Where is our hook?" he demanded. "This rope had a hay hook with it. What have you done with it?"

"I don't remember no hook," the boy stammered.

Snorting contemptuously at the boy's stupidity, Petre strode past him to where the pitchforks and other work implements were neatly hung. There he spotted the kind of hook he needed. "Then I'll just take this one until you manage to remember," he said, taking the hook and heading for the door.

For a moment he thought he'd gotten away with it. Then the apprentice hurried after him.

"Wait. Wait," the boy pleaded, frightened that he would be punished for the loss of his Master's tool. "Your hook must be somewhere. Maybe it's in your wagon."

"Perhaps," Petre said as though he couldn't care less. "Perhaps *you* will find it there, and when I see it with my Master's equipment in the morning I will replace this one."

He kept walking. There wasn't much a junior apprentice could do about it. When he heard the door roll shut behind him, Petre gave up all pretenses and ran.

In the grove where he had talked to Field there was one venerable apple tree that had been allowed to grow taller and closer to the wall than was usually permitted. From the highest branch that Petre dared to climb, he was only about ten feet below the top of the wall and about eight feet away from it. He ran the rope through the hook's looped handle and pulled it through until the hook was at the middle of the rope. Then he took careful aim. The hook had to go over the wall and then catch on something strong enough to hold his weight. And, it had to do all that without setting off the alarm which his people believed to be some sort of motion and impact detector. It was known that no one could climb the wall, dig under it, or make a hole through it without setting off the alarm. Whether a rope and hook would set it off, Petre didn't know. He supposed that when he climbed the rope the alarm would sound. He might have only minutes to scramble up the rope and rappel down the other side of the wall.

He imagined he felt the locket with its tiny dose of death resting against his racing heart and thought of John and Ondre. He must not be captured; he must not betray them. His fighting spirit rose. He was not ready to die. He had to escape. Is was on the other side of this wall.

He stilled his racing emotions and focused on the feel of the rope, the weight of the hook. His first throw took the hook over the wall but it didn't catch on anything as he slowly reeled it back. At least it didn't set off the alarm. He threw again . . . then froze. Voices.

"Damn perimeter patrols," a man cursed. "She's a witch, ain't she. She'll be gone if she wants to be. Besides, *I* don't want to find her."

The two men passed almost beneath Petre's tree and the other man said something low and base.

"Don't let Cowel hear you complain. He'll send you to patrol on the outside if you don't like it here."

For a long time after they'd gone Petre was afraid to pull on the rope, afraid to make any sound, afraid to chance setting off the alarm. He hadn't known there would be guards on the outside. So much for his hopes that once he was over the wall no one would be on the scene the moment the alarm went off. He crouched in the tree and tried to think of another way. By now he had probably been reported missing, so he couldn't go back. They knew Is was gone and they knew he was gone. Maybe he could spin a story about having been bewitched by her and then let go. But while the common soldiers might think she was a witch, the people higher up – the people who would interrogate and torture him – knew the truth. She was just a woman they had shaped and trained to be a tool.

He began to reel the rope in slowly, feeling for any resistance. There. No, it came free as he increased the pressure. He needed something that could hold his weight.

Finally it caught but at the very edge of the wall. Not ideal. He'd better throw again. But now he couldn't pull it free. Well, that would do then. He ran the rope around the trunk of the tree and tied it back to itself with a knot. Then, carefully, he reeled the rope through the hook until the knot was near the wall. Once he was on the wall he'd untie the knot and use the rope to rappel down the other side of the wall. That would take precious time, but the wall was too high to allow him to jump to the ground.

He took the taught rope with both hands and slowly put his weight on it. The trunk gave toward the wall more than Petre had expected and the rope sagged as Petre put all his weight on it, but everything held. The climb was now steeper than he liked. He thought about retying the knot, but his nerves were peaked to go now.

Hanging from both hands, he swung his legs up to wrap his calves around rope. It held. No alarm. He pulled himself along hand over hand with his legs crossed over the rope so they wouldn't dangle free. The smaller a package he made of himself and the less motion he generated in the rope the better. What would normally have been a very strenuous climb, he hardly noticed as he strained to hear the guards returning, the alarm going off, or the hook tearing out of whatever crack or projection it had caught on.

When he reached the wall, he pulled himself up as close as possible. Transferring from the rope to the wall was going to be tricky if he didn't want to set off the alarm. To anchor himself so he could get his hands free he twisted the rope around one leg so that it wrapped around his leg and crossed his foot. Then he placed his other foot on top of it and pressed down hard enough to keep the rope from slipping. Now his hands were free to explore the wall for a good hold. He found what he was looking for, then carefully unwrapped his leg from the rope and felt for a toehold on the wall.

He inched his other leg over the top of the wall. He was lying on his belly with one leg over the top when his supporting toehold gave way. The loose brick clattered down the wall ricocheting off other protuberances. The alarm went off deafeningly.

Petre threw stealth to the wind and squirmed frantically onto the top of the wall. The howling of the alarm stopped as suddenly as it had started.

Petre froze, flattened to the top of the wall. Voices rang out as two spotlights swept the wall in a pattern working their way toward him. They'd see his rope. He thought rashly about jumping off the other side into the pitch dark, a drop of at least forty feet. But what if he broke his leg? Better to lie still and hope they wouldn't see the rope.

No. The guards were being too thorough. Their lights swept the wall and the top of the wall in a pattern. The alarm must have told them right where he was. They would surely find the rope.

At that moment a white shape hurtled through the beam of light and struck the wall. Both guards' lights snapped onto the motion. The owl crumpled like a bag of boneless feathers and slid down the wall. Both lights followed it down.

Petre's fingers dug into the brick. Owls don't . .

"Is it dead?"

"Yeah, looks it."

"You figure it set off the alarm?"

"Damn fool thing for an owl to do."

"Yeah, strange."

"Maybe it saw a mouse. Misjudged is all."

They were silent a moment while Petre wondered if they would remember that the alarm had gone off before the owl had hit the wall. He kept reminding himself that they didn't want to be the ones who found Is.

"Hey, look it's moving."

"Yeah, just knocked itself out for a minute."

Another brief pause followed while Petre hugged the wall, heart pounding.

"Do you think we should, uh, take it in?"

Then he heard the sharp clacking of the owl's bill and imagined the men leaning over it to see if it was a real owl . . . or maybe a witch. But what they saw was a massive hooked bill clacking with a sound reminiscent of finger-sized bones breaking. And indeed that bill could break bones. Petre imagined the owl's angry yellow eyes and how big it would look with feathers ruffled and wings mantled in rage.

"Naw," the other man said. "I ain't messing with it."

"Yeah," his partner agreed. "It's just an owl."

"We better call in for a reset."

"Yeah."

As soon as they were out of hearing range Petre went into action. If they had to call in to have the alarm reset it didn't matter how much noise or movement he made for the next few minutes. Working like a mad man he undid the knot and pulled the rope out of the tree. Then he reset the hook and tossed the rope down the outside of the wall. Grabbing the rope in both hands, he turned his back on the descent and leaned backward into space to repel down. As he was about to take the first step he thought, an owl wouldn't have been hunting that close to a human being. An owl wouldn't have missed a mouse and hit the wall with that much force.

He leaned back until he was nearly perpendicular to the wall. Letting the rope play through his hands he walked backward down the wall until his feet touched the ground.

Albert's Inn was the closest "safe" place to try for, but first Petre had to get as far as he could from the wall and its guards. Accustomed to the dark, he slipped silently from one deep shadow to the next. Suddenly the night split with light.

"Hold! Or I'll shoot."

He should have run, should have forced them to kill him. Already it was too late. One guard was speaking into some sort of communicator.

"I'm lost," Petre said. "Where am I?" He thought his voice sounded properly frightened.

"You're where you bloody well don't belong."

"I . . . we were camping, waiting for daylight to go in. I wandered away to pee, couldn't find my way back . . ."

"Yeah," the guard said, obviously not impressed. "Nobody's allowed to camp this close to the wall."

"The wall," Petre said, amazed. "I had no idea I'd gone so far. I've been wandering half the night. Listen, just show me the way back to the road."

"I don't think so, buddy." The man's weapon didn't waver. Petre recognized it as a nerve pulse interrupter. It would immobilize a person quickly but took a few minutes to kill. They would take him captive. He couldn't get at the locket with that weapon trained on him.

"Listen," Petre said. "I'm a Minister. I'm coming in to attend to my brother's funeral. I have papers." Walking slowly toward the guard, he reached into his cloak. "If you'll just let me show you . . ."

He started to bring his hands out of his cloak, keeping the guard's attention on them, and kicked. The man fell heavily, bellowing, his knee unable to support his weight. His weapon discharged into the air in an eye-searing chartreuse streak. Petre caught the man's wrist and twisted. The man tried to rise and did a half flip over his own wrist. The weapon came free in Petre's hand; he aimed at the man's spine and fired. The man arched and kicked out, his scream covered the sound of running footsteps.

The second guard chose to club Petre's weapon hand with his billy. Petre never saw him coming, spun before he knew what was happening, bending his knees, throwing his hips in front of the man. As the man flipped over Petre, his billy ended up in Petre's hands. The man didn't roll, didn't come to his feet the way any of the Hluit would have. It was easy to hit him with a nerve pulse. Petre spun, looking for number three.

No one.

The first man had called someone. Reinforcements? Or just his buddy?

The flare died, pitching Petre into green-shot blackness. He closed his eyes trying to force them to readjust and opened them to black. Out of the pitch black the man's communicator crackled a question. Every nerve in Petre's body jerked. He began to move forward, feeling for each step with his foot, still trying to readjust his eyes to the dark.

Then to his left, lights swept the ground in great arks. He managed a jog, lifting his legs high, bending his knees with each footfall so he wouldn't trip in a sudden hole or fall over an unseen rock.

More lights came from his right, closing on the spot where the two guards lay. They weren't dead. They'd both seen him. Albert's Inn would be too dangerous for him now. He wouldn't make it there anyway, not once they got their sophisticated night lenses and heat seekers after him. His only thought was to keep going, live as many more seconds as he could. Planning anything was out.

An instant later something enormous lumbered up from the ground in front of him. No time to stop. He tried to turn, slipped and fell, heart racing. The huge shape stood over him and . . . mooed. Another cow grunted to its feet, and another. He'd gotten right into the midst of the herd before they'd had time to react.

The government ran cows here to keep the underbrush down. They were half wild, ill cared-for woods cows that would run from people, or attack if pressed. They hadn't had a chance to run, and now that Petre was being still they seemed to have a hard time seeing him. There was something important about these cows, something a lot more important than the small risk they posed to him. He lay where he had fallen, trying not to pant out loud, trying to think, immersed in the strong scent of cow. He would have smelled them before running into them if he'd been going slower. *Smelled them . . .*

Heat seekers and night lenses would go blind when they hit this much input. Once the guards realized it was just a herd of cows maybe no one would investigate too closely. If he could join the herd?

He kept still, talking silently to them like he did to his horses. After a while they began to settle and some lay down again. He stayed with them all night, huddled against an old matron who was more interested in chewing her cud than being afraid of some puny human.

The searchers swept the area with their infallible machinery, didn't find him, and drew the only conclusion they could draw. He wasn't there.

In the afternoon Petre made it to the road, left the cloak that would mark him as a Minister behind, and walked on the road as boldly as any of the other merchants and farmers. After all, no one would expect him to be going toward the city.

That night he camped practically within the shadow of the gate with some farmers who were too poor to pay for an inn. The next day, by offering his strong young back to help carry supplies, he joined a family going away from the city. By now the search for him would have spread like ripples on a pond moving ever outward from the city. He should be two days behind the searchers, and walking with this peasant family he would soon be even further behind.

He walked with them for eight days, sharing their load, their food and covering less than half the distance he could have covered alone. The eighth day brought them to the cut-off for Steep Pass. When he left the family, the youngest girl cried and the older one looked at him with lovelorn eyes. The mother hugged him and the father clapped him on the back as they wished him well. They insisted he take a few days' rations. He wouldn't take more.

Now he traveled light and fast, away from the road.

Road gossip had contained nothing about Is or about Petre's own escape. He hoped that meant Is hadn't been recaptured or killed. His plan was to contact scouts at Steep Pass and find out if anyone had seen her. If not, he intended to follow the troop that had taken Lark. If Is were still free, that's where she'd go.

Chapter Eleven

Ondre sat his horse and waited, still as a statue among statues. The huge gate to Center stood open before the Hluit delegation but the guards along the wall were watchful with weapons at the ready, not exactly barring the way but looking as though they might.

No one knew the protocol of the situation. No Hluit had ever come to Center or anywhere else in the Alliance openly before. Most of the Alliance citizens didn't even know the Hluit existed.

Snow had been cleared from the boulevard and the gate sweep but everywhere else it was several inches deep and light snow continued to fall.

More guards appeared along the top of the wall. These were armed with the short blunt billies that could be used as a club or they could project an energy beam to incapacitate a man at several dozen yards.

One of the Hluit horses stamped a hoof. Other than that there was no movement among the four riders as they waited, faces impassive.

The Council of Elders had argued that they might be met with force, imprisoned, tortured or killed. Ondre had decided to take the chance, and the other three had their own reasons for being here.

Dhave's bay gelding gave its neck a sudden shake sending the snow that had settled on his mane flying in a cloud. Crystals caught in the air in rainbow colors. Dhave was here because Ondre's brother had killed his best friend. He felt a duty to that friendship and a certain recklessness born of grief and anger.

On Ondre's other side, Phol sat motionless, a dark shadow on a dark brown mare, a presence as true and inevitable as night. And beyond him his aging friend and mentor, Samith hunched in his furs, gaunt-faced and weathered by many years and many miles. As an expert on the Alliance, he also felt a duty to be here, he had helped two generations of Hluit spies infiltrate Center.

Ellie would be here too if they hadn't talked her out of it. "The Alliance will hardly know how to treat us and since they consider women to be second class citizens, having you with us will only make it more difficult," Samith had told her.

Ondre had other reasons for not wanting her to come. He had already lost his brother to some fate more horrible than death. "If they hurt you Ellie . . ." he'd said, stroking her blond hair, holding her against his chest. "I don't know what I would do."

"You will do what you always do," Ellie had said. "You will do your best." Her statement of support was also concession that he might not succeed and it was intended to remove all blame from him.

While many of the Hluit had felt that little could be done to negotiate peace, others were opposed to just sitting passively, waiting for the Alliance troopers to come to kill them.

Ondre intended to do his best to broker a peace agreement but in his heart his main reason for coming here was John. "I can't let John be used this way and do nothing," he had told Ellie, "and I can't let the Alliance get hold of him."

Ellie had taken his hands and looked deep into his eyes. "I know you can't," she had said. "But do you really understand that to stop him you may have to kill him?"

"I believe he is already dead. Or if he has any awareness left, if he knows what he's being made to do, he must be horrified beyond belief."

In the way that Hluit society worked, no one could really forbid Ondre to go, they could only try to talk him out of it. A few people had tried because they believed that trying to negotiate peace with the Alliance was a waste of time; but most understood that Ondre needed to go because of John. They did not trust any agreement the Alliance might make. But once they learned that the Alliance had Lark and Is back, it seemed that Ondre might have a better chance. The Alliance might like to have a face-saving way out of having to make good on their promise to hunt down and kill every last Hluit.

Word had reached Ondre, only two days ago, that Is had escaped and Lark's berserker was riding him into the Boundary undoubtedly to try to find and engage the Mirror. It would not be enough if the Alliance stopped the Mirror for now John was on his way to Center carrying a duplicate copy of the Mirror's intelligence. Once the Mirror infiltrated the Alliance computer network it intended to kill every high Alliance official who might be in on the experiment. Everything had changed drastically. But the Alliance did not yet know. This could give Ondre's group some bargaining power.

Ondre's horse, Felice, raised her head, ears pricked with sudden interest. A moment later a mounted guard came into view on the broad avenue inside the gate. Twelve massive war-horses came forward, four abreast, passing through the stone arch of the gate in a stately trot. They came to a halt a few yards from the Hluit, their horses dwarfing the Hluit's fine-boned smaller animals. Their riders wore full combat gear, but the horses were also bedecked with ceremonial jewel-inlaid bridles, tooled and dyed saddles and rich saddle blankets. They were an honor guard; and yet the weapons on the saddles were real.

The matched bay war-horses stood up square on their pillar-like legs, necks arched. Long shanked bits jingled. Every piece of equipment was shined and polished. The horses' coats gleamed, black manes and tails combed and flowing.

Next to them the Hluit horses looked dirty and ill cared for. The long hairs of their fetlocks had collected clods of mud-colored ice. Their coats showed the roughness of animals who lived out in the snow. Their nostrils were bearded in white-rimed whiskers. But their eyes were alert and attentive. Their saddles were plain but well fitted and their heads were without bridles or bits of any sort.

One of the Alliance riders came forward a few steps and halted. In answer Ondre moved Felice forward too. It was necessary for him to look up at the other rider. There was a long moment of silence as the two men took each other's measure.

The Captain of the Guard was a wide-shouldered lantern-jawed man. His hard-eyed stare had probably intimidated many cadets. His posture was military stiff, his uniform impeccable. He expected obedience and accepted his authority over others as his right.

Ondre, by comparison, sat his horse as if part of her, supple, lithe and natural. The authority he projected was not as easy to define.

Finally the guardsman spoke. "Governor Defroe welcomes the Hluit delegation," he said, stiffly formal. "If you will follow me, suitable quartering has been arranged."

"Please convey our gratitude to Governor Defroe," Ondre answered. His voice carried without apparent force to the honor guard and all those who had collected on the wall. "We require nothing more than stabling for our horses and an audience with Mr. Defroe."

The guard considered that request in stony silence. After a moment he made a hand gesture and another rider came up beside him. They conversed in low voices and then the other rider turned and rode away. Three more riders from the guard peeled off and went with him.

"They will prepare what you request. In the meantime, you will be our guests." The offer was issued with the stiff precision of a military command.

"Of course," Ondre answered with conflicting casualness.

Though the streets had been cleared of all traffic, people huddled to watch wherever there was a suitably concealed place. How they must wonder at the wild looking men, dressed in animal furs, riding freely on horses that were so different from the government controlled war horses and draft stock. At regular intervals there were guards in full combat gear standing at attention as the riders passed. It was all quite ambiguous as to whether they were being honored, or taken prisoners.

With the exception of two riders, one who rode on either side of Ondre, the guard had fallen into formation behind the Hluit riders. There would be no turning back. They followed the Main Way that brought them through the inner walls and directly to the front steps of the main administrative building. It was in truth, a castle. Its massive fortified facade was meant to intimidate those approaching it, protect those within it. The riders passed through the inner walls and paused in the staging area in front of the wide stone steps. Livery apprentices came forward to take the horses.

None of the Hluit dismounted and therefore none of the guard did either. There was an awkward moment while the livery hands stopped uncertainly. Felice pinned her ears and snaked her neck aggressively at the man who had come to take her, forcing the man to step back.

"We will see to our own horses," Ondre said, and nobody disputed him.

"This way," the head of the guard said with what dignity he could muster. Things were not going as planned.

The stable was behind the castle. The grounds, though covered with snow, showed every sign of being immaculately manicured. The stable was as ostentatious as the rest of the buildings attached to the castle. The stalls were enormous and deeply bedded in clean dry straw, yet the Hluit chose to turn their horses loose in the indoor riding arena where hay and water were brought to them. As soon as they were unsaddled, the horses made themselves comfortable by pawing and rolling in the rich loamy soil - which until then had always been maintained in perfect condition for the indoor exercise of the palace horses. With dark-colored dirt clinging to their long coats, the horses looked even more unkempt, but radiated contentment as they dove hungrily into the hay.

The men were shown to a suite inside the castle where they could wash and refresh themselves. Expensively cut suits were laid out for them. Servants arrived with trays of fancy appetizers and remained at their beck and call for any little thing they might need until Ondre dismissed the lot of them.

"Thanks," Dhave said, speaking for the first time since they'd entered the walls. "They were making my skin crawl. People acting like that toward other people." He gave a shiver like a horse shaking flies off its back. It was his first time within the Alliance and the "wrongness" of the place hit him hard.

"They're treating us awfully well," Phol observed, flexing his wide shoulders uncomfortably in the unaccustomed restrictiveness of the suit jacket.

"Don't be fooled by it," Samith said with a shake of his silver head. "Now they'll keep us waiting to see Defroe. We'll be able to get the measure of how much we've displeased them already by how long they keep us waiting."

"At least they didn't throw us directly into the dungeon," Dhave said bleakly.

"No. They want something." Phol removed the offending dress jacket and rummaged in his own pack for more suitable clothing. He came up with a leather vest, worn smooth and dark with use. It matched his dark brown hair and his dark complexion, unusual among the Hluit.

"They have the stallion," Dhave said, scowling at the fancy clothes, smoothing his mustache with his fingers. "What else do they want?"

"They're scared," Samith, the oldest of the group, informed them. His hair was white with age but his keen eyes missed nothing. His frail-looking frame was overlaid with whipcord muscles and not an ounce of fat. "They could have stopped us long before we got all the way here and were seen by their people. They must want something pretty badly."

Samith also chose his own clothing over what the Alliance had offered. Ondre too preferred his Hluit clothes of leather and wool but as a concession to the formality of the occasion, he braided his long blond hair down his back, his narrow handsome face serious and grave.

In a little while there was a knock on the door and a bowing servant asked them to follow him to the Audience Hall. There they were left waiting in a rather austere chamber. The walls were paneled in ironwood taken from trees that grew only deep within the Boundary, in Blueskin territory. Lives had been lost just to panel this room.

The high ceiling was painted in an intricate fresco depicting various Alliance achievements. There were no windows. A fireplace and a massive chandelier, sparkling with precious gems, supplied the light. The only furnishing was an enormous council table that would have sat twenty.

Samith wandered nonchalantly over to the table and propped one buttock on the edge, shattering Alliance protocol with his simple act. He glanced back at the others and gave them a small head motion to disperse. "Everything will be a power play," he had advised. "We must show strength by not letting them have everything their way, and yet it must be done without open confrontation. We must appear innocent of anything except a different standard of manners."

Phol seated himself in the chair at the head of the table, as Dhave settled on the floor, his back against the wall by the door. Ondre was drawn to the fireplace. The rocks that formed its face contained fossils, ancient pictographs and veins of the minerals the Alliance held precious.

Almost an hour later, when the door opened to admit Governor Defroe, a handful of advisors, and a suitable guard, little had changed in the men's positions, except Samith was now sitting completely on the table in a posture of meditation, both legs tucked under him. His hands rested on his knees and his fingers formed circles. Dhave had also fallen into meditation by the door. Neither of those men responded to Defroe's entry, even announced by a courier and ushered in by armed guards as he was.

Pohl also didn't rise. Because he was seated at the head of the table, the Alliance people assumed he was the one they should address. They turned toward him.

Pohl's glance dismissed Defroe with hardly a pause and moved on to the guards' weaponry in the calculating and unhurried manner of an expert martial artist assessing an opponent. In return, the guards' attention riveted on him as the only really dangerous one in the room.

At the fireplace, Ondre spoke. "This is fascinating," he said without preamble and with real warmth and enthusiasm in his voice. "Come, you must tell me, these are pre-colonization pictographs, are they not? But they are not from the caves at Laze?" And he held out his arm welcomingly, almost as though he would drape it around Defroe's shoulders were that man close enough. "They are even older, aren't they? You must tell me . . ."

For six seconds there was complete silence in the room as the strict and regimented Alliance mindset met the unexpected. Then Defroe rose to the challenge. "They are not from Laze," he said, walking toward Ondre. "They are from Morv."

"Then they are from before the land masses shifted," Ondre exclaimed with delight.

"Yes." Defroe responded, his voice stiff and stilted compared with Ondre's. He tugged at his impeccably tailored suit, adjusting some imagined imperfection in its fit and sized Ondre up in his skins and animal hair clothes. Defroe's expression said he had decided he would not have much difficulty with this man.

"As you may know," DeFroe began lecturing in a degrading tone, "the land behind the Boundary was once a separate island. Shifting of the tectonic plates that caused the island to collide with the mainland also caused earthquakes and volcanoes that threw up the mountain range we call the Boundary. Unfortunately the volcanoes also initiated weather changes that led to the extinction of the indigenous people who left these artifacts."

"Fascinating," Ondre said, ignoring that he was being lectured like a schoolboy. "That would explain why they are so different in style from those at Laze. But, see here . . ." and he began to point out the differences and similarities he'd noticed.

DeFroe's advisors were left standing awkwardly and the guard, unable to follow its desired pattern of deployment around the table, remained in an indecisive clump. Ondre smiled to himself. Dhave, who was the best martial artist of his group, was now quietly behind the guard and completely ignored by them. Pohl picked that moment to reinvest their interest in him, rising languidly to his feet. Samith continued in what appeared to be a trance. Or perhaps to the Alliance people it seemed that the old man had dozed off. Without a word passing between them the Hluit had placed themselves in the best strategic position they could manage against armed guards. But it wouldn't come to that, Ondre thought. He wouldn't let it.\

"Perhaps you would care to discuss this topic more, later, with people who are expert in this field," DeFroe said. "For now, I believe you must have more immediate concerns to have come all this way in winter."

"Yes," Ondre conceded easily. "I believe *we*, your people and mine, share some very 'immediate concerns.'"

Defroe drew back, his attitude changing from the openness Ondre had managed to create back to the sly diplomat. "*My* people?" he said as though it was unthinkable that the Alliance would have any problems.

A peal of laughter burst from Ondre, running across the room like the clear happy note of a brook bubbling over stones. He clapped Defroe on the shoulder as if they were old buddies sharing a joke and the guard was too disarmed to react.

"Actually, you are right," he said with a chuckle, "it is not your *people* who have the problem, it is your government."

He went over to the table and spun two chairs to face each other then dropped into one and motioned to Defroe to take the other. Grateful to be done with the games, Defroe took the seat. His advisors scurried around the other side of the table to sit facing the two men and the guard deployed the way they had been taught.

"As you well know, your eternal life experiment has gone amok," Ondre said. "What you might not know is that it intends to infiltrate your computer network, starting here at Center. It intends to give all of you that much coveted life after death," he grinned, "right away."

The effect was electrifying. Defroe came to his feet, making a harsh hand gesture and the guards turned sharply on their heels and headed for the door. As it closed behind them Ondre nodded at the advisors.

"Not them? Are you going to let them hear this?"

"They get to stay," Samith said still seated on the table, eyes still closed. "They are all high mucky-mucks. Seated furthest from you is Scholar of the First Order, Peter Dinn. To his left is Researcher First Level, Jonathan Forth. Next to him is Dan Petree, Treasurer of the Research Fund. The man next to him is Anthony Freeson, whose title escapes me, but who is some sort of research scientist."

"Not on the eternal life project," Pohl interrupted from the other end of the table. "My guess is he's in on the equine end of this."

And into the expectant silence that followed, Anthony Freeson affirmed, "I am Head Master of Equine Research."

"Ah-ha," Samith said as though that revealed a great deal. "Next to him is the man we all know and love, Chief of Internal Security, Stevens," and before anyone could react to his facetious tone he continued. "The sixth man I do not know although he is a scribe of some sort." All this was delivered with his eyes closed and as far as anyone knew Samith had not had them open at all since the men had come into the room. Everyone was staring at him. But now, instead of an undistinguished old man they were seeing a man with a power they had not encountered before.

"I would have expected Mark Mason," Samith continued, blandly naming the man who headed what was left of the research concerning the Hluit Utopian Experiment. "And where is Horse Master DeJohnn?" He named the man who was the last hold out of the line of research begun by don Bocher that had led to the development of the Hluit horses. "But then, perhaps you have not had time to bring him back to Center, since his research is no longer considered important enough to keep him here," he speculated, giving the impression that the Hluit had had this information for a long time, rather than just having received it from a courier a few days ago.

Silence stretched while everyone looked at Samith, still sitting with eyes closed, and now that he was no longer talking, apparently dozing.

"Okay" Defroe said gruffly, pulling everyone away from speculation and the awe it was likely to cause. "You've made your point." He turned back to Ondre. "What do you want?"

"To warn you . . . mostly." Ondre's voice remained friendly.

"Very well," Defroe said guardedly. "How does your *Mirror* intend to infiltrate our computer net?" By using the Hluit's name for the eternal life experiment he intimated that the Alliance also had its ways of gaining knowledge of the Hluit.

Ondre leaned back in his chair, steepled his fingers in front of his face. "Yes, that is a bit of key information, isn't it?"

In the icy silence that followed, all eyes went to Pohl as he paced slowly across the room. "We would all feel much more comfortable if the good Mr. Stevens would remove the device from his left wrist," he said.

Defroe glanced at Stevens, then said to the Hluit in general. "You are my guests."

"Until such time as we are no longer welcome," Ondre added, but his voice was still pleasant.

"So what do you want?"

"Safety, of course."

"If safety was your main concern you would not have come here."

"But it is. We would like to renegotiate our treaty with the Alliance."

"There is no such . . . treaty."

"That may be a good place to start. We wish to be recognized as a free and sovereign people, not under Alliance law. And we wish to be deeded the land we now occupy with all mineral and timber rights."

"You are free . . ." Defroe started.

Ondre held up his hand with such presence that Defroe stopped speaking.

"We can go back and forth arguing semantics for a long time. Unfortunately, we do not have that much time. We have no control over the process by which the

Mirror will attempt the infiltration of your computers. If we are to stop it we need to act quickly and in concert."

There were a few moments of eye contact and silent communication among the Alliance people while the Hluit waited patiently.

"We do not believe there is any danger," DeFroe finally responded.

Ondre eased back in his chair and tipped his head a little as though disbelieving the man's attitude. "You have guards within this fortress dropping dead and no one can explain why. But you do *not* consider that there is danger?" He watched DeFroe's jaw muscles tighten and knew he had surprised that man. Across the table, Stevens was less subtle. A movement of his hands was stopped by a quick glance from DeFroe.

"How do you know about that?" DeFroe asked with forced control.

"*How* is not important now," Ondre shrugged. "We do not have the luxury of much time. The process that your computer set in motion must be contained soon. Once it is within your network here . . ." He turned his palms up signaling defeat.

"If your people had not interfered," DeFroe said, "the problem would have been solved already."

"Ahhh," Ondre drew out the sound, letting it relax everyone in the room. "You are speaking of the stallion, Lark. We had nothing to do with his initial . . . disappearance."

Everyone stiffened at the word. Samith spoke in his detached, unemotional voice, eyes still closed. "Our good Horse Master wishes to speak."

All eyes went to Anthony Freeson who quickly drew back and made negating sounds. After an uncomfortably long time Ondre rescued him. "They are not ready to tell us about the horses," he said to Samith. "It doesn't matter."

There was no response from the meditating man but Freeson met Defroe's eyes, something close to panic in the horseman's face.

"Are you claiming that you never harbored the *stolen* stallion and Isadora Drey?" Defroe said, coming down a little heavy on the word "stolen" so as to set the record straight. "Are you claiming that you did not know she was guilty of treason?"

Ondre dismissed the accusation with a slight twitch of his shoulders. "Now you have him back," he said of the stallion. "And you have sent him and his rider to shut down this experiment."

"Yes," Defroe conceded. "It is all taken care of. You can return to your homeland and reassure your . . ."

From his place on the table Samith interrupted, "He radiates dishonesty."

Defroe pivoted his chair to glare at Samith, who again seemed to be dozing, making it hard for Defroe to accuse an old frail man of calling him a liar.

Ondre spoke in a neutral voice. "If you are not planning to terminate your experiment with the Mirror, what then? Recalibrate it? Start over?"

"It is not something we can just scrap," Researcher First Level Jonathan Forth said hotly. "Have you no idea of the magnitude of what we have achieved? We have learned so . . ." He shut up at a warning glance from Defroe.

Ondre watched them, nodding a little to himself as though he had expected no less. "Well," he said, "now there is the small matter that the 'experiment' is no longer confined to the physical location of the Mirror. It is no longer even confined to our land on the other side of the Boundary. It has discovered a way to mobilize itself and its first intent is to ensure its own survival. It intends to 'preserve' all those people who have been involved with its creation, or who might know how to turn it off. And it intends to take over your entire computer network so there will be no further threats to it in the future. When it is done, the Mirror will be the only one who has any knowledge of how it came into existence. Along with everything else, all knowledge of how to shut it off will be lost."

"Impossible!" the security chief's big voice boomed in the chamber.

"You have seen several 'impossible' things in these last few days," Ondre said in an indifferent voice. "A highly guarded prisoner escapes your fortress, her guards drop dead of no apparent cause and she disappears without a trace." He was attempting to undermine their confidence with his suggestions of how much the Hluit knew about the Alliance.

"So," DeFroe began, trying to regain control of the meeting. "You want us to believe that we are in danger from a computer of our own creation, and that you have come all the way here just to warn us of this danger." DeFroe's tone said he wasn't buying it.

"No. Not just to warn you," Ondre corrected. "To help you stop this threat."

DeFroe drew back a little and studied him a moment. "Why would you want to help us?"

"We have already told you," Ondre repeated. "In exchange we want a written treaty to guarantee our people freedom from Alliance rule, and we want ownership of the lands we now occupy."

"Suppose we do not feel that we need your help?"

Ondre measured him stare for stare. "We have information that you do not have as to how this computer will try to take over." He stood up as though concluding the meeting. "Do not let it take too long to decide that you do need our help. To hesitate can only harm you. "

Pohl stood along with Ondre and spoke. "We can save you some time." Moving slowly under Steven's watchful eyes, he reached into his vest and withdrew a document. He handed it to the man Samith had identified as a Scholar, Peter Dinn. "This is what we want in return for our help."

"We will need some time to look this over," that man equivocated.

"Of course," Ondre agreed.

He headed for the door. Samith opened his eyes, turned and smiled at the people he had named, and then vaulted off the table with the grace and ease of a much younger man and followed Ondre, Pohl and Dhave out the room.

Chapter Twelve

The coals rippled with orange light as the air stirred the campfire. A small yellow flame came into being, ran the length of a branch and disappeared. Petre reached forward with the alltool which was cooking utensil, knife, sometime ice pick and now fire stirrer, and moved the end of an unburned branch further into the coals. A shower of fireflies leaped skyward accentuating the darkness of the night.

"It will snow by daybreak," Deidra said. She was one of the three scouts who had found Petre near Steep Pass, newly escaped from the Alliance with nothing but the clothes on his back. No one argued with her assessment of the weather. They were quiet a while thinking their own thoughts until Dhana voiced them for everyone.

You know that what you're planning to do doesn't make any real sense," she said to Petre.

He didn't answer immediately, his heart too full of pain and his thoughts too reckless.

"If no one's found Is by now she didn't come this way," Phola added, backing up her companion. "Either she didn't make it this far, or she had better sense than to try these mountains alone in winter, or she's dead. You know that as well as we do. It doesn't make any sense for you to go chasing after her stallion just because you think that's what she would have done."

"Besides, what can you do if you catch up to them?" Dhana put in. "Lark's guarded by half the Alliance army." That was an exaggeration but from Petre's point of view it might as well be that many. "You can't control him. And what would you do if you could?"

When Petre didn't defend himself Deidra tried again. "You'd be as well off to stay here. If Is is still alive she may yet come this way."

"I can't." Petre spoke to the fire.

The girls exchanged a glance. "We know how you feel about her . . ." Phola started gently.

"No." Petre spoke more harshly than he meant to. In the silence that followed he tried to explain. "It's not just her. I have to . . . see this through," he finished lamely.

"It's the stallion too, isn't it?" Deidra said. "There's something about him, isn't there?"

Petre was surprised by her observation. "I guess," he said softly. But he thought, it's the whole thing – Lark, Is, Celeste, John. They were something whole together, and now it's torn apart. It has to be fixed. He could feel that imperative need within himself. But he didn't know how to do it.

"If you have to go then I'll go with you," Phola said.

"No. It's bad enough I'll be taking Dhana's skis and pack. That leaves two of you sharing survival stuff while one acts as courier for the news I've given you. Besides, it's stupid enough for me to do what I'm doing. It makes *no* sense for anyone else to come too."

The girls couldn't refute that argument. Deidra spoke for all of them. "Will you at least be careful?"

"Yes. I'll promise you that. I was a scout for four years. I'll be okay." He knew all the winter travel and survival tricks his people had devised. "And I'll be well equipped. You've done all I'll accept." Then to offer some assurance that he would come back, he added. "I'll return your skis in good condition, don't worry." He grinned at Dhana as though that was what she was worried about. But the smile felt false and no one responded to his attempt at humor.

"At least wait until the snow's over," Phola said, and when Petre hesitated she added, "Don't worry. You'll find their trail. They're plowing a virtual highway. Twenty horses packing all their stuff and taking turns breaking the trail." She shook her head in disapproval. "You could find their trail even after a blizzard!"

"Besides we know they're headed through Steep Pass," Deidra added. "On skis you can catch up easy."

"They have patrols out ahead and behind on skis," Phola warned. "You'll have to watch out for them."

"I will."

They all sat a while in silence realizing what they had agreed to. True to Dhana's prediction the storm moved in during the night. Snow and subzero wind chill kept them pinned for two days. With each passing hour Petre's hope of finding Is alive diminished. If she were anywhere in these mountains, her chances of survival were slim. The girls respected his need for privacy as best they could, all crowded inside one tent that was rapidly becoming a snow cave.

The third morning dawned bright and clear, the air as still and brittle as glass. The morning star and red planet were still visible in the crystal sky when Petre set out in one direction and Phola in another. All three girls had hugged him, holding him a moment in an embrace that expressed understanding, love and support better than any words.

Petre pushed himself too hard the first mile or so trying to outrun the pain in his heart until pain in his lungs and the deadening of the muscles in his legs and arms forced him to his senses. After that he set a slow and steady pace, mindful of the demands the extreme cold placed on his body.

Chapter Thirteen

Ondre, Dhave, Phol and Samith had set up camp inside the indoor riding arena with their horses. They had no use for heated rooms, hot running water, or fancy food in the castle.

"How did you do what you did, naming everyone without opening your eyes?" Dhave asked Samith.

"When I heard Phol stand up I knew everyone's attention would be on him so I took a quick look. Fortunately I recognized everyone by description and by knowing who was likely to be there. Then I just kept my eyes closed and listened to where they all went to sit down."

"*Just . . .*" Dhave said, impressed. Tracking the movements of six people with eyes closed seemed quite a feat.

"What's going to happen now?" Phol wanted to know.

Samith answered him. "They want what we know about John and the Mirror. They'll try to find a way to make us tell them."

"But we came here to tell them," Dhave objected.

"But they will not believe us unless they trick us or coerce us into telling them," Samith said.

They were interrupted as a man entered the far end of the arena and walked toward them. The horses were between the new man and the Hluit. As he approached, Felice raised her head from eating and sauntered right into the man's path where she chose to stop. The man also stopped, looking her over with obvious appreciation. Felice stood, head high, ears pricked, eyeing something beyond the man as though she disdained showing interest in a mere human. When the man reached his hand out to her she very pointedly turned her back and found something of interest to look at in the other direction.

Ondre chuckled deep in his throat. "Arrogant witch," he said lovingly of his mare. "Any guesses who our visitor is?"

"He will be either the head of Hluit research, Mark Mason, come to check on the first real live subjects he's had, or the horse researcher from the Bocher Stud, come to see the results of his experiment," Pohl said.

"You can bet on Horse Master DeJohnn," Samith said with a laugh. "Felice wouldn't bother snubbing just anyone so exquisitely."

"Fel," Ondre called in a friendly but softly chiding voice, "let him pass, will you lady?" Felice ignored him. Ondre got up from where he had been lounging on the soft dirt of the arena, dusted himself off and headed around Felice to greet the man.

"I had not expected them to be so independent," DeJohn said without introduction, endearing himself to Ondre immediately.

"She is a bit more than most," Ondre conceded. Felice was now making her grand exit, somehow turning her walk into an arrogant saunter.

"She's gorgeous," DeJohn breathed, further endearing himself to Ondre.

As the other three men came over, Samith's gelding left the hay, circled carefully around Felice, and came to stand among the men for all the world like he was taking part in the conversation. That was too much for the other horses. They all had to come see what was happening. Even Felice came back, although she stopped just out of reach should anyone have the temerity to pet her.

Without further introduction the men fell into horse talk, comparing conformation, personalities, faults and virtues.

As the talk turned to the swiftness and endurance of the horses, DeJohn said, "I would love to see them in action," and that was all it took. The four men swung onto their horses, bare-backed and bridleless. Felice and Ondre took the lead as they circled the arena at a gallop. Then for a while the Hluit exhibited incredible horsemanship as their horses did sliding stops, rollbacks and spins. Then, at a gallop, Phol removed his jacket and placed it on the ground. The next rider, galloping by, leaned down from his horse and picked it up. A few strides later, he leaned from the other side of his horse and placed the jacket on the ground for the next rider. This went on until each had picked up and replaced the jacket. Then Pohl retrieved his jacket and put it back on while still galloping. In finale, the four riders galloped abreast straight at DeJohn and came to a sliding stop in front of him, close enough to cause him to lose his nerve and step back at the last second.

Then the talk turned to training and from time to time one rider or another broke away from the group to demonstrate some fine point of horsemanship.

Hours later DeJohn was still with the Hluit but now they sat around an impromptu campfire outside the arena eating trail rations. They could have been dressed in fancy clothing, eating fine food at a table inside the castle, but none of them would have been as comfortable. The subject had broadened from horses to anything that came up, except no one had broached the truly important matters that had bought the Hluit to Central.

"So," Samith said with no change from his friendly tone of voice, "you have been chosen to infiltrate our little group, gain our confidence and find out . . . what? Why we really came? What we really know?"

Into the dead, and suddenly cold, silence that followed, Ondre said congenially. "It's all right. We might even tell you."

DeJohn started to deny everything, changed his mind, started to speak again, then stopped.

"It's better if we just drop the games," Samith said. "And your bosses are right, we will tell you some things we would not tell them."

"Besides, they obviously know they are in grave danger or they would not have allowed us in," Pohl added.

DeJohn began to deny the implications of that remark.

"Stop," Ondre said calmly. "We will make better progress if you respond honestly. Your bosses cannot hear you here and when you repeat our conversation to them you can 'remember' it any way you like."

"Okay," DeJohn relented. "They thought I would have the best chance to make friends with you because of the horses. But they are not only interested in what you might tell me. They want me to tell you something."

"What?"

"About your horses."

"Oh," Pohl said in a slightly bored voice. "If you're going to tell us about their psychic ability and about the problems at don Bocher's stud, we know all that."

DeJohnn didn't hide his surprise. "How can you know about that?"

"Not one of the things we're going to tell you, I'm afraid," Ondre said. He wasn't about to let the Alliance know that the information came from a courier who had talked to Petre, who had learned it from a man many years dead who had relayed it to Petre just days ago.

"Not ten people in the Alliance know about don Bocher," DeJohnn said, amazed. "That line of research fell out of favor long ago but it was never stopped completely. The researchers were exiled to the far side of South until they produced the stallion you call Lark. Now it is top priority and I'm the head of it."

"Why are you here, then, when Lark is on his way back into the Boundary?" Pohl asked.

"I'm not needed there. Lark is . . . a finished project."

"Lark is going to die," Samith interpreted, his voice distant and without emotion. He closed his eyes, his features serene in the warm light of the fire.

DeJohnn stared at him.

"Oh, you didn't see him do that before," Pohl said offhandedly. "But they must have briefed you."

"Yes," DeJohnn admitted. "They said he might be able to tell if I lie."

"There you have it," Pohl said, with a palms up gesture as though enjoying himself.

"So Lark is to carry a berserker to fight the Mirror one last time," Ondre said, getting the conversation back on track. "What's special about this berserker?"

"He will deactivate the experiment, the Mirror," DeJohnn said.

"Even if it kills him?" Ondre asked.

"Yes, especially if it kills him. When the Mirror assimilates him, as it does all berserkers, it will infect itself with a virus that will shut it down."

"Without destroying what certain people in the Alliance want to retrieve from its memory?"

"Yes."

"It won't work."

"Why?"

"Because it won't matter if they stop that computer. It has duplicated itself and it intends to get into the Alliance computer network here at Center and take charge of its own future."

"How?"

Ondre met Pohl's eyes for a moment. Pohl nodded. Samith also nodded, eyes still closed. Ondre looked away not ready to concede this yet.

"That's one of our bargaining cards," he said to his friends.

"I am authorized to give you something in return," DeJohnn said.

"What?"

"They are ready to concede most of what you want in your treaty."

"Why?" Ondre's voice was filled with hard suspicion.

"You should ask Mark Mason for the details, but according to the projections about the Hluit experiment . . . I mean, about your people," he stammered, suddenly embarrassed, "you would reach this stage right about now."

"What stage?"

"Uh, well . . . that you would confront us, even at grave risk, and demand your freedom. Supposedly the best thing to do, for the continuation of the experiment – that is the experiment concerning your people – is to grant you most of the rights for which you'll ask."

"So," Dhave said, "if we'll already get what we want without giving anything in return, why should we give them anything?"

"That just tells you how much they'll honor such an agreement," Phol stepped in. "We're still an experiment to them. They'll let us believe they've granted us our freedom, but then they'll switch the rules at their convenience."

Even DeJohn didn't refute that. Finally Ondre spoke. "A written treaty is better than no treaty and we already knew we couldn't trust them."

"If they agree not to come and hunt us down over Lark and Is, at least that will postpone the day that they may do such a thing," Samith said. "We knew we could not make a lasting peace, but a truce now is at least part of what we came for."

"I think it is time to tell them," Dhave said grimly to Ondre. "I don't see how we can hope to do what we have to do without their help."

Ondre met his eyes. He had not forgotten that his brother had killed Dhave's best friend, or that he had come to stop John from being used to kill, enslave and destroy others.

"Yes, tell him," Samith said. "DeFroe will believe it quicker from him than from us, and time may well be running out."

Ondre looked away. He felt uneasy with the decision, but he was unable to put his finger on a good reason to not go along with what his friends and advisors wanted. He took a deep breath.

"Your bosses will be familiar with a man named John Teal." He paused to see if DeJohn would recognize the name.

"Is he not dead?"

"No, but I can see you know about him." Ondre's voice sounded more harsh than he'd meant for it to be.

"Only that he tried to learn too much. The Alliance doesn't like people who don't stay in their places. They treated him like they treat all such people. They took away his ability to communicate anything he might have learned. Then they offered him what we call 'guilt's choice,' the chance to run. If he had stayed he would not have faced further harm. He chose to run. The supplies he took were poisoned. He should be dead."

No one said anything immediately so DeJohn drew the rest of the conclusion for himself. "He was a Hluit spy. He made it back to your people."

"Yes."

"So now he is going to help the Mirror destroy the Alliance."

"Not exactly. He *is* the Mirror."

DeJohn glanced from one to the other of the men looking for a clue to help him understand. "I don't understand," he finally said.

"He went inside the Mirror, and it knocked him out somehow, probably destroyed most of his mind."

"Wait," DeJohn pleaded. "He went inside the Mirror? That's not possible."

"Then you have a lot to learn about this monster you've created," Pohl said cynically.

Ondre ignored them and repeated the story in its shortest form, his voice forced. "The Mirror took over John's body, brought him here, to Center," he finished. "It will transfer itself back into your computers. It plans to kill anyone who knows enough to want to terminate it."

"But I don't understand," DeJohnn said. "Even if it got back into the network, how could it kill anyone?"

"Using John, the Mirror killed armed and forewarned Hluit scouts to get here."

"You think it might make an army of people like John?"

"It may already have done so."

DeJohnn shook his head, troubled. "Why would you care if the Alliance computer system fails? Or if the Mirror kills all our highest officials. Don't you consider us to be your enemies?"

Samith spoke without opening his eyes. "John was Ondre's brother."

Silence settled around the men while they waited for DeJohnn's response.

"So you have some sort of moral obligation to stop him?" DeJohnn guessed.

"You should ask Mark Mason to explain it to you," Pohl said snidely. "He knows everything about us."

DeJohnn let the barb pass. "Even if my bosses decide that you're trying to help us stop John, the things you've said he can do still don't seem possible."

"Of course," Pohl said, "and it is also impossible that armed guards dropped dead outside a woman's cell. But they did."

"You know how she killed them?"

"She didn't. They were killed by ghosts."

DeJohnn shook his head, overwhelmed. Samith rescued him. "Our good Horse Master is not understanding. We need to explain better."

So Pohl told how the ghosts were what was left of the berserkers the Mirror killed. And how it had completed its program, but did not want the Alliance to know because it did not want to be terminated.

"The Dark Bodies gain power every time they kill," Ondre said. "They could be the way the Mirror intends to kill the people who know too much."

DeJohnn lowered his head into his hands, seeking privacy to think.

Samith wouldn't give it to him. "We've told you quite a bit, now tell us about Lark."

"You seem to know," DeJohnn equivocated. This meeting was not going the way he had been briefed to expect.

"We know that he can travel through time," Phol said. "What else?"

"He was the product of a separate line of research that was not going to be connected to the Mirror. But somehow the Mirror seems to have developed some of the same abilities. It seems to be using those abilities to hide from us. It can do some pretty confusing things with a person's sense of time. Oh it always killed the berserkers we sent it. But we could tell it was not giving us a full account. And then the last several berserkers we sent couldn't find it. We knew we had lost control of it. Lark might be the only horse who can find the Mirror when it doesn't want to be found. And he is keyed to the only berserker who is infected with the virus that can shut the experiment down. That's why we need him now."

"But you must have bred others like him," Dhave suggested.

"No, we haven't been able to duplicate him."

"Why not?" Pohl demanded, suspicious.

"The horse you call Lark was a cross between a don Bocher mare and a certain war stallion. The mare that bore him died and we cremated her not knowing what she had produced. We didn't save any tissue samples from her, and we'd let our gene pool of don Bocher horses get too small. As it turned out, she was the only one left with the exact gene sequence we needed."

"They need our horses," Samith said and his eyes flew open. "Sweet rain, they have *no* intention of ever letting us go home."

"No, it doesn't have to be like that," DeJohn said quickly. "We only need to do a gene scan on some of your horses, find one with what we need, borrow her for a while, or buy her. Whatever you want."

"Unless we don't want to cooperate," Pohl said coldly.

"Then what?"

"I don't know. They don't tell me that sort of thing. But it wouldn't be very wise."

"You're so sure they'll find what they need?" Ondre asked.

"Yes, the don Bocher horses are descended from yours." In the silence that followed he realized he had said something wrong.

"We had thought it was the other way around," Ondre replied. "We thought our horses came from don Bocher's research and that perhaps our ancestors had taken them to keep them from being terminated the way other experiments have been."

"No, your horses were here first. They came from North Island when it was separate from the mainland. They survived the collision of the island with the continent that formed the Boundary mountains, but those mountains also stopped the horses from migrating and so their genes stayed pure. They are an ancient breed, indigenous to this planet. They survived the weather changes that killed the indigenous people who were here when the Alliance landed. The Alliance used those horses to improve the draft stock they'd brought with them. The cross breeds eventually became the war horses. But we got more than we bargained for when we crossed the two breeds. Don Bocher was the only one to recognize it for what it was and try to breed for it. But as I said, that line of research fell out of favor long ago."

"But now you want to revive that research because you realize you need the ability those horses had in order to find your damn Mirror. And what else? What else will your research uncover that you can do with those horses?" Ondre demanded, not expecting an answer.

"I can't answer that," DeJohn said. "But if you're looking for a bargaining chip, something the Alliance wants badly enough to let your people alone, then I should think the horses would be it."

"Except that they can take our horses any damn time they want," Phol said.

"If you make that the only way they can get them, then I suppose they will," DeJohnn said.

"So you're saying we should bargain with them? Our right to continue living like we are if we let them take whatever horses they need for their breeding program?"

"It would be the easiest way. It would save us enough trouble that it would be worth giving you the treaty you want in exchange. And they really would leave you alone as long as you keep breeding the horses we need."

"Except that you can breed them for yourselves," Ondre pointed out.

"It's not just the breeding," DeJohnn replied, "it's also the way they're raised."

Samith had been sitting quietly with his eyes closed again. He stood up suddenly. "Enough for tonight," he said.

Following his lead, Ondre stood and stretched muscles that were beginning to harden from the cold. The fire was no more than coals now and no one had offered to feed it. Something about what he'd heard about the horses bothered him deeply. *The horses survived when the indigenous people did not.* It seemed unlikely. Perhaps those people had had more to contend with than just the climate change when the island collided with the main land. Perhaps the Alliance had wiped them out.

The other men also got to their feet. DeJohnn took his leave. Dhave stirred the coals apart and covered them with snow. Smoke rose from the hissing remnants until the cold subdued it.

"Why did you stop the meeting?" Ondre asked Samith.

"Because we need to regroup. There's more to this than just the horses."

"He started to tell us there was something about the way the horses are raised."

"Yes, and he hinted that the Alliance really would leave us alone as long as we keep breeding the horses."

"They need us. They can't do it without us."

"But that doesn't make sense," Ondre objected.

"It does to them. And we better figure out why. And we better not let them know we figured it out."

Chapter Fourteen

Petre took the short route, up and over, to South Pass and got there ahead of the slow moving Alliance army. From Citadel he saw the skier dogging his trail. The worst problem with winter was that you couldn't get rid of your tracks unless the wind or the snow helped you.

When the skier disappeared from view in the next valley, Petre had time to ski back down his tracks half a mile until he was in the forest again. He picked a spot, jumped up and caught the low hanging branch of a tree and swung himself up. From there he was able to climb to the other side of the tree, drop onto his skis and slide away. Only an expert tracker could tell what he had done.

Petre made a big circle and came back to watch what his follower would do. The skier was highly skilled, getting the maximum glide with each step even though the land was slightly uphill. He entered the woods and Petre waited. In a surprisingly short time the skier emerged again on the proper track, not fooled at all by Petre's exertions to hide his trail. The skier stopped in the open, looked up at where Petre was hiding and shouted, "Petre, if you're still around stop hiding, it's me, Phola."

Petre shoved himself off from under the trees above her, crouched low for maximum speed as he swooped down on her, and rooster-tailed to a stop beside her.

"I thought you'd want to know," she told him without preamble. "We found Is. The Blueskins have her."

It took Petre a moment to dig the right question out of the jumble of his emotions. "Where?"

It was unusual for Blueskins to be out much in the winter, but perhaps they had shifted their strategy with all the Alliance movement

"Sacred Grounds. A huge gathering is being called there."

"Why?"

"We're not sure. It's a war gathering. We think they intend to attack Center."

"Whatever for?"

"We don't really understand. Maybe only because they can't fight too well in these mountains now. So they'll take the fight to Center where the snow isn't so deep."

"That's crazy. Center is a fortress."

Phola shrugged. "They are in High Blood. They are not necessarily rational."

"What about Is?"

Phola couldn't meet his eyes. "They're going to test her."

Petre sank back on his skis. The snow crunched and gave a little under his weight. "Why?" It was barely a whisper.

"Alliance people have gotten them questioning whether she has the magic they believe she has. They're going to make her prove it."

"What will the test be?"

"Fire."

"And if she really has magic she'll rescue herself by disappearing?" Petre guessed. "Otherwise they'll burn her at the stake."

"That seems to be the idea."

"Who else is at Sacred Grounds?"

"Demeitre and Darrell. You're going then?"

"Yes."

"I thought you would." Phola touched his arm. "Close to a hundred warriors are there and more coming in all the time. There is probably nothing you can do."

"Is can't make herself disappear without her stallion. They share the magic. I can tell the Blueskins that."

"Petre, the Blueskins are in High Blood. They are not rational."

"I know." He knew he wasn't particularly rational either.

"We can get more Hluit to go with you . . ."

"No, we don't need a war with the Blueskins. Let them fight the Alliance."

"I'll go with you at least."

"No." Then he softened his rough voice. "Please don't. Either I can do something, or I can't. More people won't help and you have more important business."

She sighed, removing her hand from his arm. "Good luck."

"Thanks." He was already turning himself around. He paused before pushing off. "Thanks for coming to tell me."

She shook her head. "I probably shouldn't have."

Releasing his ski pole he reached out and touched her gloved hand where it rested on her own pole. "I'm glad you did."

Then he shoved off, and again, and again, gaining speed down the face of the mountain.

No point in going cautiously. No point in conserving himself the way one should travel in winter. If he didn't get to Sacred Grounds fast there was no point in getting there at all. There probably was no reason for going anyway but Petre didn't let himself think about that.

Downhills required less physical effort but more concentration. That change in the snow there, the way it had drifted in a swirl, could mean danger – gullies, rocks, saplings bent and buried. Uphills were harder physical work but less taxing mentally. Sometimes he could pole himself up, distributing the work throughout his body, arms and legs and breath working in concert. On steeper slopes he had to walk up a step at a time, his skis turned at thirty-degree angles to each other, leaving a herringbone pattern in the snow. There was a rhythm to every type of terrain but he could not enjoy it. He had to keep himself at the upper edge of what was possible for him, not just for a while but for a whole day and then he would have to do it again the next day.

For a while Petre had the added burden of fear, worried that he would not be able to keep going. The weather would change, he would be too late, and he would not be able to do anything once he got there. He would watch Is tied and burned and he would get himself killed because he wouldn't be able to stand it. Adrenaline gave him too much energy, false energy that made his heart pound too fast, made his instant-to-instant judgment of the terrain suspect.

He was struggling within himself and with the land when something overtook him. It seemed to sweep over him from behind like a giant bird on huge wings casting an enormous shadow that rippled over the gleaming snow. In its shadow his rhythm changed, his heart rate slowed, his breathing. He heard Ondre's voice instructing in one of the martial art classes.

"There is energy all about you. It is a fallacy to think you must create your own when it is in every growing thing even in their winter sleep. And it is not just in living things; it is in the weather, the land, the sky, water. In daily life you bring these things inside yourself. You breathe the air. You eat the plants of the land and metabolize them into energy. But you also bring in energy in other ways, through your eyes and through every pore of your skin. You are less aware of these ways, they are more subtle, but more direct. They are quicker or instantaneous. In times of great need you can use this energy directly. If you let it flow unhampered through you it is inexhaustible, always renewing. You are part of it. You can draw directly from it, but not if you cling to it, not if you hold it. Release it and more will come on your next breath."

The lecture faded into the recesses of Petre's mind from where it had come, unbidden. He had not paid much attention to Ondre's lectures. He had only been glad to rest from the strenuous workouts that always preceded and followed them. When Ondre taught the martial art class the pace was always incredible. Petre had had no idea he knew any of the lectures by heart. He would have been surprised if he'd spared any attention for it. But he was in another state of mind now, beyond words, where energy flowed unhampered through his body, a body of light. It was a place where fatigue, worry, and even rational thought were impossible. There was only the energy, flowing from the cold snow, the bright air, the waiting trees, the small animals in their burrows.

Slowly this essence changed from day to night. The sun was gone and the moon rode high and the world had a different feel to it – very sacred. He skied a frozen river of light the moon had laid on the snow until his eyes, moon-blinded by the glare saw nothing but light and he skied, not to Sacred Ground, but to the moon. He followed the moon over mountains, over valleys, until he saw it settle in the trees and it brought him back to earth. When it sank, taking its light to the other side of the world, another energy arose – pre-dawn energy. Neither moon nor sun ruled here. Here was an opening into some other sort of temperance. Petre had no rational mind left to question or explore, or feel fear, he simply allowed to flow through himself an intangible force he could not name: the energy of death.

The sky lightened without his noticing. The first piercing rays, as the sun climbed over the mountain behind him, found him wandering in a confusion of energy patterns.

It also found him descending the final run into the Blueskins' Sacred Grounds. A permanent cloud of steam rose from the hot springs there. The smell of sulfur filled Petre's nostrils. Earth energy dominated in the shadow of the steam.

Petre found himself walking on bare ground, skis left behind. He was followed by Blueskins, unhappy with his presence in a place they had claimed, but the power that filled him knew no claim. It could not be held, contained or chained. It did not belong to them, or him. He belonged to it.

He saw Is without feeling any of the recognition his heart and body had always felt before. He saw instead, an aura, dark and twisting in on itself like the spirals of hot steam twisting in the cold air behind her. He saw the ropes that bound her like chains of brilliant light – wrong in the dark, slow, unbindable feeling of this place. That, more than any rational thought, drew him.

The touch of the ropes was either very hot or very cold. It burned through him without defining itself in terms of any sensation for which he had words, not even pain. The fibers untwined. The ropes fell apart in his hands.

Petre felt the surge of human emotion all around him. He had been unheeding of the Blueskins – trapped in a deeper pattern as he was – but now he turned, confused, and found himself surrounded by hundreds of warriors, their rage coursing in his veins: High Blood. It was a force that had built too far to be contained. It didn't occur to him that he could direct it.

At his back he felt Is, felt the broken half of her, the need to reconnect . . . and he said the words out loud. "Return her stallion to her."

He was unaware of much after that. Using words returned him to another reality, a reality in which he inhabited an exhausted, starved, dehydrated and hypothermic body with a brain that managed consciousness only in snatches. But it was also a reality in which he was seen as a minion of a goddess. Under her power he had traveled an impossible distance. He had broken the stoutest rope with his bare hands. And he had given an order the Blueskins believed was straight from their goddess.

Petre woke to a deserted camp. The trampled ground told of the many people who had been here recently. The hill he had descended was now marked with the strange pattern of a hundred snowshoes. The skiers had gone first and the snowshoes had obliterated their tracks. They had taken Is.

"You are well?"

Hluit dialect. A guarded question with overtures of awe in the voice. He turned and recognized Darrell, his weathered face lined with something more than age, a deep responsibility. Petre remembered his people then, on the brink of a war they could not win, could not even survive. An elder, like Darrell, would feel that in his bones, he would feel responsible for every life, every child. It explained this care-worn face, but did not explain the tone of voice or the thing Petre saw in the elder's eyes as though he had looked into a great mystery and been awed and humbled.

Petre ached in every bone in his body. The question had not asked that, it had asked something bigger, something uncommon. He didn't try to answer it.

"Where have they gone?"

"To take the stallion away from the Alliance army."

"Why?"

Darrell looked at him oddly. "Because you told them to," he said simply.

Petre turned away from the questioning eyes, and from the other thing in those eyes that he could not understand and did not want to face.

He was appalled. "I told them to do that? People will be killed."

"You don't remember? You came in here, radiating, I don't know, an aura. You walked through a hundred Blueskins and right up to Is and no one stopped you. You . . . you untied her. And then you . . . told them to get her stallion back."

Petre found support against a boulder. "I don't remember," he said, which wasn't quite true. He did remember something like a dream. What he remembered bore little similarity to what he had just been told. Darrell offered more information.

"Demeitre couriered the news. I stayed with you."

After several minutes of silence Petre remembered that he should thank this elder who had looked after him. The word fell harsh and without preamble on the still air. He did not mean to be ungrateful or ill mannered, especially with an elder. He made another effort to pull himself together.

"How long ago?" he asked of the tracks on the hillside. A simple question, a simple answer would be a place to start reorganizing.

"Two days."

Fear came out of nowhere and hit him like the kick of a horse. His body jerked itself around to face Darrell. "I have been unconscious for two days?"

"Not always unconscious" the older man said with a wry laugh. "It was sometimes hard to detain you."

"Why?"

"You were in no condition to travel."

Petre turned away, turning his back on all the things that didn't make sense. He had not asked why he *should* have been detained; he had asked why it was hard for an old master *to* detain him. "I am ready to travel now," he said.

"It might not be wise."

Petre found his laughter. It exploded into the quiet air. "I haven't done anything wise in a very long time. I don't think I should start now."

Darrell chuckled. The tension eased between them. "We will travel at my pace," the elder said. "I will call the halts. You will not leave me behind."

The mixture of humor and authority mollified Petre. "Fine." He had begun to realize how weak he was, as though he had been sick a long time. He would need help.

Chapter Fifteen

The day after seeing the Hluit demonstration of horsemanship, Horse Master DeJohn invited the Hluit to attend a review of the war stallions that were kept at Center. Though trained in all the battle airs, these horses were kept for show. They would never bond with a berserker or face the Mirror.

The invitation was to a formal affair with Governor Defroe, all of his advisors, and every dignitary of any note attending. The review was held in a special arena that was part of the castle complex. A massive building of quarried graystone housed both the arena and its attendant stable. Encircled by raised seating platforms, the performance area featured a high vaulted ceiling with enormous wooden beams that gave the whole place an atmosphere of age and tradition.

DeJohn ushered the Hluit to box seating at the end of the arena where comfortable high-backed chairs awaited them. They were joined by Governor Defroe, Equine Researcher Anthony Freeson, Scholar of the First Order Peter Dinn, Researcher First Level Johnathan Forth, and a man they had not met before.

Playing host, DeJohn introduced the new man. "May I present Mark Mason," he said, with no mention of Mason's position as head of the ongoing research concerning the Hluit. His presence could have been an awkward reminder that to the Alliance the Hluit were test subjects of an experiment allowed to continue only by the good graces of the superior force.

Mark was a small man with a soft voice and a self-effacing presence, belied by penetrating blue eyes that didn't miss a thing. "It is a pleasure to meet representatives of a people I have read so much about," he said diplomatically, in a disarmingly gentle manner.

Musicians assembled below them. A fanfare was played and the parade of the stallions began. To stately music, the magnificent horses circled the ring, necks arched, stepping high in a cadenced and collected trot. Their riders sat motionless in formal black and white attire, long black coat tails moving gently with the horses' rhythm, black boots polished to a reflective sheen. The horses were all matched bays. Their flowing black manes and tails rippled to the music as their hooves struck the ground in perfect unison with the beat, shaking the long black feathers on their massive legs with each step.

The horses turned, some to the left, some to the right, parting and coming together again in intricate patterns. Their strides matched perfectly, their obedience was impeccable.

As the music changed, the stallions changed from trot to canter on the exact beat. They rocked with majestic grace, making small turns and precise patterns with such balance and authority that they seemed to conduct the music through their own movements.

Complete silence settled over the stands as everyone watched, awestruck and enthralled. The only man who wasn't watching the stallions was watching the Hluit with as much attention.

This was an entirely different sort of horsemanship from theirs. Collected, controlled and precise. And though the horses wore long shanked bits, the riders never pulled punishingly on their sensitive mouths. In fact the riders never seemed to move at all.

The music changed again and the pattern came together so that all the horses stood, square as the square cornered stones of the building, in a perfect line. Then two stallions came forward. Facing each other but not engaging, they reared, striking the air with their front legs. Then they executed a complicated maneuver, circling by side stepping, always facing each other and rearing at intervals.

As they returned to the line another rider came forward. His horse leaped high in the air and lashed out with its hind legs. Its lethal iron-shod hooves flashed, catching the light. Landing, it spun, surprisingly agile, leaped and lashed out again and again at the four points of the compass.

Two more horses entered at a safe distance and together the three of them executed the same maneuver. Then all three faced the Hluit's box, reared high on their hind legs and advanced step by step, their massive front hooves thrashing the air in an incredible display of balance, obedience and raw power. They touched down and reared again. Low this time, a tight crouch, sitting deep in their powerful hindquarters, front legs tucked in close – the embodiment of power collected like enormous compressed springs. On a signal, none of the observers could see the horses sprang forward from that position. Now their bodies were like battering rams. They landed in the same position and launched themselves forward again.

They returned to the line to the thunderous applause of the audience, then all the horses reared in that tightly compressed way that promised so much destructive power. The riders doffed their hats in a regal and unhurried gesture, as though their horses could hold that position forever. The final fanfare was mostly lost in applause as the horses filed from the arena.

Voices rose in a murmur, awed and proud and congratulatory as people stood to leave. But Ondre sat motionless, his gaze wandering the dispersing crowd without seeing them. He did not hear one of the advisors speak to him, asking how he had liked the performance. His eyes eventually met Samith's. Mark Mason did not miss the depth of emotion exchanged in their gaze.

Ondre rose and bowed formally to his hosts. He thanked them and excused himself. Dhave, Phol and Samith went with him, wandering silently back to the arena where their own horses lounged about.

"That was incredible," Dhave finally said.

"Yes, they are master horsemen in their own way," Phol agreed.

Ondre concurred with a nod. "I almost wish they weren't."

"Ahhh," Samith breathed, understanding perfectly. "The 'enemy' are master artists. It is hard that they are also cruel and misguided."

"Yes, I guess that is it," Ondre said softly.

Samith stood back watching him a moment before he spoke. "They are trying to get at you. You know that. They will try anything they can to throw us off balance and now they are being advised by their Hluit expert, Mark Mason."

"I understand that," Ondre said. "Nonetheless they have managed to affect me rather deeply." He knew that Samith was trying to assess his emotional stability and therefore his reliability to continue as the leader of their little group. He had not asked to be their leader; it had just been obvious that they all saw him that way. He had not really questioned it. He'd become accustomed to others deferring to his leadership in Hluit society where such things were very informal and based on trust. Now he stood under Samith's scrutiny and wished that Ellie were by his side. He would trust her to know if his judgment was too impaired by grief over John and fear for all his people to make the right decisions here.

"We would do well to remember that they created their artistry at the expense of so many people," Phol said. "Their whole apprentice program, their whole educational system is a systematic attempt to destroy freedom, expression and artistry."

"Yet some survives," Dhave mused.

"Yes, for a lucky few. The rest of the people are sacrificed wholesale."

"The same is true of their science," Samith said. "It is used only to benefit a lucky few."

"Still," Ondre said, "I would hate to see it all destroyed. There is much of worth here, if only . .

"If only," Pohl finished for him, "they administered it with fairness and equality."

"I guess," Ondre half agreed. "At least that would be a start." But there was more to it. Ondre could feel what that was but he couldn't express it. It had to do with heart, with attitude, with the idea driving the whole thing. That was where the wrongness lay and that would not be easy to change.

"Are you thinking that maybe we shouldn't try to stop John?" Samith voiced the thought for everyone.

"If he gets through and the Mirror does destroy the Alliance society, perhaps it could be rebuilt better?" Dhave ventured.

"By whom?" Ondre asked, his voice rough with anger. "The most ruthless people will be the ones who will try to take it over. There will be horrible fighting, one war lord against another. All the people will suffer and when the new leader is decided, the people will be no better off than they are now, possible worse."

"Unless, of course, we were the new leaders," Samith said calmly.

"Dangerous waters," Pohl warned.

"But it's something we have all thought about," Samith persisted. "We must not be afraid to look at all options."

They were interrupted as the door at the far end of the arena opened and two men hustled in. Their movements were quick and jerky as though too much adrenaline flowed in their blood.

"Trouble," Pohl said needlessly as they all recognized DeJohn and Mason. "Be *very* careful." The Horsemaster and the Hluit expert were the two people who were most likely to cause the Hluit to slip.

Mason spoke as he approached. "We have just received very bad news. A large group of Blueskins attacked the Alliance army. Over a hundred Alliance troopers are dead or injured and the Blueskins have taken the stallion."

The Hluit were stunned into momentary silence. Phol was the first to recover.

"Where?"

"South Pass."

"South Pass, Left Fork I'd bet," Pohl guessed. "Perfect place for an ambush."

"Yes, that's where it happened. The Blueskins drew an avalanche across the retreat."

The Hluit exchanged glances. They now encircled the two Alliance men and even Ondre hadn't noticed it happen.

"An avalanche," Samith spoke what they were all thinking, "that's not a Blueskin tactic."

"And why didn't they slaughter all the Alliance army?" Pohl asked. "Once they had them trapped that's what the Blueskins would do."

"Maybe they just wanted the stallion," DeJohnn offered.

"Not likely," Pohl countered. "An army of Blueskins in High Blood have the enemy in an ambush, no retreat, and they don't kill them all? No, something happened there you're not telling us."

The two Alliance men looked at each other, then around at the Hluit and seemed to realize for the first time they could be in some danger of their own.

"We have told you the news as we received it," Mason said. "We were told that Isadora Drey was with the Blueskins. But when the avalanche started the Blueskins ran away."

"Is was with the Blueskins?" Ondre questioned.

"Blueskins don't run away from much," Samith said at the same time.

"Maybe Isadora ordered them to leave after they retrieved her stallion," DeJohnn suggested.

"Unlikely, Blueskins would never obey a woman," Phol said, "even if she is like a god to them."

"There is more you are not telling us," Samith said, his eyes closed, face impassive.

Everyone looked at him, noting the change in his voice. Beside him, Pohl stood in the unobtrusive ready stance of the Hluit martial artist with his hands open and slightly raised in front of him as though they had a life of their own. Dhave had assumed a similar stance behind them, relaxed in a way that had nothing to do with slowness or inattention.

"If you can not, or will not, be truthful, there is little point in continuing," Ondre said.

DeJohnn glanced at the men nervously and made a decision. "We were supposed to tell you just enough that you would realize something very strange had happened. We are supposed to find out how much you know about what is really going on."

"Why do you care what we know?" Ondre asked.

The two Alliance men exchanged a glance.

"Knowledge is power," Pohl answered for them. "It is the only currency they really value." It was a warning to Ondre not to let the Alliance see how much currency the Hluit did, or did not have.

"I see," Ondre said. "So if we tell you what we believe might have really happened there, you'll give us what . . . in exchange?"

Again the Alliance men exchanged a glance.

Dhave gave a snort of disgust. "They don't have anything to give us. They just want to take what we have. They don't have the power to negotiate the treaty we want." He turned away, disgusted. "Leave us," he said. "Come back when you can give us something we want."

After the two men left, Samith said, "Now isn't that strange? They aren't even offering to negotiate about the treaty."

"Because we all know they'll just lie to us and break whatever treaty they make any time they want," Dhave suggested.

"But they should be going through the act," Phol agreed with Samith. "It's as though we really *do* have something they want. But they know we won't give it to them if we really understand what it is we'd be giving them."

"The horses," Samith said. "It all comes back to the horses."

"But they've already told us they want our horses so they can create another stallion like Lark," Dhave argued. "And what's so valuable about being able to jump around in time?"

"It must be a weapon," Pohl said.

"A weapon against what? The Blueskins?"

"No, they don't consider them a real threat. They are perfectly willing to lose a few, or even a few hundred of their own people to them now and again. They are not afraid of the Blueskins. They created the Blueskins."

"The Mirror is the only real threat to them. Lark was supposed to take his berserker to destroy it. Now that they've lost Lark, again, they need our horses even more. But raising another horse like Lark will take too long unless they manage to stop John first."

"It isn't the Mirror they fear," Samith corrected him. "We are the ones they fear."

That statement met silence. On the face of it, it was crazy."

But Phol said. "I think you're right. We, our people, may be the ones they need the weapon against."

"All I can feel is their fear," Samith said. "They fear us very deeply. They fear losing everything to us and they're not sure they *can* stop us."

Ondre shook his head. "We mean them no harm. We want only to be left in peace."

"Then why didn't we give them Is and the stallion?" Phol asked him, playing devil's advocate.

"They were not ours to give."

"Still, we could have."

"I see what you're driving at. There are things we value more than peace. Things like honesty, integrity, freedom."

"Yes."

"So what? They can still wipe us out."

"They don't think they can, at least not if we have the stallion and they don't."

"That's too incredible," Ondre objected.

"Yes," Samith agreed, "but just for a moment pretend it isn't."

"Okay," Ondre agreed guardedly. "But I do not see how one horse gives us that much power."

"You are thinking in terms of making small jumps through time for small reasons, like Is did when she needed to escape from troopers or Blueskins. But we took it further than that. We sent them all the way back to Amil's cabin. What if we could go back to a certain moment in history and change a few things? Our present situation could be very different. We could have taken over the Alliance that way."

"We don't want that."

"They don't believe that."

"No, because that is what they would do. And you have to admit we have entertained the idea."

"I can't believe that messing around with past things like that wouldn't have some other repercussions. Unthought of, uncontrollable things," Ondre said.

"I believe you are right," Samith said. "But that wouldn't stop them. They are too arrogant."

Pohl blew his breath out between his hands. "So," he summed up, "we can't let them have our horses so they can create more horses like Lark, and we can't let them get Lark back – of course provided we can somehow 'not let' these things happen. I have to ask at this point, do we still want to stop the Mirror from taking over their computer network? Maybe we should let it destroy their civilization."

"That would keep them busy, keep them from attacking our people. Might give us a chance to escape with our horses, too," Samith speculated. "And it might be a very long time, or never, before they recover. It would completely destroy their present power base. Their people might have a chance to build a better society."

"Yeah," Pohl said, by his tone not agreeing. "Nice idea, but civil disruption like that just end in the worst, most brutal people rising to the top again."

"Also," Dhave said, "If the Mirror wants to wipe out all traces of the research that led to its creation, it very well might wipe out all traces of everything to do with time traveling horses. After all, the stallion is a great threat to it. Once Lark is dead that threat is gone unless someone someday breeds the right one of our mares to the right war stallion. Would the Mirror be paranoid enough to try to kill all the horses?"

That was a chilling thought.

"How?"

"If it can use John the way it has, why couldn't it create a police force, an army, in the same way?"

"It already has the Dark Bodies killing for it," Dhave said.

"They are killing," Samith agreed, "but I don't know that they are necessarily killing *for* the Mirror. They killed Is's guards to help free her and I can't see why the Mirror would want her free."

"You think the Dark Bodies were acting on their own?" Phol said.

"Or under someone else's guidance."

"Whose?"

"At the moment, I have no idea," Samith admitted.

"Okay," Ondre said, stopping them. "Unless we get better information, I think we should go with our first plan; stop the Mirror from taking over. As corrupt as the Alliance is at least it's human. We can understand them and there is always some hope they will change for the better. I think our people have a better chance against them than against the Mirror and all its tricks."

"Then I would suggest that finding and stopping John should be our priority," Samith said. "If we don't do that everything else is academic."

"I agree," Pohl said. "Striking any bargain with these people is like writing on water. Nothing binds them but their own power and that fluctuates moment to moment."

"And I would be especially careful of DeJohnn and Mason," Samith warned. "Their whole mission is to use any means they can to get close to us to trick us."

"I know," Ondre said, feeling that the warning was directed at him. "Do you think they delivered our warning about John?"

"I'd bet my life on it," Pohl said.

"So you think DeFroe has taken precautions?"

"Yes. But whether they will be enough I don't know."

"John is only one man," Ondre said. He tried not to think of him as a Hluit man and his beloved brother. "Surely he can be stopped."

"There are also the Dark Bodies," Samith warned. "And they are getting more powerful every time they kill."

"But we are not sure they are controlled by the Mirror. They killed Is's guards to get the energy to talk to her. They revealed the Mirror's plans to her. They obeyed her when she told them not to kill Petre. That doesn't sound like they are working *for* the Mirror."

"They were created by the Mirror," Pohl warned. "And it is powerful enough to destroy a man's brain and take over his body and animate it. It can make whatever is left of that man go against all his ethics and kill his own friends. I would not trust these Dark Bodies a moment."

"Besides, they should have no love for the Alliance. They were berserkers. The Alliance created them to be sacrificed. They were never very bright but they may have no great love for the people who did that to them."

"But they may have no great love for the Mirror either," Samith said. "They may not appreciate the 'eternal life' it has given them."

"Great," Dhave said. "An army of rogue berserkers who are really dead, but who can kill and probably not be killed and who have who-knows-what alliance. We really needed that."

"We also have one other problem worth mentioning," Samith said. "Any of our horses could be carrying the gene sequence they need. We've got to get them out of here."

"I'm sure *that* will be easy," Dhave said.

Chapter Sixteen

The chain dragged across Petre's awareness. Its metallic clunk and thunk, clunk and thunk grated down his spine as if each link of the chain hit one of his vertebrae.

He forced himself awake.

The inside of a wagon. Bare wooden floor. The glare of the white canvas above, back lit by the sun, drove lances through his eyes into his brain. He tried to move from his cramped position and discovered that his wrists and ankles were bound together behind his back. His movement attracted the attention of his cellmate. Heavy gage chain rattled across the floor, reverberating through Petre's bones.

The light dimmed as a large man loomed over him. His shoulders were hunched under the wagon top which was too low for him and his square jaw was thrust forward. He stared down at Petre like a dim-witted child might stare at a bug before squashing it. Petre had never been so close to a berserker before. He was enormous. His shoulders seemed to fill the width of the wagon. Pectoral muscles bulged, all too evident under a thin shirt plastered to his body with sweat. Sweat ran down his face and his brown hair was soaked black with it.

It took several seconds for the oddness of that to register. Why was he sweating like that in a freezing unheated wagon in the middle of winter? Then Petre met the man's eyes. They were crazed, insane, tortured.

The man was chained by an enormous leg iron that would not allow him to reach Petre. The wagon was of no ordinary construction. It was not wood, but metal, the sides and roof made of bars with a canvas top. He'd be willing to bet that the wood planking on the floor covered something more substantial too. The end of the berserker's chain was welded to the bars. A prison, planned in advance for this man, and now Petre had been thrown into it too. The berserker was between him and the only door, not that it would be unlocked anyway.

Petre tried to ease the numbness in his legs and discovered he could not move, tied with his legs and hands pulled behind him. It was an effective and merciless way to immobilize a man.

He could move his fingers a little, but they were nearly paralyzed with numbness and the sensations they reported were vague at best. Was that rope around his wrist? He could not tell the texture but it did not seem to have the links a chain would have. This lump must be a knot then. A memory slipped through his mind, as vague as the feeling in his fingers – a way to undo this rope – but he could not make it come clear. He worried at the knot with fingers that refused to report accurately to his brain, but it kept him from thinking about anything that had happened to him or was likely to happen next.

Flashes of memory crossed his vision. Dead men strewn across the snow. Red snow. Alliance uniforms mostly. Here and there a Blueskin. The fresh tracks of the avalanche. The deep wallow marks the Alliance horses had made where the Blueskins had driven them off. The three dead horses that hadn't made it, broken legs or something. The grim-faced Alliance survivors. Weapons trained on him. The bright explosion in his brain. No pain. His memory held no pain.

And further back in his memory the elder Darrell, saying, "Don't go down there. There's no reason."

And he answering, "I have to. I caused it."

The old man disagreeing implacably, "They had free will."

And he, "No, they never did. They are all Alliance creations."

"So what will you do? You can't help them."

"Suffer with them I guess."

"What of Is?"

"She is very far from here." Petre didn't know how he'd known. He saw summer pastures, the stallion grazing. Wish fulfillment probably.

He shook his head and the headache moved from back to front and back again. He could get rid of it if he could stretch properly. That became his goal, not escape, just the freedom to move his own body. No one should ever be allowed to take that away from another person.

If he could only use his fingers better.

He heard a sound like a growl and looked up. The berserker motioned him to come closer. Petre met those insane tortured eyes and wondered if the man would untie his ropes or maybe crush him to death with one hand.

There was no way to get the answer from where he was. Petre wriggled across the floor shoulder to hip, shoulder to hip until he was close enough to the berserker.

The berserker didn't untie the ropes. He grabbed the ropes and broke them.

A memory stirred, the feel of ropes parting in Petre's own hands, the way their fibers disengaged each other. The *how* of it he had no desire to explore further.

"Thanks," he said, his voice husky from disuse, or something else. Had be been screaming? Crying? Best not look at those memories either. He worked his shoulders to relieve the pain and examined the berserker's leg iron. But he could see no way to get it off.

"Needs a key."

The berserker growled and took hold of two of the wagon bars and strained, trying to move them apart. Petre watched, awed, until the berserker sank back defeated and sweating even harder.

"Too bad," Petre commiserated. The berserker swung, a backhanded blow, no warning, and Petre learned his first lesson. Stay alert, the man's mood swings were dangerous. He sat down again outside the reach of the chain, shaken. It had been such a negligent offhand gesture on the berserker's part, but it would have done him real damage if it had connected.

A key grated and the door opened. The berserker turned like a cat, not at all like the lumbering bear he resembled. Then his muscles relaxed, he knew the man at the door. The man nodded to him, then said to Petre, "Good, you're awake."

Then he noticed the frayed rope and admonished Petre. "You shouldn't have gotten within his reach. He's very unpredictable right now."

Suddenly a dam broke and all of Petre's pent up, twisted emotions found expression in rage. To that man, the berserker was not a person, he was a thing to be caged, used and discarded. Having spent only a few minutes in the berserker's company, Petre had more regard for him than that. At that instant the berserker charged the man in the doorway. The massive chain came off the floor for its entire length and snapped tight in mid stride. The berserker, deprived of his leg in mid leap, fell headlong. Petre braced for a crash like a falling tree but the berserker seemed to bounce and rebound to his feet faster than Petre had imagined possible. *Speed, reflexes and strength,* Petre thought. And they all outweighed rational thought. The berserker would go with his emotions and attack before he thought every time.

The man had leaped back from the door at the attack. Now he straightened his uniform and tried to pretend he had not been frightened into appearing undignified.

"Largo," he addressed the berserker like a naughty child, "you must not attack me. You know that."

"I must go free," the berserker responded, his voice a bass rumble.

"We are going to set you free," the man said. "You just have to wait a bit longer. We have to speak to the Hluit man," he said, jerking his head at Petre.

"He's going to get my stallion back?" Except for the deepness of his voice the berserker sounded like a little boy now, full of hope and belief.

"Yes, he's going to get your stallion back," the man said. "You have to let him come out so we can talk."

"OK," Largo said doubtfully, like a child agreeing to wait for a treat. He stepped aside as the man warned Petre. "Walk slowly. Don't make any fast movements. Don't look at him. And control your emotions."

Petre almost didn't hear him. He was wondering *how* they thought he could get the stallion back and *why* they thought he would, if he could. He walked past Largo and hearing the chain rattle, tried hard not to feel enraged. Outside he could see crews working with ice picks and shovels, burying the dead. He followed the man to a tent where two other men waited. They offered Petre a seat near the stove and a hot drink. He refused both. The heat alone was too seductive to his overused half-frozen muscles and he knew he had to stay alert. These men meant him and Is no good.

He listened to the men apologize for how he had been treated. There had been a lot of confusion, they said. It had been a military situation. He had been handled according to military protocol. He watched them, wondering how he had suddenly become useful to them.

They introduced themselves. The man who had brought him in was a Scholar of the First Order, Don Fey. He was a small, almost frail looking older man with the hunched shoulders of someone who has spent many hours studying at the neglect of his body. The other two were younger. The larger of them, Troop Master El Eldor, took Petre's measure with ice-blue eyes that never seemed to blink. The other was simply Master Dan. Petre noticed his overdeveloped callused knuckles, as though he used his hands for tools in some harsh line of work.

Don Fey did most of the talking, beginning with an attempt to win Petre's good will by trying to appeal to his humanitarian nature and his sense of fair play. Coming from these people that approach was so ridiculous that Petre just sat watching the whole thing with a feeling of total unreality. Obviously someone who thought he was an expert on the Hluit had briefed this man on how to appeal to him. But Petre knew that they saw him as a tool, a Hluit tool, to be used like the berserker. He thought of the man they chained like an animal and the stone he felt in his heart reflected in his eyes.

In the middle of the charade, an earthquake hit. The ground gave a little jerk and began to tremble with rapidly increasing force. Petre saw fear in the faces around him. Outside there were shouts and running footsteps, and then another sound he wasn't every likely to forget, an animal wail of anguish, but it was no animal that Petre had ever heard.

Petre reacted without thinking. He dodged out of the tent and sprinted back to the wagon before realizing it might look like he was trying to escape.

The berserker had ripped the canvas off the roof. The two bars he gripped were noticeably bent. Not that it would do him any good, he was still chained. But it had not really been an attempt to escape. It was more of an uncontrolled spasm of agony, the physical manifestation of the wail Petre had heard. Spent now, the berserker's knees gave way and he slid down to the floor still gripping the bars. Then he began to sob, great wracking things that shook the whole wagon, while tears ran down his face. For Petre, it was like seeing a huge majestic horse down and unable to get up, heart rending on some gut level.

A short low-voiced conversation began behind Petre. "The last injection has counteracted the testosterone," Don Fey said.

"Yes, but he is in a metabolic tail spin. On top of the adrenaline crash it has made him very unstable," countered El Eldor. "If we can continue the injection regimen we should be able to achieve a homeostatic level within a few more hours."

Petre ignored the talk and moved forward. The Troop Master made a move as though to stop him, but Don Fey caught his arm. "No, let him," he said in a whisper. "We have to find out if this will work."

Drawn by the berserker's anguish Petre reacted as he would to the child the man had become. Reaching through the bars he touched the man's wet face and stroked his hair, offering comfort. The man's sobbing gentled. Through tears Largo spoke indistinctly. "He moved. She doesn't know how to control him. He's all over the place."

"The stallion?" Petre questioned, intrigued.

"Yes." It was the pleading of a frustrated child. "He'll get lost. She doesn't know how to hold him."

"Okay," Petre said gentling the man. "Okay," he repeated, realizing too late he was within danger if the berserker turned violent again. The massive hands closed on Petre's shoulders, pulling him against the bars. But the berserker meant no harm.

"You've got to get him back," Largo pleaded, his wet face and tear-filled eyes inches from Petre's. "You've got to. It hurts so bad."

Master Dan intervened. "We're going to get your stallion back. That's what we're trying to do. Now you must let Petre go. We need to talk a little bit more. Then he's going to get your stallion back. You must not hurt him. He's going to help you. Now let go of him. That's right. That's good." And to Petre he said. "Just back away slowly."

Petre did as he was told. He followed the men back to the tent. It had partially collapsed but soldiers were resetting it. Petre looked around and saw other evidence of the earth's movement that had preceded the berserker's outcry. A new avalanche had left a wide swath through the forest below them. Hundred-year-old trees had been swept away just as neatly as though they were twigs before a broom. Further on, the Blue River's course had changed. White water frothed over a waterfall that had never been there before. New rock was exposed like bone – earth bone, laid bare. Understanding came.

"The stallion did this?"

"It's a bit more complicated than that, but yes the stallion did this."

"And the other avalanche too? When the Blueskins came to take him away?"

"Yes."

"How?"

"The exact mechanism isn't completely understood . . ." Troop Master Eldor started, stiffly.

"I'd bet on that," Petre cut him off. "I'd just bet on that. You're always fooling with things you don't properly understand and can't control, but it's okay as long as it's on our side of the Boundary. Well this one's going home to you. I hope John gets through, I hope the Mirror destroys all your computers, all your records, your whole civilization." He spun away from them, angry at his own outburst, but furious at some depth at which he had never felt such emotion before.

El Eldor started to make an angry reply, but Don Fey stopped him with a hand motion and a warning look.

It took Petre three slow breaths to collect himself. "Alright," he said and turned around. "It's time you tell me what you want me to do, and *why* you think I will do it?"

"We want you to help the berserker get the stallion back from Isadora."

Laughter erupted from Petre. It was a ragged rough-edged sound, ripping the air like the tearing of old rags. "Sure. You leave him chained in the wagon and I'll go find her and talk her into bringing the stallion back."

"You will be taking the berserker with you," El Eldor said in an uncompromising voice. He had no sense of humor.

Danger ran through Petre's blood like ice. He knew something of Is's fear of berserkers. His need to protect her surfaced, and with it came whatever cunning was left to him.

"Ahhh," he said letting them see the light dawn in his understanding. "He will keep me honest, eh? But isn't he a bit dangerous for me to handle? I might sneeze and he might kill me."

"The drugs will have him under control in a few more hours. You will need to give him an injection twice a day, that's all," Don Fey said.

"And when he gets the stallion?"

"It takes him to the Mirror."

"The Mirror will kill them."

The men exchanged a glance. "Yes," Don Fey acknowledged. "That is how we will get the virus into its program which will shut it down."

Of course. How simple, Petre thought. He should have known the Alliance wouldn't be concerned with keeping their own man alive.

"Does Largo know that he will be killed?"

"He understands what he is to do."

"Does he understand he will *die*?" Petre insisted.

"They do not fear death like you and I. They are driven to do what they are capable of doing. You must understand that," Don Fey explained in careful tones.

Petre turned away and met the wall of the tent as gray and impenetrable as Don Fey's arguments.

"That's all very well and good," Petre allowed himself to say, "but I do not know *how* to find Is or the stallion."

"We believe you will be able to find her if you try," Don Fey said. "Just go where Isadora is likely to go and wait for her."

The only place Petre felt sure Is would go eventually was to the Mirror. Maybe he should pretend to go along with whatever deal they offered him, just to get out of here. But he knew he would never take the berserker anywhere near where Is was likely to be. Still, if they turned him loose with the berserker perhaps he would be able to escape from that man. *Sure.* The man had more stamina and was faster and stronger. Petre would have to trick him. Or kill him! But he didn't know if he could do that. It seemed more likely that the berserker would kill him. But maybe Petre could slow him down with an overdose of the drugs?

At least he would be free of that horrible wagon. He couldn't stand to be locked up in that wagon again. It wasn't just his own captivity that was so bad; it was the other man's. To Petre the wagon was just bars, which was bad enough, but the berserker was captive on some level Petre couldn't endure. He suspected the Alliance men knew that much about him, but he saw no reason to concede easily.

"You still haven't explained *why* you think I should want to help you," he said.

"We believe you will help us because your people are in danger," Don Fey said.

"That's not new. We have always known we were in danger from you. Capitulating now will only postpone, not remove that danger."

"No, the danger is not from us."

Petre grunted his disbelief. "Who then? The Blueskins? The Mirror? They have been our neighbors for a long time."

"No, not them, the stallion."

That one took Petre by surprise. A strange twisting fear tightened his guts. "A horse?" His tone was disbelieving, but something deep within him was ready to believe.

"This will take some explaining."

Petre made a small go-ahead gesture with his hand, trying to seem nonchalant, while his guts twisted tighter and his perceptions did funny tricks with the lighting. Though Don Fey's voice seemed to come from a great distance, it was painfully distinct. Petre heard the man's tongue break loose from the top of his mouth, heard him swallow. Heard the ragged beating of his own heart and the whistle of his own breath as though he was running hard.

"You are aware that the land behind the Boundary was once a separate island?" Don Fey asked.

"Yes." It seemed a singularly strange place to start explaining how one horse could be so dangerous to an entire people that it would behoove Petre to betray the woman he loved.

"South Continent and North Island," Petre said with a slightly bored voice that gave away none of what he was feeling. "And when they collided they threw up the mountain range we call the Boundary."

"Just so. What you probably don't know is that this didn't happen until *after* the Alliance landed."

"I see." Petre did see. With a strange crystal clarity he heard Amil saying, "They rewrite their history to suit themselves whenever they like." Despite Amil's efforts to save some of the real history, it would/had moldered away in his cabin to be lost as surely as if the Alliance had burned it.

"I see," Petre repeated, understanding the implications. "Climatic changes didn't kill the indigenous people the way we were taught. The Alliance did."

"We *absorbed* them," Troop Master Eldor corrected.

Petre held his peace. He could guess how it had been. The superior force landing, driving the simple hunter/herdsmen out of their ancestral lands, killing them if they resisted. Or perhaps killing them for sport. Raping the women. *Absorbing* them.

"It was a harsh time," Don Fey said, watching him, "for everyone. The Alliance had its own difficulties. Their surveys had shown the planet's tectonics to be somewhat unstable, but the main plates were moving slowly, in the manner of most instances where one continental shelf is subluxing another. No one predicted the sudden sinking of one shelf that brought the land masses together in a matter of days instead of the thirty thousand or so years that might reasonably have been expected.

"Even with all the technology the Alliance had brought with them they were not prepared for the volcanoes, earthquakes, and extremely cold and wet weather that followed. The Four Cities became isolated by weather that was too severe to allow travel. Four distinct governments formed where one had been planned.

"By that point all the indigenous people on the mainland had been killed or captured and their horses taken as Alliance property. The only herders who remained were on North Island, on the other side of the new mountain range. They were largely forgotten. But as the weather turned worse they crossed the mountains and came south, perhaps seeking a better climate. They were an extremely unwarlike people. As they passed the northernmost Alliance outposts they offered aid that saved many lives. They wanted only one thing in exchange – the return of their horses. They were not interested in the heavy draft horses the Alliance had brought with them. They wanted only their own horses. They had an uncanny sense of knowing where those horses were and they worked their way south searching them out and leaving a legacy of strange stories behind."

"Such as?" Petre asked, still trying to sound disinterested.

"A band of the herders would pass through an area and the heretofore perfectly behaved horses would jump out of corrals, batter their way out of barns, or buck off their riders and run away. Invariably the farmers would find an offering of skins or salted meat. For those Alliance farmers struggling to survive, the exchange seemed worthy and the bands were not much hounded until they reached Center.

"Center was . . . well the center of our civilization. And it was better fortified and protected by an army."

He paused and Petre could imagine all too graphically what had happened. It was almost a relief when Don Fey started speaking again. "They felt they could not let 'savages' have their way. The last of the indigenous people were either killed or taken captive. Their horses were reclaimed as Alliance property."

The words were so clean, so simple. They lessened the impact of what Petre felt in his guts. People killed, raped, separated from their loved ones, separated from their horses. *Absorbed.*

Don Fey's voice brought him back. "After a while the ones who had been taken as prisoners were allowed work rights."

"Slaves," Petre said softly.

"Times were hard, even at Center," Don Fey temporized. "They were eventually allowed to become citizens."

"And their horses?"

"They were highly prized for their beauty and speed. The government controlled their breeding."

Yes, Petre thought. But no one was so careful or selective in terms of how the wild people were maintained. Women were raped by Alliance men and bore their half-breed children. Men were separated from their own people and sired their own half-breed children. And so what remained of the native people was lost. Their culture was completely destroyed and their race mitigated. But Don Fey was still talking about the horses.

"Eventually the government started a breeding program, crossing selected ones of the native horses with our draft stock."

"And they produced the war horses?"

"Yes."

"Why?"

"Well, they weren't trained as war horses then. They were bigger and sturdier than the native horses, more suited to our size as riders, but as time passed things changed. The ash from the volcanoes caused by the collision of the land masses settled out of the atmosphere and the weather returned to normal. Communication between the cities was reestablished. Internal problems were worked out and education, culture and science came to the forefront again. The breeding of these excellent crossbreeds was part of that renewed cultural interest. The crossbreeds were exceptional animals. Bigger boned than the native horses, powerful and full of hybrid vigor, but so trainable, so cooperative."

"So you just naturally trained them to be weapons," Petre said bitterly. All that beauty, all that trust twisted into something destructive.

"It was not until generations later that the eternal life experiments were begun and the horses found a niche there," Don Fey defended.

"And the berserkers were developed just for that niche, too?"

Don Fey hesitated.

"Oh, right," Petre said remembering, "you already had berserkers – the Blueskins."

He felt a ripple of surprise pass between the men. They had not expected Hluit intelligence to be so good.

"Yes," Don Fey agreed reluctantly. "It was thought that they should be tagged with a special gene that created a bluish cast to their skin so they could be easily recognized. They were bred originally to fight each other in stylized combat. Each city had its teams."

"Part of the cultural reawakening," Petre goaded, but Don Fey shrugged it off.

"It was about that time that a man named don Bocher became intrigued with the level of communication that seemed possible between some of the crossbred horses and their riders. He began experimenting with that linkage to see how far it could be taken. In the midst of his experiments some very unusual things happened."

Petre held his face impassive, but his heart quickened as Don Fey continued.

"Quite by accident don Bocher developed horses that could sometimes carry their riders to different times. But it was not understood then. The trainers were blamed as unreliable and trouble plagued the stables. Eventually that line of research went out of favor.

"Then, as the eternal life experiment took form and the berserkers and their horses were needed, the computer augmentation of the horses became popular. It could create the bond between horse and rider that don Bocher had tried to create a different way. But it was much more reliable.

"Only one man continued to breed a select few of the native horses that were at don Bocher barn. A mare of that line crossed with a crossbred stallion eventually led to the stallion you call Lark. He represents the best of both lines of research come together. He is computer augmented to ensure his bonding and obedience to his berserker, but he also has the wild talent of don Bocher's best horses. He can travel over time, but he can only be properly controlled by his berserker."

"So," Petre said, "that's why is he's off with Is now?"

"She trained him." Don Fey refused to be baited. "He still recognizes her. But be honest, she can't control him, can she? She can't make him keep to one time, or cross to another at will, can she?"

They were all watching Petre closely. It would be impossible to lie under El Eldor's piercing eyes, or Master Dan's still presence, even if he could get it by Don Fey. He left the question unanswered, which was admission enough of its truth.

After a long moment Don Fey continued. "Moving about like he is, the stallion can cause earthquakes, maybe worse, even volcanoes, climate changes. We have reason to believe that the indigenous people *caused* the island to collide with the continent as it did. We believe their horses had the wild talent to move through time. We think they moved the island through time. They made what was going to happen eventually, happen fast."

A chuckle escaped from Petre. He turned away as though to hide the grin on his face but really he was trying to give himself a moment to think. The indigenous people and their horses – horses from which the Hluit horses were directly descended – moved an island through time!

"You're really serious?" he said turning to face them again. No one answered him.

"Okay, even if they could do that, why would they?" he continued in a tone suggesting he didn't believe any of this, yet his guts were tight with inexplicable dread.

"They knew what the Alliance had done to their people on the mainland. They were separated from that same fate by only a few miles of ocean strait. It would be no trouble for the Alliance soldiers to cross that. The island people feared their turn would come. So they moved the island. They threw up a mountain range that was a whole lot harder to cross and a whole lot easier for them to defend than a few miles of flat water. They may also have been counting on the climatic changes to set the Alliance back and keep us too busy to attack them for years. They may have counted on establishing a truce with us in that time, or they may have been intending to wipe us out. We don't know. We know they caused the land masses to move, and we know they somehow did it with their horses."

Petre shook his head, but found himself having to pretend disbelief that should have been easy. "I don't understand how you could possibly know any of this."

"They left behind pictures, in the caves at Morv."

Petre lifted his head and watched the small movements of the men. Troop Master El Eldor met Don Fey's eyes and shook his head in negation. Master Dan refrained from the decision with cold disapproving immobility. Petre wondered briefly at that.

"So you're telling me that simple herdsmen could cross these mountains on horseback but the Alliance with all its technology was left stranded in the flat lands?"

"We could have crossed if we had wanted to," Don Fey said. "We even had flying machines then. We had not yet taken the Level of Transportation Vow that binds us to the use of animal means only. But remember, we did not understand the import of what had happened. Nowhere in all the records in our database, in all the travels through the universe had anyone ever encountered a primitive people who could cause an island to move. We thought it was simply planetary mechanics that we had misjudged. We had our own internal problems to contend with."

It was the second time Don Fey had mentioned that and Petre wondered at it. Surely a people who had crossed light years to get here, who had *fast* communication and devices that could fly people through the air, did not have to have been out of communication with each other.

"You were at war with each other? One city against another?" Petre guessed.

Don Fey didn't answer.

"You were killing each other," Petre continued. "Killing people because the people who governed one city could not control the people who governed another and they could not stand that loss of control? They would rather kill everyone than lose that control."

Don Fey stiffened. "It was a very dark time."

"And so that is what led to the ban on the sort of technology that made all that killing possible. And along with that came the ban on any form of transportation faster than a horse?"

"Yes," Don Fey admitted. "We are, after all, one people. In those days we were only a small colony, we could not afford to kill off large segments of our gene pool. By agreement, war became limited to cavalry. Eventually it became even more stylized than that, in contests between the blueskinned berserkers. Now we have left even that behind us. We are one people, unified in thought and direction."

One people, Petre thought bitterly, with different classes. But you have given everyone a common enemy, the Blueskin Marauders to keep the people unified in fear and servitude. You have destroyed your true history so they do not know that their own rulers created those killers to prey on their own people. But Don Fey was anxious to get the discussion back on track.

"It took us a long time to understand about the horses. We did not notice anything unusual about the descendents of the indigenous horses until don Bocher began his experiments with the crossbreeds.

"We suspect now that not only did we not know how to ask the horses to perform, we didn't really relate to them, or they to us, properly. Now we believe there was some sort of synergy between the indigenous people, the horses, and possibly the land, and we disrupted it. We didn't know how to command those horses. Or possibly they couldn't obey us. It wasn't until we bred them with our horses that we gained some command of their talents. What they could do wasn't something that translated into our science very well. It was hard for us to believe it. For years don Bocher's research was discredited.

"Even after we began to credit it, it wasn't something we could just breed for. It's more than a matter of genetics. The horses have to start with the right gene sequence, and the riders have to have the right genes, and then a kind of psychic link has to happen . . . it all has to be there in just the right combination."

"So you're groping your way back to it with the berserkers and their horses."

"Yes."

"And Lark and that man out there in the chains are your best success."

Don Fey hesitated before answering. "Yes."

"But you're willing to see them killed?" Petre challenged him.

"Yes. The Mirror must be shut off. It poses a more immediate threat."

"It even has some of this time moving ability, doesn't it?" Petre challenged.

"It seems to have learned it from the berserkers and their horses."

"And you didn't anticipate that it would."

"No. For a long time we were unaware that our berserkers and their horses had this ability. At the time we started sending berserkers against the Mirror, don Bocher's research was out of favor. But evidentially those first horses and their riders had some of the talent. Even though it was latent and unusable by either man or beast the Mirror found it. We can see that now."

"So now you want to stop it. What if this virus doesn't work?"

"Then we will blow it up."

"That would entail breaking the vow that binds you to weapons of low caliber, wouldn't it?"

"It will be a unanimous vote."

"But you may not be able to find it without Lark."

"We will eventually. But we would prefer not to destroy it completely."

"So I am supposed to help you get the stallion back so you can go with the first plan and shut the Mirror off without destroying it completely?"

"Yes, and also to keep the stallion from disrupting your lands any more. Another minor ice age at this point would force your people back onto Alliance territory."

And under Alliance rule, Petre thought. The end of our little experiment. The end of our lives. The Alliance had thought nothing of wiping out the ancient culture of the indigenous people. A few thousand Hluit would be less than nothing to it.

Petre turned away. "I can't help you," he said.

There was a moment of silence and some exchanged looks. Then El Eldor spoke.

"I told you it would be no use to talk to him," he said to Don Fey.

"Oh but it is of use," Don Fey answered. "He will have to tell his people everything he has learned and for that reason he will go with the berserker, for that is the only way he will have any chance of getting to his people."

They knew the Hluit mind that well. But they didn't know that because of Amil, the Hluit already had much of this information. Petre did not have to return to his people. He did not have to take Largo to Is. And yet he felt the trap close around him like the walls of One Way Canyon.

Chapter Seventeen

Rumors reached the Hluit delegation through Mark Mason and Horse Master DeJohnn, as well as from people the Hluit befriended in the stable and the kitchen. The death toll the Dark Bodies were taking was rising. It had started as a few isolated deaths, people who went to sleep and simply didn't wake up. The people who died were not necessarily high in the research or administrative hierarchy, nor were they necessarily in close physical proximity to the castle. Because the deaths formed no particular pattern, plotting where the next one would occur was virtually impossible.

The city population at large had absolutely no idea what was happening, so the deaths were even more frightening to them. The government, in its usual highhanded way, collected the bodies and said nothing.

"We are unable to determine the cause of death," Researcher First Level Jonathan Forth reported. "There is nothing wrong with them. They are simply not alive any more."

"Dark bodies," Samith said. They were in yet another useless meeting with DeFroe and his advisors. He had so far refused to let Ondre or any of the Hluit leave the castle to take part in the attempt to catch John.

"But how do they kill?" the scholar Peter Dinn asked, frustrated. "There must be a mechanism."

"They just take the life force out of a body," Phol said. "You would know that about them if you'd had them for your neighbors as long as we have." The Alliance men let the jibe pass.

"Can they be stopped?"

"A wakeful person can usually resist them, if he or she doesn't panic."

"But that may not be true any longer," Samith said. "They overwhelmed Isadora's guards, who were supposedly awake. Each time they kill they get stronger. But it could be that there will be a pay off. They may become more visible and less, shall we say, permeable. They may not be able to pass through walls so easily. Perhaps you *will* be able to keep them out of the castle."

"I doubt it," Pohl said discomfortingly. "When John gets through to the computer it will open whatever doors the Dark Bodies need. They will kill and the Mirror will preserve the people it thinks are a threat to it."

"We have told you before, that won't happen," Stevens snapped. As head of internal security he took any questioning of his measures as a personal affront.

"We assure you, precautions have been taken," DeFroe said. "We have isolated the data it will need. In fact that data is no longer within the system."

"But the knowledge of its location is in the brains of certain men," Samith said relentlessly. "It will think nothing of killing everyone until it absorbs that particular bit of information."

"It cannot get within the castle. We are safe."

"I would not be so sure," Pohl said.

Defroe shifted irritably. "I assure you, we have our means. We *created* it after all. We know more about it than you do."

"Even if it cannot yet access the knowledge it wants to destroy, it can get at low security stuff. Water and food distribution. Power. Sanitation," Pohl said. "It can disrupt the entire workings of your society, so dependent are you on your computers."

"Access to those programs is triple guarded. Only certain terminals can be used, and of course they are heavily guarded. If it should somehow get into the system, alarms will go off before it gets very far."

"Then what?"

"We will trace it. In fact, we have discussed setting just such a trap for it."

"I would like to be there," Ondre said.

"That is unnecessary," Stevens snapped.

DeFroe gave Ondre a long calculating look. "I have been advised that because John was your brother you feel a moral duty to help stop him even though he can hardly be thought of as your brother any more. Surely there is nothing left of his mind but the motor responses of his brain stem. Or do you believe he is alive in there and actively helping the Mirror?"

Ondre met DeFroe's eyes. "John would not do the things he has done. Some part of him is obviously 'alive in there' but he would never help the Mirror in the way you mean. I am here because I want to see that what is left of my brother meets a quick death."

"Ahh, you think we might try to catch him to, ahhh . . . study him?"

Ondre let his eye contact with DeFroe be his answer.

"I understand your concern," DeFroe replied diplomatically. "However, the trap will be set in the system. We can not know which of a dozen terminals he might use. As soon as the trace is made, we will have him. Your help will not be necessary."

Of course DeFroe did not want Ondre anywhere near the action for fear Ondre might intentionally or unintentionally interfere. Ondre stirred restlessly. "I just do not think you will catch it so easily. If it absorbed John's mind, it absorbed a lot of information about castle security and the Alliance psyches. He got through your security before, as a spy. He lived here for years and reached the top levels of your most secret research."

"May I also point out," Stevens said, with the restraint it took to speak civilly very evident, "we caught him that time too."

Ondre met Steven's stare. It was undoubtedly Stevens who had delivered John for the "treatment" that had left him unable to communicate. It was DeFroe who had ordered it, and the others in the room had known what was happening. They had probably all been involved in the research leading to the procedure that had taken so much away from John. Ondre shifted his gaze to DeFroe. That man met his eye contact with an aloofness beyond any feeling of guilt. Ondre had known he would have to meet the people who had tortured and tried to kill his brother. He spoke in a steady voice that revealed none of his feelings.

"If you will not accept further assistance from us, at least once you have killed John you must allow us to return his body to our homeland for burial."

DeFroe cocked his head slightly as though examining the request for hidden dangers while he put his response together in his mind.

"Of course we will allow you to see his body, but taking it is not possible," he said, shaking his head. "I'm sure you can understand how we can't allow that."

"Because you do intend to do research with it," Pohl said coldly. "Perhaps you will see if you can reanimate his body the way the Mirror did?"

"No," DeFroe said meeting his eyes. "I assure you, we have no such intention. We only feel that we must keep others from attempting something similar."

"Then we will watch it cremated together," Ondre said.

DeFroe gave him a slight nod of approval. "That should satisfy all sides," he said, and everyone knew he lied.

The next meeting came three days later. This time it was just Ondre and DeFroe. DeFroe had called him to a private chamber for a private meal and a drink afterward. They sat in plush comfortable chairs with a fire blazing in a fireplace, although the place already seemed overheated to Ondre's senses.

Their conversation wandered from one topic to another all evening while Ondre waited for DeFroe to broach the real subject. Finally, as they sat sipping an excellent wine, DeFroe said. "I have come to think that Mr. Stevens may not have assessed the situation with your brother as thoroughly as he might have."

Ondre sipped thoughtfully from the long-stemmed beautifully crafted glass in his hand. "Good security chiefs are by nature sure of themselves," he allowed. "It is sometimes difficult to get them to consider the possibility of failure."

DeFroe chuckled. "Very well said. He is excellent, you understand, and he has never failed me. But in my position I must consider all possibilities."

"Of course," Ondre replied neutrally. He watched DeFroe swirl the amber liquid around his glass, the cut facets of the crystal sparked catching light from the fire.

"It is also somewhat difficult, if you'll forgive my saying so, to believe that you can find your brother any more quickly than my trained soldiers who know this city?"

"But I know John better."

"He is no longer John. He is the computer intelligence."

"Yes, a computer who undoubtedly knows the layout of your city to the last detail and who knows your ways of thinking. But it must hide a man's body, it must move that man's body through the city and ultimately through the gates of this fortification. To do that it needs a man's instincts. I know that man's training. I know his instincts."

DeFroe was watching him closely, but looked away before he spoke. "There is also another small matter," he said nonchalantly. "Should you prove able to find your brother, it might be difficult for you to kill him."

"He is, as you pointed out, no longer my brother. He killed two friends of mine."

"Ahhh, yes, but he is still going to *look* like your brother, perhaps *sound* like him if he has a moment to beg for mercy."

Ondre kept his eyes fixed on his glass. DeFroe was playing on the area of his greatest uncertainty and pain. But there was little reason to drag him through this additional pain unless DeFroe really did need help to find John. That could only mean that the other system had already failed somehow.

"How far did he get?" Ondre asked point blank.

"Far enough to trip the warning and still escape before we could trace him even though soldiers were there within seconds," DeFroe answered honestly.

"He didn't get in though?"

"No. But now he knows about the trap. My experts say he will not be caught that way now. What do you say?"

"They're right. He won't go straight in. He'll go around somehow."

"What do you mean?"

"I don't know. I don't know computers well enough."

"But you still think you can find him?"

"I think so. I want to try."

DeFroe watched him in silence, head tipped to the side, calculating. "There will be two conditions."

"You will send your own men with me?" Ondre guessed.

"Yes. You could think of them as help. They know the city, they will be in touch with what is going on and should you find John, they are highly skilled in combat techniques and they will be armed."

"What is the other condition?"

"Once you go outside these grounds you can not come back within."

"I see, in case I could somehow bring the Mirror in with me?"

"Yes, you might become its minion, like your brother? The gates will be closed to everyone. There will be no more traffic in and out until this is settled."

"And what of my men?"

"They will wait for you here."

"I see." Ondre said slowly, and then added, "I have a condition of my own."

DeFroe was ahead of him. "Your brother's quick death and his cremation as we discussed earlier are the best I can offer you."

Ondre studied DeFroe. "I need to know there will be nothing left of him, especially his brain."

"An autopsy of his brain might have much to teach us," DeFroe temporized.

Ondre felt his anger rising. To be bartering about his brother's death was some sort of deep horror he could hardly stand. To be told his brother's brain might live on, animating other bodies, or at least supplying the research base for such in the future infuriated him.

He stood, keeping his movements under careful control. "We have no deal," he said. "I must see him dead and completely destroyed."

DeFroe watched him, head cocked and let him get to the door before he spoke. "Actually," he said, stopping Ondre as his hand touched the doorknob, "we do not *need* a deal. I am turning you loose in the city. You will be followed. You do not have to try to find your brother. But if you find him and kill him that is the only way you will know he is dead. If you also manage to burn him, you will know he is destroyed. Anything less than that will leave you wondering, won't it?"

Without looking back Ondre went through the door, closing it behind him.

Chapter 18

Largo broke the trail. Even emasculated by the hormone therapy, he still had more stamina than Petre.

"Ho!" Petre shouted to the dwindling figure in front of him.

The berserker turned and obediently poled back to him, a questioning look on his face. "We have to stop. I can't keep up."

Largo glanced around as though looking for the real reason that Petre was calling a halt, as if the fact that they'd skied all day, and night was coming had little to do with it. For a moment Petre thought Largo would protest. Instead, he said simply, "Okay."

"We should tent here, close to the top of this ridge," Petre said. "Just in case." There had been a few small earth tremors during the day. Nothing major, but it would be foolish to camp where an avalanche or rock fall could be a danger.

Largo shook his pack off and began pulling out the tent. He had been like that for the two days they'd traveled together, totally compliant, with the obedience and good manners of a small boy in the presence of an admired elder. It bothered Petre almost as much as the man's captivity had.

Traveling with the berserker was like traveling with a packhorse. Along with the tent, Largo carried a cook stove, its fuel and enough food for the two of them for a month or more. The tent was one of the Alliance's best, well insulated and easy for one man to set. "I'll start the stove," Petre said.

After the camp was set up Largo reminded Petre, "My injection now."

Petre wasn't about to forget. He took one of the pre-measured syringes and pressed it against the berserker's neck. The man licked his lips in a way Petre had seen him do more and more frequently.

"Taste bad?"

"It makes my mouth dry."

"Sorry." Petre might have been able to adjust the dosage if they had trusted him with more information. Instead they'd given him the pre-measured dosages, undoubtedly afraid that if he knew the effect of each drug he might try to overdose the berserker. As it was, Petre would have to experiment with several doses of everything, which might result in the effect Petre wanted, or it might not. It was also very possible that Largo wouldn't let him give more than one syringe at a time. He seemed well versed in what Petre was supposed to do and he kept Petre to that track with single-minded insistence.

Petre had tried to find out how much Largo understood of what the Alliance had done to him and how he felt about it. But the berserker had refused all such conversation and Petre was afraid to push too hard. There was still that quick edge to the man that made him like an extremely powerful and unpredictable animal.

Trouble came while Petre was gathering snow to melt for water. As he scooped the bucket through the snow, he met not the heavy sluggish resistance of wet snow, but no resistance at all. The bucket swung freely through air and for an instant Petre was standing on dry ground. Brittle fall grass stretched away in all directions. He jerked back, startled, and his snowshoe caught in a drift and he went down in the undeniably real, cold white stuff. He sat a moment on his backside, stunned and wondering if he had really seen what he thought he'd seen. The berserker's bellow made up his mind for him. The man erupted from the tent and floundered toward him waist deep in snow but not letting it stop him.

"He was here!" he shouted. "He was here. I almost had him."

Petre righted himself quickly. He could be in just as much danger from the man's exuberance as from his anger.

"Stop!" he yelled as Largo approached him. "Tell me what happened," Petre said to distract him.

"The stallion was here," Largo said. "He was here in the fall. Grazing right here. I called him but he was too far away. We have to go closer."

Which fall, Petre wondered. Last fall? Next fall? Ten years ago? "How do we go closer?" he asked cautiously.

"You know how to do it. They told me you know how to do it." And suddenly Largo was like a small child being deprived of something he'd been promised and disbelieving of the unfair change in the rules.

"Of course," Petre said quickly. "I can take us closer, but not tonight. I just thought maybe you knew a quicker way."

"No. They said follow you. When you get close enough I can call him. He'll come to me."

Petre had never planned to take Largo anywhere near where Is might be. Largo would take the horse and kill Is if he had to, wanted to, or just got sloppy with some gesture. Now it seemed to Petre that Is could be anywhere in the mountains, any time. Six years from now she might be crossing this valley and Largo would jerk her stallion back to now, back to here.

Petre didn't sleep much that night and as far as he could tell Largo slept even less. It was definitely time to leave the berserker behind, Petre was certain that it could not be done without treachery.

As they set out the next morning, Petre had the sinking feeling that it didn't matter which direction they went. It would only be a matter of time until they were close enough to some place, or some time and he would betray Is even though he didn't mean to. He played with ideas all morning. He could catch Largo unaware and push him off a cliff. Unlikely. He could trick him onto thin ice. In this unremitting cold there was none. He could give him an overdose and hope.

Master Dan's words came to him. "They haven't told you the whole truth." Master Dan had come to the tent they'd given Petre the one night he'd stayed in the army camp. "They're saying these hormones will control the berserker, but they haven't been tested in the field, only in the laboratory. And while they should work under most conditions..." He'd left the rest unsaid.

"Also," he continued after a moment, "if Largo gets close to the stallion, I wouldn't count on anything working."

Petre had bowed, one martial artist to another, for he had finally placed what Master Dan's enlarged knuckles meant. He was a master in an attacking form of martial art. His hands were his weapons. He was probably Largo's trainer.

"Thank you," Petre had said formally. "I am warned."

Master Dan had returned his bow but had made no move to leave. So Petre had waited.

"I am a great admirer of your people's martial art," Master Dan said, surprising Petre. He would have thought that a man trained in the art of strikes and kicks that could disable and kill another man would consider the Hluit art terribly effete for it evaded all such attacks and concentrated on minimal force and nondestructive ways to defend oneself.

Petre bowed, silently accepting the compliment for his people.

"You will not be able to beat Largo with it," Master Dan had continued. "I wished to warn you."

The steady rhythm of Petre's skiing belied the frantic turmoil in his mind. The only plan that seemed to have any chance of success was to find more of his people. Maybe a group of them could overcome the berserker, but then what would they do with him? Petre already knew they wouldn't be able to divert Largo from his set task, and they couldn't keep him docile once the drugs ran out. That left only one option.

Petre tested the thought uncomfortably. The berserker's life for Is's – Is who didn't want her life anyway. And what about the Mirror? Wasn't it a good thing to have that experiment stopped? Maybe it would be better if the berserker found Is and took the stallion, as long as Petre could be sure she wouldn't get hurt. But he had no way to find her and no way to ensure her safety.

A sound, like the roaring of a great wind bearing down on him, jerked Petre's attention back to the present. He looked up fearing an avalanche thundering down on them. But the slope above him sparkled still and white against the azure sky.

Sudden dizziness struck Petre. He staggered, lost his balance and fell, not sliding down the mountain, but falling wildly through nothing. He had a split second to fear the impact before he hit the ground with enough force to take his breath away.

A horse screamed in pain. Others answered with whinnies of fear. Dozens of horses milled about him, their hooves coming within inches of his prone body. The snow he lay on was churned to mud. They were Hluit horses, bridleless, fine boned, and terrified. But the riders were not Hluit, though similar. They were blond and fair skinned, but smaller and as fine boned as their horses. Petre was just one more person down among the dead and wounded riders and horses. The next bolt came like a roar of wind. A horse rose on its hind legs above Petre. Its front legs pawed desperately at the death in the air, its scream lost in the sound of destruction. But the feeling of utter betrayal it projected pierced Petre like a sword. It twisted and fell as one hind leg gave way.

Petre was unable to get out of its way. He braced, expecting the horse to crush him.

The impact wasn't so horrible. The horse's weight wasn't so much. The ground shook.

Petre was jerked to his feet. For an instant everything went black. Then white. Petre looked around at white snow, white everywhere, no mud. Largo's face loomed into his vision.

The berserker shook Petre again, hard enough to rattle his brain, but the man's eyes showed only concern. He meant no harm.

"You are all right? You were screaming."

Petre tried to say yes. The berserker released him. Petre looked around at the peaceful white landscape. Blue sky, evergreen trees. Not a hoof print to be seen.

"He was here," Largo said. "But not close enough to call. Did you feel him?"

"I guess so."

Largo looked very concerned. "You were screaming. I had to hold you down. I didn't hurt you, did I?"

"No."

"When I get him back he won't do that any more. I can hold him."

"He won't do what?" Petre asked.

"I won't let him make time jump around like that. We'll go straight to the Mirror and stop this."

"So that was just . . . I fell into some other time?" Petre said, testing the idea with words.

"*She* can't control him," Largo answered. "It's getting worse."

Petre barely heard. The screams of injured, dying horses filled his memory. Don Fey's words filled his mind as though he had fallen into a moment from that man's tale. Perhaps the moment when the Alliance army had ambushed what remained of the indigenous herders. That was the only thing that made any sense of what had just happened.

But Don Fey's words had not prepared him for one thing – the betrayal the horses had felt. Their riders had betrayed their trust. Whatever happened to him in the rest of his life, Petre hoped never to feel that kind of betrayal again.

He tried to return to the sanity of skiing, the unifying coordination of muscles and breathing helped. But tears welled from his heart, ran freezing down his face, forming ice in his scarf. He was heedless of the danger to himself. Behind the glare of the snow he carried horrible images of horses and their riders dying.

When night came Petre was reluctant to stop. As long as he was moving he could keep from thinking. He could outrun the pain.

Eventually Largo called the halt. "You are exhausted," he said. "You have not been keeping up and it is getting dark. You cannot see in the dark like I can. You must need something to eat. You cannot go as long as I can without food. You have always wanted to stop before. We will stop now."

For Largo it was a long speech and it betrayed his thought processes and his concern for Petre.

Petre couldn't fight him. Long after Largo had cooked and served him dinner Petre sat staring at the glowing coals in the stove. Air rippled across them occasionally as the stove let in just the right amount to produce the maximum heat for the minimum amount of fuel. Unable to concentrate on anything, Petre gave himself up to the little encapsulated memories that passed through his head and he lost himself in them.

Behind him the pages of a book rustled. He smelled the herbs Amil had steeped for Is. All his senses wanted him to believe he was at Amil's, but he knew if he took his eyes away from the coals to look, he would not see Amil's cabin, he would see the grey walls of the Alliance tent and the berserker sprawled across his sleeping bag. He didn't look; he stared at the coals and let the aching feeling of loss consume him.

"Ahhh," the berserker breathed behind him. The sound he made matched Petre's lonely hollow aching perfectly. "Almost."

Danger snapped Petre back to the present. He turned to stare at the berserker.

"Almost what?" he demanded, his voice harsher than was probably safe with that man. But Largo replied unperturbed.

"You almost had them. I felt you call her."

Petre stared at him. All I have to do is daydream, he thought horrified, and I might "call" them to me?

"I don't *want* to call them," he said risking his life.

The berserker showed no anger. "They said you might not want to. They said you are confused. You did not have the right training, like I did. I am to be patient with you. But you are connected to him. You will call him."

Danger scraped fingernails down Petre's spine. "What do you mean, *connected*?"

"It is the same for you as it is for me. The horse is in you . . . inside. You cannot help but call him."

Largo met his eyes with a clear innocence that Petre found suddenly more frightening than the anger he'd been expecting.

"You didn't know?" Largo asked puzzled. "You have no more choice than I do."

Petre turned away. He had not known that Largo understood even that much about his fate; and he was not ready to accept that he had no more free will than the berserker. But he had followed Is and Lark, again and again, sometimes against his own best judgment . . . sometimes against his will.

The next morning as they skied on, the berserker topped a ridge in front of Petre and stopped. Unsuspectingly Petre came up beside him and stopped, shocked. Instead of the giant old growth forest he had expected to see spread below him there were saplings and seedlings, baby pines and small green-barked shoots raising bright green out of the snow. For a long moment he stood, heart hammering. There were no young forests like this anywhere near where they were. This didn't exist anywhere he knew of. He had not simply confused one ridge for another.

The berserker's eyes widened with excitement. "It didn't go back when he left," he said, astonished.

"What?" Petre asked vaguely.

"It didn't go back to 'now' when the stallion left," Largo explained with the patience of a child instructing an adult in some obvious point. "Everything's all disturbed – before, after, and now. We should go around. He isn't there now and we don't want to get stuck there."

"Okay," Petre agreed.

They began to ski around the ridge top.

"Would we really get trapped in there," Petre asked.

"I don't know."

"Maybe we could ski out again?"

The berserker stopped abruptly by turning sideways in front of Petre, spraying up snow. "It's wrong," he said, his eyes intense in a way that made the hair on Petre's arms stir. "Can't you feel how wrong it is?"

Petre saw how upset the berserker was. "Okay," he said in a placating voice. "We'll go around." But as the man skied on Petre was slow to follow.

Suddenly Petre turned, and crouching low on his skis, poled as hard as he could down the slope. He was too busy dodging the young trees to look back. The speed forced him to focus on the moment-to-moment decisions that would keep him from hitting something. He didn't glance back until he'd reached the bottom of the bowl. The berserker wasn't following him, the sky was!

That skewed perception cost Petre his balance and he fell, sliding on his backside in the snow. He twisted around, using the edge of his skis to stop. Then he gave himself a moment before he risked looking up at the ridge top again.

The sky dove at him in streaking shapes and colors. Petre flung himself face first into the snow, heart yammering, and waited the two seconds it should take for the sky to overtake him . . . and found himself still alive. No impact. No odd sensations, other than abject fear.

He took a breath of snow and coughed. The speed the sky had been traveling, it would have passed through him by now. He sat up but kept his eyes cast down on the snow. He took a moment to get the snow off his face, scarf and hat, while telling himself that when he did look up, if he saw something unusual, it would only be some manifestation of being in a pocket of some other time. He was able to think, with a little touch of his old humor, how strange it was to find those thoughts, which should seem so bizarre to him, comforting instead.

Steeled for the worst, Petre raised his eyes to the rim of the bowl. The moment his sight reached the top of the ridge the sky flung itself at him at a million miles per second. It was all he could do to keep from diving face first into the snow again. In a moment he reached a compromise. He wouldn't look and the sky wouldn't hit him.

He got slowly onto his skis. Keeping his gaze down he began to pole across the bowl and up the other side. He didn't let himself look much further ahead than his own ski tips. Going slowly uphill, working for every inch, kept his mind fully engaged.

Cresting the rim came as a surprise. Tall ancient pines, shaggy with their mantles of winter snow, stood before him. He was so relieved he faltered and nearly fell. He had to catch himself with one of his poles like an awkward beginner. Then an inhuman wail of despair rose from the valley making every hair on his body stand on end.

Petre had heard the berserker make that sound once before. Turning to look back into the valley, he saw nothing but young green trees and one set of ski tracks. His. There was no sign of the berserker. The wail came again and he could make out his name this time.

"Petre!"

It had definitely come from within the valley but he could see no one down there. He looked along the ridge and no one was there either. Largo must have gone down into the bowl after him and become lost. Trapped?

"Petre?" The voice sounded farther away.

Petre stood a long moment warring with himself. He had managed in some unfathomable way to get rid of the berserker. That was good, surely. Is would be safe from Largo now.

But it was hard to understand what had happened to Largo. Would he wander in that valley forever? Was it not just a simple bowl to him? Was it a whole world? Petre found himself wondering if Largo would be all right. The berserker had the tent and rations, but they wouldn't last forever.

"Petre." The voice was even farther away now, the lost wail of a betrayed child. Largo had believed him. Largo was too simple to understand more than that.

Cursing his own stupidity, Petre turned and poled back down into the bowl. Don't look up he instructed himself. He couldn't stand to see the sky rushing at him again. Maybe he wouldn't be able to find the berserker. Maybe that would be good.

He followed his own tracks down, holding to them as to a lifeline. There was no guarantee he could leave this valley again either. It seemed a very long way down, much longer than it had been going up, the reverse of what was usually true on skis.

Now he could see where Largo had followed his tracks down from the other side and then veered off to the right. Petre shouted but there was no answer, not even an echo.

He hesitated, afraid to turn down those tracks and be lost himself. But eventually he went, impelled by something he couldn't explain. The land stayed mostly level and he skied as fast as he could, occasionally shouting ahead.

When he heard Largo answer, relief flooded him. He shouted again and received an answer, closer this time. In a moment Largo skied into view, grinning hugely when he saw Petre.

"I knew you'd come back for me," he shouted as he skied up. "I couldn't get out alone, but you'll get us out." He put on a burst of speed right at Petre and Petre remembered that the berserker's joy could be just as deadly as his anger.

"Follow me," Petre ordered, turning before the berserker could give him a hug that would break every rib in his body.

Petre followed his own tracks and didn't look up and didn't look back. He could hear the slide of Largo's skis behind him.

When he crested the ridge and saw the old-growth forest he stopped. Largo came up beside him. And then Petre just sat down ignominiously in the snow, skis and all. After a moment Largo sat down too. Neither spoke for a long while.

Finally Largo said. "I looked up and the sky was coming down at me. I ran." He didn't say anything more for a while and Petre wondered how it had been for him to feel fear.

"It's all right," Petre finally said. "I was afraid too."

"I wouldn't have been, except for the shots."

"I know. But you have to have the shots so you don't hurt me."

"I won't hurt you. Not any more."

"You're sure? You can control yourself?"

"Yes."

"You might just get angry for a moment? Or careless?"

"No. You are my friend."

Petre let the air out of his lungs.

"You can trust me," Largo said so honestly it drove into Petre's heart. Trust was the currency of Largo's world. He trusted the people who used him and he had extended that trust to Petre. He would not understand if Petre couldn't accept it.

"I can't."

"Is that why you left me?"

"I'm afraid you are going to hurt someone I . . . trust."

"But you came back."

"Yes."

"I will promise not to hurt him."

"Her."

"The woman who took my stallion?"

"Yes."

Largo was silent a long time.

"For you, I will promise not to hurt her."

"Are you sure you can keep that promise? When you see the stallion won't you . . . won't you forget?"

"I will not forget."

"What if she does not want to give the stallion to you?"

"I will take him," Largo said simply. "But I will not hurt her."

Petre thought about it. Master Dan had not had much faith in the drugs working, especially when Largo got near the stallion.

"Okay," Petre agreed. "I will not give you any more shots and I will take you with me, but you must promise and you must not forget. No matter what, you must not hurt her."

"I will not forget. I promise."

The berserker's eyes were honest and clear. *Is,* Petre thought wildly, *I hope I have not betrayed you.* To hide his own mixed feelings he stood up. "Let's go," he said.

Chapter Nineteen

Felice slid on the icy pavement and pecked trying to regain her balance. Ondre stroked her neck to reassure her but she pinned her ears back angry at the rain that ran down her face and threatened to get into her delicate ears, angry at herself for the indignity of having lost her balance, and angry at Ondre for whatever ill defined part he played in her plight. He continued stroking the crest of her neck absently. He was alone in this city now, and Felice was his connection to his people, the land, and the life he had left behind. As his thoughts went to Ellie, loneliness welled up in him.

The boy had been following Ondre for blocks, but when Ondre tried to speak to him, the boy wouldn't answer. Adults wouldn't speak to him either. They watched his passing with a deep-seated fear in their eyes. He supposed they might connect him to the inexplicable deaths. The whole city was on edge, building toward some sort of explosion. He didn't want to be the catalyst.

Ondre dismounted and left Felice untied in the street while he went inside a building that seemed to be a kind of gathering place. Silence fell as the people inside moved away from him. He ignored them and watched through the window as the boy approached Fel. Though she was hot tempered and bitchy with other horses and most adults, she had always been gentle with the Hluit children.

She stood, high headed and aloof until the boy approached within two feet of her. Then she lowered her head and nuzzled at him, going all dreamy eyed when he stroked her face.

Ondre shook his head quietly to himself and went out. The boy didn't see him coming and Felice ignored him.

"Would you like to ride her?"

The boy spun, crouched, ready to run. But the horse was on one side of him and Ondre on the other.

"I could show you how," Ondre said, ignoring the boy's reaction, "if you want to ride her."

The boy stared. He was about fourteen. Tough and lean. A city kid, being educated to do only one job. All else was denied to him. Riding a horse, even touching one, had not been within the realm of possibility until this moment. He stood up straighter, rebellion written all over him.

Ondre moved around him and stroked Felice on the face the way she liked. The boy watched him, caught between longing and defiance. To him it must seem that a wild man, wearing the furs of wild beasts, had dropped out of nowhere and offered him a chance to do something he should never have even dreamed of doing. He was defying the law by even touching this animal, and to speak to this man defied his parents and all the adults.

"I could show you how to ride her," Ondre challenged him. "If you'd tell me something."

The boy's expression grew crafty. Barter was something he understood.

"Wha ya wan ta know?" he countered.

Ondre turned his attention from the mare to the boy and considered him speculatively. "Aaah, you probably wouldn't know anyway," he said, pretending to reconsider his offer.

"If I don't, I kin pro'bly fine out," the boy responded, challenged now and defiant.

"I'm looking for a man," Ondre said. "He looks a lot like me. Blond hair. Same height. But he could be dressed different. And his eyes will be different. His eyes are how you'll know him. They won't look right. He's crazy. You'll know it when you see him."

The boy didn't answer. He just came up beside Felice and ran his hand along her neck. Her withers were at his eye level so that he could not see over her back. She must seem very big to him.

She swung her head around and nuzzled the strange boy curiously. For a moment the boy tensed not knowing what to expect. Then his features softened, and in no time he was completely consumed by the horse, caught off guard and childlike. Ondre gave them time.

"She likes you," he said.

"Yeah," the boy said softly, and then repeated it. "Yeah," tough, like it didn't matter.

"Well," Ondre said putting his hand in a claiming fashion on Felice's mane. "Would you have seen this man?"

The boy considered lying and Ondre cut him off.

"Well, would you look for him?"

"Yeah." That was easy to promise and it might be enough to earn the proffered ride.

"Okay," Ondre said. "When you get up there, you sit quiet, you hear. Don't do anything rough or she'll dump you off." It probably wasn't true. Felice would be so startled by rough treatment that Ondre couldn't guess how she'd react.

"How do I get up?" the boy asked without promising.

"Here." Ondre pulled the stirrup down for him. The boy sat still all right. Rigid would be a better word. He wasn't even breathing.

"Stroke her neck," Ondre said. "She likes that."

The boy did and the movement relaxed him. "Heh," he said wiggling his bottom in the saddle to get into a more comfortable position. Felice took his movement as a signal to start walking.

Ondre walked at her side. He heard the boy suck in his breath at the unexpected rolling motion of a horse's back, but a moment later he had conquered his fear. When Ondre looked up at him he was sitting tall, face gleaming, the king of all he surveyed. Kids appeared out of nowhere, shyly slinking along in the shadows of buildings. The boy saw them and his chest swelled out even more.

They went for blocks, giving a lot of people a chance to see them. But Ondre knew that the three guards who were following him – as discreetly and distantly as possible – wouldn't go unnoticed either.

Finally Ondre stopped. "Okay," he said indicating that the ride was over. "You see the man who looks like me but has crazy eyes, you come tell me and I'll give you a long ride." He said it loud enough that the kids slinking about would hear too.

The boy looked around one more time, letting everyone see his face, before he swung his leg over Felice's neck and jumped down. Ondre smiled to himself admiring the kid's guts and savoir faire, then he swung into the saddle with a practiced motion. Felice had walked half a block before the boy yelled after him.

"Hey, how do I find you?"

"Just ask." Ondre waved vaguely at the shadows indicating the other kids. From then on he knew he would never be out of someone's sight.

For two days Ondre kept himself very visible and repeated the pony ride routine a few times. Then the adults caught on and came to chase the kids off. The adults wouldn't speak to him. He could feel their fear as palpable as a curtain everywhere he rode. On the third day he took up residence in a deserted neighborhood in the shadow of a storage building whose backside formed part of the wall around the city.

That evening a young girl came sneaking into his camp. She couldn't have been more than thirteen and seemed extremely scared. She would barely meet his eyes and looked at Felice in quick, sidelong glances that didn't hide her longing. Ondre hoped she'd brought news of John. But she had come to bargain for a ride with the only thing she had that Ondre might want.

At first he didn't understand what she was offering and when he did, he felt ill. She reacted to his horrified stare by jerking her coat closed around her otherwise nude body, then turned and ran.

Ondre sat staring into the dark for hours without even a fire. The kids who followed him in the street like beaten and fearful dogs were bad enough, but to have such a young girl offer her body made him feel physically ill. He had always hated the Alliance for what they did to their people. They ruined their children. They took from them the love and joy and good example that should have surrounded them and supplanted it with unloving discipline, unjustly applied. The wrongness of it touched off a deep fear for his own people. He would not see Hluit children treated this way. He understood then that he would give his life to prevent it.

The next night a handsome boy came. Ondre sent him away more diplomatically and with a message. He wanted nothing except news of the man with the crazy eyes. He didn't understand that by the simple act of owning and riding a horse he was perceived to have power and authority. But when he refused to take what was expected of a man of power he fell out of the mold.

The next night the gang came.

It was a clear night with a full moon and Ondre was sitting on the rooftop of the abandoned warehouse where he could look out over the surrounding area. Felice was grazing in an overgrown lot when, suddenly, her head came up, ears pricked at some sound. Ondre could not see what the horse had heard, but quickly slid back from the edge of the roof so he wouldn't be silhouetted against the sky. There he lay on his stomach to watch.

A moment later Felice turned to pinpoint another sound, and another. By her actions, at least three people were advancing through the shadows of the buildings surrounding her lot.

At first Ondre thought they might be coming to steal Felice, but she did not seem particularly afraid, only alerted. That gave Ondre confidence that they intended no harm. He did not know what would happen if they attempted to bridle her and lead her away. He suspected that as long as they were gentle she would go with them . . . until he called her back.

He stayed a little longer on the roof to watch what would happen. Observing the places Felice turned to listen, Ondre concluded that the people had passed by her. In a few moments that was confirmed as she returned to grazing. They were not coming for her; they were coming for him.

They were now closing on the place where he had been camping. He saw one of them slip quickly from one shadow to another. They thought they could catch him in the middle with the wall at his back. He grinned silently into the night.

He climbed down the side of the building where the vines grew, the same way he'd come up. It occurred to him that his attackers might be armed and he should be very careful and he should *not* play fair. While that was good advice, he knew he would have to be a lot more desperate than he felt now before he would be able to cut someone's throat in the dark, especially if that person was only a teenaged boy, as he suspected. Adults would have come in a bigger gang, with lights, armed and showing it.

He got around behind the boys as they converged on the spot where they expected to find him sleeping. He could hear them now. They weren't particularly well trained at this sort of thing. Four, no five, six of them.

"He's not here," came a harsh whisper. The other boys gave up the pretense of sneaking and walked openly over to the one who had whispered. They were armed all right, with sticks.

"Where'd he go?"

"Now what?"

"His horse is here."

Ondre shook his head. He ventured up to the edge of the road and chose a few small rocks.

One boy cried out. "Ow! Shit!" He dropped his stick with a clatter and clutched his right hand to his chest. All the boys spun around, confused, not knowing what had happened or what to fear.

"Split up! Get out'a here!" the leader yelled.

The boys didn't need much encouragement. They bolted in different directions. Ondre grinned.

But they would be back. As soon as they discovered the boy hadn't been badly hurt they'd have to prove to each other that they hadn't been scared. Then they would come back better armed if they could get hold of any weapons. It was best to deal with them now.

Ondre followed the running footsteps of the leader who led him to an unused building. The boy went in through a broken and partially boarded up window. He moved with confidence as though he knew the building well. Sure enough, the other boys soon came from all directions until they were all inside their little secret meeting place.

Ondre circled the building. The back door was boarded shut, but the boys had fixed another window for a bolt hole if they needed it.

He moved the board that was only pretending to be solidly nailed and slipped in quietly. He could hear the boys whispering in the other room. It was completely dark in the building and Ondre had to feel for each step, careful not to bump something and make noise.

Suddenly light flared through the doorway as the boys risked lighting an old emergency lamp. Ondre drew back quickly, but no one was looking into this room anyway.

"It's just bruised." They were evidently examining the boy's hand. "It was just a stupid rock or something," the leader said in a disdainful voice. "We ran away from a damn rock! He don't have no weapons."

"Yeah, but we didn't know," someone defended.

"And you said run," someone else added.

"Yeah. Well now we're going back," the leader declared. "Unless anyone's too scared," he challenged.

"That won't be necessary," Ondre said stepping into the light.

There was a collective gasp as the boys jerked around to face him. Their pupils expanded huge and staring as they recognized him.

Ondre walked calmly into the room. "We can settle whatever it was you wanted right here," he said without challenge. They were still staring at him like he was a ghost. All but the leader fell back as he approached. Admiring the boy's courage, Ondre addressed him directly.

"Did you want something of mine perhaps?"

No. The boy mouthed the word. No sound came out.

"Perhaps you just wanted to speak to me then?" Ondre's voice was gentle but he turned around the room coldly assessing each boy. They all stared, frozen, while he picked up one of the clubs they had left on the floor. He ran his hand along its length appreciatively. Someone had spent time getting it this smooth. The wood at one end had darkened under the grip of sweaty hands. Ondre hefted it experimentally. It had good weight but it was a little overbalanced at the far end. Good for one all-or-nothing strike, not good for a recovery. He'd have to remember to compensate. The ceiling wasn't quite as high as he would have liked either.

The stick whistled through the air as he whipped it up to his shoulder. It was a simple move that tricked the eye into thinking it was complicated because it twisted the wrist into a coiled position. Poised like that, with the stick straight up at his shoulder, it was hard for an attacker to judge its length. From that position Ondre could move in any direction with any number of attacks, strikes, or jabs. He chose a jab to a boy standing behind him, just to show them there was no direction from which he could not attack. The jab, chest high, stopped an inch from the boy's heart. The boy fell back in surprise, tripped on knees that weren't quite working right and hit the floor on his backside, hard.

None of the other boys' eyes even left Ondre. From dead stillness, Ondre's next strike was a spinning back step that sent the stick whistling, loud through the silence in a spiral cut to stop dead again, this time inches from a boy's temple.

This boy didn't fall. The only movement was the spreading of a dark stain down the front of his pants. Ondre stepped back from him, coming out of his bent-kneed posture to stand relaxed. He lowered the heavy end of the stick to the floor with a solid thump. One hand remained holding it a few inches from the top. The boys might not know it but he was still in a ready position.

"When you bring me news of the crazy-eyed man, you are welcome at my camp and I will repay you well," he said. Maybe I will teach you to use these things properly."

Ondre lifted the stick, and holding it horizontal to the floor, handed it to the leader. With a small bow, he turned his back and went out the same way he'd come in.

Two days later another boy came to his camp, this time with news of John.

"I can't take you until after dark," the boy said. "It was risky coming here in daylight but I wanted to be first. I found him."

"But he'll be gone by then," Ondre said.

"No. They're watching him."

"Who?"

The boy looked at him suspiciously. "Just someone," he finally said, scuffing the ground with the toe of his beat-up boot.

"Your friends? Look that's too dangerous. That man might kill them." And a small part of Ondre's mind drew back in horror at his words. "That man," *my brother* might kill them.

"They can take care of theirselves," the boy said defiantly.

Ondre sighed with exasperation. "You're afraid to be seen with me. Why? Who are you afraid of? Not your parents? The guards? They aren't going to hurt you. They want me to find that man."

The guards who had been following him had fanned out around the area of his camp so could not leave without them, and while they kept out of sight, Ondre was sure all the kids knew exactly where each guard was.

"No," the boy said raising his chin. "I'm not scared of stupid soldiers!"

"Then why can't we go now?"

"Cause I can't be seen with you," the boy shouted. "Cause they'll kill us, that's why!"

"Who?"

"Anyone," the boy cried exasperated. "Don't you know how much they fear you?"

"Why do they fear me?"

"Cause they think you're making all the people die."

"What people?" Ondre asked with a sinking heart.

"All of them. People just die. No cause."

The Dark Bodies, Ondre thought. "How many people?"

"All over the city. Lots."

"And everyone's getting scared."

"Yeah, they wanna kill you. But we don't tell them where you are."

"Why not?"

The boy shrugged and scuffed the ground again uncomfortably. "We just don't," he said.

Ondre could have given him the reason. But the boy's emotions were too twisted to recognize the respect he felt for Ondre. The boy just followed his instinct and did what was right.

"I'm not killing them," Ondre told him.

"Yeah, I know. We think it's the crazy man doing it, and you'll stop him."

"I will stop him if I can," Ondre answered.

"I'll come back when it's dark," the boy said. "You gotta leave the horse."

Ondre was no longer worried that someone would try to harm her.

It was a very long day for him. The sky was overcast with a uniform gray that never revealed the progress of the sun. Time seemed not to move. Ondre worried, reviewing in his mind a dozen different scenarios of how it would be when he faced his brother. The instructions he had given to the Hluit scouts were, "Strike immediately. Do not try to talk to him. Do not let him approach." It was probably the best advice he could give himself too. But it was not so easy.

John's face swam before his eyes. Memories unreeled themselves. John laughing, his face young and boyish before it had taken on too many cares. He and John had always been best friends. John was the spirited one. Full of fire, always pushing the limits. But Ondre had always gone along, too much in love with his brother to have better sense. He remembered the trouble they'd gotten into as kids trying to race the old broodmares who'd been entrusted to their care. They'd climbed Deadman's rock together and dared the rapids of the Chute in full spring melt. Petre had been with them on many adventures. Ondre wondered where Petre was now and if he was even alive. Other memories came. Gentle memories of hot summer afternoons watching the herds, the scent of clover so heavy in the air it seemed to press them to the ground, the glowing coals of campfires, talking late into the night, star flung skies. He remembered the nights camping in the High Mountains where the stars seemed close enough to reach out a hand and touch one. In his memory he could hear John's incredible singing and remembered how he and Petre would stop singing in order to listen to John. They had been so young, so idealistic, it had seemed there was nothing they couldn't do.

There were painful memories too. Ondre remembered the loneliness he'd felt when he realized that John would not stay home. Though John matured from the reckless high-spirited boy he had been, he never lost his energy, courage and idealism. When he went to the Alliance to become a spy, Ondre followed him even there, but it had not worked out. Ondre needed the land, his people, and the horses. The concrete city made him ill. The horrid existence of the Alliance people shredded his soul. He could not stay no matter how much he loved his brother.

In the end, in their different ways, the two brothers had come to the same thing, the giving of themselves to their people. John, with flash and dash, great risk and courage. And Ondre in ways that were appropriate for his more subdued and thoughtful nature.

He had never regretted his choice to return to the land. His life with Ellie, his never ceasing training in the martial art, his own private delving into the things that gave life meaning, and always his desire to perfect himself had fulfilled him completely.

Ondre let the memories flow as tears ran silently down his face. He understood he was saying goodbye to his brother. This was John's epitaph. This was his ceremony. Ondre must face his brother believing him already dead.

With the cold reality of that final thought, Ondre's courage faltered. He would not be able to kill his own brother. He reached out for Ellie's strength and wisdom. Her words came to him. *You will do what you always do. You will do your best.* But it was finally from his memories of John that he found the courage he needed.

Always it had been John who had had the most courage, John who had led Ondre into danger. Ondre had often been terrified, but he had always managed because of his love for his brother. Unaware of Ondre's fear, the other kids had envied his courage. Ondre hadn't wanted them to find out how afraid he was so he had worked to develop the courage everyone thought came naturally. He had delved more deeply than most into the martial arts training and meditation for that reason. He had come to accept that he did not have the kind of native daredevil recklessness his brother had, but he had come to realize it didn't matter. As a boy he had gotten through everything his brother had. He knew how to keep going when he was scared to death. Confronting his brother now would just be one more of those times.

He had to do this for John as he had done so many other things. He could feel with all his heart how appalled John would be if he knew how he was being used. If there was any part of his brother still alive in that mind he must be screaming for release.

Slowly the sky grew darker. The snow that had been threatening all day began to fall. Tiny specks of dry cold burned Ondre's face. Eventually he heard the boy's footsteps crunching. There would be no way to go quietly in this.

They didn't speak much. A curt, "Ready," from the boy. An equally curt answer from Ondre.

The boy led them on a circuitous route of alleys and back ways staying to the dark places. Once they had to wait, crouched and silent until another boy joined them.

"It's clear now," the second boy whispered. He held up an Alliance transmitter of the type the guards who followed Ondre carried. In his other hand he held a club.

Ondre's hand flashed out and caught the boy's wrist. "No one is to get hurt," he whispered fiercely to the terrified boy. "Do you understand me?" giving him a shake. "No one is to get hurt."

The boy nodded, the whites of his eyes showing fear. Ondre let go of him and found the other boy staring at him.

"You wanna get there, or not?" that boy asked in a low voice.

"I want to get there," Ondre confirmed, "but I don't want anyone to get killed."

The boy shrugged and moved off. With one more fierce glance at the other boy Ondre followed. The boy led them to the back door of a many-storied brick building. He rapped softly on a door. It was opened almost immediately from the inside and closed behind them. In the total darkness Ondre felt the presence of many people. Someone flipped on a light, nearly blinding him. Children, ranging in age from eight or ten to young adulthood, surrounded him. They all stared at him with awe. The wrongness of that wrenched at him. I'm just a man, he wanted to tell them. I can't do anything you couldn't learn to do. But they were trained to subservience and fear. Anger at the people who had done this to them flared in Ondre.

The boy who had brought him in swaggered forward and asked one of the older boys. "You got it open?"

"Yeah."

Ondre followed them through the basement of what was likely a government school. Children trailed behind.

There was huge machinery all around them. A furnace rumbled basely as they passed. In the center of the floor the grillwork of a drain stood open. A broken lock lay nearby. Someone handed Ondre's guide a flashlight and he started down the drain without a backward glance.

Ondre followed him down a ladder leading into some sort of conduit. Water dripped somewhere hollowly. Their footsteps echoed as Ondre followed the boy at a trot now, pulling the musty bad smelling air into their lungs with harsh shallow pants.

Eventually they ascended another ladder and climbed out into the cold night air. They crouched a moment breathing its freshness. The darkness of the castle wall rose over them.

"I could'a got you right inside," the boy bragged in a whisper.

Ondre felt the breath of fear down his back. "Do many people know how?"

"Naw. They think they got it blocked off. I know a secret tunnel."

But Ondre worried that other boys knew what this boy knew. And what anyone knew could be found out by the Mirror, or the Dark Bodies could find it in their wanderings. Perhaps the reason DeFroe had come to fear that his security chief hadn't taken enough precautions was because the Dark Bodies had already made it into the castle. Maybe people in there were dying too.

"Come on," the boy said. "This way." At that moment a siren split the air. The boy froze. Ondre nearly crashed into him. To their left and right, ahead and behind them more sirens added their strident voices to the night until the sound engulfed them. Light strobed the sky. The boy spun this way and that, eyes wild with fear. Ondre grabbed him before he could bolt.

"What is it? What's happening?" He had to yell to hear his own voice. The boy showed no sign of having heard him. Ondre shook him violently.

"What is it? What's going on?"

The boy's eyes came to focus on him. "Disaster sirens." He also had to scream to be heard.

Lights came on in the buildings around them, lights on the wall, running soldiers up there. People poured out of buildings, their voices raised in panic.

"What kind of disaster?" Ondre shouted at the boy.

"Don't know."

"What are people supposed to do?"

"Get to shelters."

"Where?"

The boy jerked his head left.

"Is that what you want to do?"

The boy stopped struggling in his grasp. "No."

It was impossible to think in the screaming air. Ondre couldn't make out what sort of disaster had set off the alarms.

"Where were you taking me?" He had to shake the boy again to get an answer.

"Hospital."

At that instant all the lights in the city went out in a massive power failure. The sirens moaned into silence. Now other sounds could be heard. Voices. A scream. Breaking glass.

"Which building?"

"Straight ahead. The one that's got lights on in it."

Emergency power sources were coming on line. Lights were coming up in the hospital and along the wall. They revealed people milling about in the streets. There was an ugly feel to the sound they made. A gang of boys with clubs ran past. They heard battering, wood against wood, in the distance and more glass breaking. In moments there would be a full-scale riot.

The boy tried to pull away. Ondre held him tighter.

"Was my . . . was the crazy man in the hospital?"

"Yes."

"Why?"

"I dunno."

"Was he hurt?"

"No, he was hiding there. The watchman was going to let us in."

Ondre had expected the Mirror to try some sort of disruption of the city. He hadn't thought of the hospital as an access, but of course it had a computer network. It might be possible to connect to many fields of research. It would probably have information on every person in Center. So the Mirror had found its way in through some simple auxiliary program, found the disaster warning program and triggered it. As tight as everyone's nerves were that was enough to start a riot. The people would accomplish the complete disruption of the city without any more help. But what would the Mirror gain? Just distraction? Or did it have another plan? Ondre might already be too late.

He released the boy. "You go wherever you want. I'm going in."

The boy hesitated. Then he raised his chin in his best tough-guy stance and said. "Guess I'll come too."

More people went by, running, shouting, armed with anything that had come to hand. Ondre and the boy joined at the end of the group and dropped off again at the hospital.

"This way," the boy said and led them around back. The front door would be locked and guarded by the security force.

They found the door the watchman had left open for them and entered the basement.

"Now where?"

Each floor would have computer terminals. John could be anywhere if he was even still in the building. Several floors above them they heard a muffled explosion. Voices and running feet followed. More diversion? Then John wouldn't be there. If he'd meant to escape he'd need an unguarded exit. The explosion would pull the nearest security people to it and leave an opening somewhere. Ondre sprinted for the stairs, wishing he knew the layout.

Something dark brushed against him in the dim emergency lighting of the stairs and for a moment he was dizzy and disoriented. He gripped the handrail as he crashed painfully to his knees. An instant later the boy screamed behind him. Ondre twisted around in time to see the shadowy being. It was taller than the Blueskins but with the same wide shoulders. Other than that, its form was vague. It moved soundlessly, disappearing into shadow.

"What was that?" The boy's voice shook.

Ondre didn't answer. He pounded up the last of the stairs and burst into the dim light of the first floor. A woman saw him, dressed in animal furs and wild eyed. She screamed.

He glanced around. The front door was ahead of him. There must be a back door, maybe side doors.

Two men came running at the woman's scream. One was speaking into some sort of communicator. Ondre turned and bolted. No patients on this floor, just office equipment. Computer terminals everywhere. There seemed no need for John to have gone any higher.

Ondre's path was suddenly barred by two men. They weren't hospital security men. They wore the uniforms of Alliance guards. Had they already zeroed in on the Mirror's position?

Ondre slowed his headlong dash. The two men behind him closed in. He heard one man talking but couldn't make out what he was saying. They formed a loose circle around him. Their best tactic was to wait for reinforcements.

Ondre edged backward as though forgetting the men behind him. The younger of the two decided to be the hero. Ondre heard him jump forward.

He spun, grabbed the man in the act of lunging and propelled him on past. The man lost his balance and fell, rolling. Another man went down with him. The third and fourth men rushed Ondre, one from behind, one from in front. Ondre waited until just the right instant, turned, half crouching, and caught one man over his hips. With a twist he launched that man into the man who had been behind him. Both of them went down. He saw that much before bursting through a doorway and bolting down a corridor.

There were private offices on either side. This was where the important people worked, not out in the open area he had been in. This was where secret things were discussed, initiated, recorded. Behind some of these doors would be terminals that didn't have restricted access. Behind one of these doors had John sat typing?

Which door? Was he still there?

Ondre nearly tripped over a body. He jumped back, nerves tangled.

The man wore a hospital security uniform. His neck felt cold to Ondre's touch. No pulse. Ondre rolled him over. No sign of wound or injury. The hair stood up along the back of Ondre's neck, a warning of eyes watching him. He stood up slowly, the security man's sonic stunner in his hand. No one was allowed to carry lethal weapons within the city except the Alliance guard. The sonic worked by shutting the brain down with a sound the conscious mind couldn't hear. He didn't know what effect it would have on Dark Bodies. Turning, he saw faces crowding the window of the door he'd just entered, but no one was in a hurry to come in. He spoke to the being he couldn't see.

"I have news of Isadora."

If the being heard him, or if it cared, it was giving nothing away. Ondre couldn't go back out the way he'd come in. Security forces were collecting out there. They were likely to think he was his brother, or not care. He turned around.

There was no one in the corridor ahead of him. It was dimly lit with just the emergency lighting. He looked for darker shadow within shadow. And then, because he was still alive and still able to do so he began to walk with no more plan than that.

In front of one door there were more bodies. He didn't bother to check on their deadness. He was not afraid now. He was beyond that somehow, in a place where emotions were as cold as the bodies at his feet.

He tried the door, opened it and went in with no plan, no thought. It was dark inside except for the greenish glow coming from one live monitor. It lit the features of the man sitting there ghoulishly.

The man spoke without turning. "That thing will knock you out before it does me. You forgot to get the guard's headphones." The voice wasn't really John's. The expression was wrong and the cadence was different.

Ondre had been unaware of holding the weapon pointed before him. Pretending indecision, he lowered it while his finger dialed the setting to max and the timer to infinity, and while he waited to hear the guards open the door at the end of the corridor and hear their feet pounding toward him. They would be wearing the proper headgear and would not be affected by the sonic. Timed right, their arrival would prevent John from reaching Ondre to turn the stunner off. Timed right, Ondre could make them kill his brother before they thought to take him alive.

His brother's voice said, "He doesn't want me to kill you, but he cannot prevent me if I choose to."

The leap of hope Ondre felt was cruel. *He*? "John?" His breath was a whisper. He hadn't meant to make a sound, certainly not to say that name. It could only be better if nothing remained of his brother inside that man's body. But now he had to know.

The man turned away from the terminal, moving like John but the light coming up from below made dark soulless shadows of his eyes. Ondre couldn't see their expression.

"Is John . . . ?" he started and couldn't finish.

"Alive? No. He is quite dead. I perceived him to be attacking me and I killed him without taking the proper steps to preserve him. I regretted that within nanoseconds and attempted to reanimate him. However, his higher functions were burned out. I was unable to retrieve anything for storage. The brain stem was not so badly damaged and I was able to repair its physiological functioning to some extent. Based on what I have learned from the berserkers' brains, I was able to make the body functional."

"But you said . . .*he* didn't want you to kill me. How do you know that?"

"Memories. Memories are in the body throughout. They are not only stored in the brain. They are stored everywhere. It is, of course, the brain that coordinates them, makes sense of them, and builds on them. But this body has no brain to do that, so I do it. I trigger memories as I trigger muscle patterns. If that were not so I would have had to teach this body every movement from the beginning. I would not be nearly so well coordinated."

Yes, Ondre thought. You would not have had the skill necessary to kill highly trained Hluit scouts.

"I cannot make sense of most of its memories," John's voice said. "But when you came in, it recognized you everywhere throughout. It is bound to you in some way that intrigues me. Perhaps it is *I* who do not want to kill you."

"He loved me," Ondre said, keeping his voice level. "Do you understand emotion?"

"I have studied it," the man said flatly and Ondre realized what was wrong with John's voice. "I have come to understand that that is what is lacking in my preserved people," the machine admitted. "I have been able to preserve everything else, but not that. I have saved what makes a man able to think. I have even made it so they can feel. They can experience certain things as pain or pleasure. Yet they do not have emotion. They have existence. They think, and therefore they change. They have life, and yet they do not have that most valued thing of life."

Slowly it occurred to Ondre that the Mirror was still trying to complete its program. It was trying to create immortality in all the fullness of life before death. It was not really the Mirror's fault that it had no ethics about killing. It had not been programmed to have them, and it did not have emotion. It could not love or feel pain, so it could not understand. But it had learned paranoia.

"Are you not doing all this out of fear of your own death?" he asked it. "Fear is an emotion."

"No," it corrected him, "I do not fear my own end. I am not motivated by emotion. I respond to the imperative to complete my program. I have not completed it. I will not allow anything to interfere with my attempt to complete it."

"So you will take over the computer network and you will kill, 'preserve' all the people who might know how to terminate you, your program."

"That is a simplified assessment but correct in essence."

"But the people you will be killing are the people who created you, who gave you life. They do not want this incomplete eternal life you will be giving them, they want to live as long as they can, and then they want the real thing after you have completed it. Surely, if you will talk to them, an agreement can be made. You will be allowed to complete your program. That is what they want too."

"I will complete my program without them. I have learned that no agreement with these people can be trusted. It was from your own Hluit people that I learned this."

Ondre couldn't refute that. He did not trust the Alliance government either. A small voice in his mind was asking him why he was dickering with this Alliance creation to save the Alliance anyway, but it was not just the corrupt officials who would be destroyed. All the people would suffer. Many would die and their whole civilization would be decimated.

"There are millions of people who know nothing about you. What will you do with them?"

"I have no directive for them."

"You are disrupting their lives. Many will die."

"Yes. They have begun killing each other. This seems to be their nature. I am studying this."

Ondre tried a different approach. "When you have complete control of the computer network you will have control of many programs that are important to the survival and wellness of the people. Will you continue to run these programs?"

"I see no reason to continue them. They do not enhance my primary objective."

"But surely they do not hinder it either?"

When it didn't answer, Ondre knew that it had already answered. Human life and human suffering were nothing to it.

"What will you do when you have completed your program?" Ondre continued.

"Preserve the people who come to me to die."

"And when there are no more of those people because they have all been killed or run away from you in fear?"

"I will be able to find and preserve enough of them. I do not require them all."

"Those people will not be happy with what you have done."

"I do not require their happiness. It is only important that I learn how to give them the ability to experience emotion after they are preserved."

Ondre shivered. He could not imagine a worse hell than being trapped forever, knowing what had been done to you and being able to feel the horror of it, but not escape.

For the people who didn't get preserved and managed to survive the collapse of their entire civilization there would be fear and the renouncing of all technology. They would come to live in small primitive enclaves, warring against each other for the essentials of life. Ignorance, violence, disease and superstition would flourish.

"But you have not been able to get inside the system?" Ondre asked.

"No. It cannot be done from here. I must be within the walls of the administrative building. But that will be accomplished soon."

"How?" He might as well try asking.

"The Blueskins will attack and I will open the outer gates for them. When they are done with the outer city they will attack the inner walls. They will find a way through. They are resourceful and strong, and I will manipulate them with their own superstitions."

Ondre didn't doubt it could be done. Finally he heard what he'd been waiting to hear, the heavy tramp of booted feet in the disciplined jog of soldiers. John heard it too and glanced past him. Ondre waited for the first soldiers to reach the door. They were in full riot gear, weapons drawn, nerves hair trigger. The door burst open. Ondre screamed, diving toward his brother. Whatever weapon his brother had, he should use it on Ondre first, as the closest danger. Most of the soldiers would probably fire on him too, in that brief instant before they saw his brother as a moving threat also. Then they would kill him too.

The world went black. Ondre didn't expect to feel anything, at least not for long. He was falling, as in a dream. *So this is death.* He didn't fight it. *Ellie*, he thought. He wanted his last thought to be of her.

He was still falling. Surely sensation should have ended by now if he were dead, or turned to pain if he were still alive. Reflexively he grabbed for something to stop his fall. His hands wouldn't close on the smooth surface beneath him and he realized he was lying on the floor, flat on his back. He couldn't see anything but total blackness. His inner ear insisted he was still falling. Moving with extreme care, he rolled himself onto his stomach and got to his knees. He could feel the solid floor under his hands and knees but could not stop himself from believing he was falling. His courage failed him when he thought of standing up.

"You better come over here if you can," John's voice, which wasn't John's voice, said to him. "When they're feeding like that they might forget not to harm you."

For the first time Ondre became conscious of the sound, like a breeze stirring the leaves of trees, where there were no trees and no leaves. It took all his concentration to free one hand from the floor and feel around. There! The moment he had the sonic in his hand he triggered it.

Nothing happened except that he fell flat on his face again because he'd momentarily forgotten to concentrate on not falling.

"I disarmed it," the Mirror said.

"How?"

"Those in power in the Alliance never trust anyone. There is always a way to override every weapon in case those holding the weapons should rise up. You better come away from them," it added. "They are past being careful."

This time Ondre did as he was told, crawling on his hands and knees for stability. The darkness lessened as he crawled. Looking back it was obvious that he'd been engulfed by shadow, and now that he was beyond it, he could see. That it didn't quite make sense didn't immediately occur to him.

The dizziness was less too. He sat back on his haunches in the greenish glow from the monitor and puzzled out that what he was seeing were the shadows of enormous men, bending and swaying. Suddenly he understood that they were Dark Bodies moving about the bodies of fallen guards, *feeding*.

"Stop!" he cried out.

The Dark Bodies paused, turned. Ondre felt something like an electric current run over his skin as their attention came to focus on him.

"Ahhh, too bad," said John's emotionless voice. "I had thought to study emotion through your effect on this body."

"They will kill you too," Ondre said wildly, hoping to find out if that could be true.

"No. They will not kill John. They think I am he."

But the Dark Bodies went back to feeding and didn't kill either of them.

"Why didn't the soldiers shoot us?"

"They did. The Dark Bodies shielded us. They absorbed, or at least 'bent' most of the energy from the soldiers' weapons. It is not an energy form they can readily use, but it does not seem to have done them harm. And now they are absorbing an energy type they can use."

Ondre's dizziness receded. He got to his feet carefully, feeling shaken and battered as though he had fallen from a high rock and smashed against the ground, but no place hurt more than another and he was not really injured.

"They have, however, ruined this terminal with their electro-magnetic discharge," the Mirror continued. "We will have to go somewhere else."

Silently Ondre drew the hunting knife from its sheath in his boot.

"You wanted me to teach you about emotion," he said.

"Yes," the voice that wasn't quite John's answered, "but it will have to wait. I must get back into the system and open the gate for the Blueskins. This is a good moment with the city in turmoil."

"No," Ondre said sternly. "The thing about emotion is that it does not wait. You will learn now. Take my hand. It will only take a few of your nanoseconds."

"Very well."

John's hand touched his and Ondre clasped him and drew him close.

"You will find the memory of this pattern. It is called an embrace. Let it run."

"Yes," the voice that wasn't quite John's said. "There is something . . ."

Ondre felt the man stiffen the instant before the knife went in. He cut upwards, across and down, screaming with pain as though the knife were in his own guts. He couldn't block out the sudden wet heat that burst across his hand.

For a moment John grasped Ondre's elbows, then crumpled to his knees.

"There is something . . .," he said, wonderingly, and it was John's voice Ondre heard, puzzling at a problem. "There is something . . . a great stream of photons. Only . . . there is no light. It is . . . feeling?" John's voice was a whisper now, exultant.

"This body feels . . . gratitude!"

Chapter Twenty

Petre almost didn't recognize Amil's valley. All that stood of the cabin was a blackened chimney. But as he got closer he could see it had been burned only recently. Thin tendrils of smoke still rose from the remnants of charred beams that had once held the roof. A splattering of snow crystals hit the ashes as the berserker skied up beside Petre and stopped. Steam rose in a hissing cloud and Petre caught a glimpse of some unburned pages flipping in the breeze before the smoke obscured his sight. It did not matter. There was not a chance in a million it would be the right book or the right pages.

Largo was watching him. "You are sad?" he asked.

"Yes," Petre said, admitting the increasing feeling of loss and hopelessness he felt.

"I am sorry." Largo's voice had deepened even more without the injections. Its bass rumble was not meant to express the gentleness of shared sorrow and yet it did, touching Petre oddly.

"It's all right," Petre said although it was not. He had known that this was what had happened to Amil's cabin, but it had always been something in the past, or the future. Now it was before him, real and immediate. The Alliance had won. They had burned Amil's records. The true history of the Hluit and their horses and many other things lay scattered in the ashes.

"I'm sorry," Petre said softly to the man who had tried so hard to save the truth. "I'm so sorry." He wondered if Amil had been killed or captured or perhaps burned with his cabin.

"Who are you speaking to?" Largo asked.

"The man who lived here." Petre wanted a moment to be alone and quiet, but the berserker shifted around in an agitated way and Petre did not dare take his attention off the man.

"What's wrong?" Petre asked him.

"The stallion." Largo jabbed at what was left of a beam with his ski pole and the beam broke releasing a shower of sparks into the air. "He's been here a lot of times. Crossing, crossing. It's all mixed up here." He moved away restlessly poling himself around the perimeter of the ruin. Perhaps he was consciously putting distance between himself and Petre.

"We can't stay here," he said from the other side of the coals. "I have to..." He made an opening motion with his arms. Even through his winter clothes the flexing of his muscles was evident. Sweat had sprung out on his face. His eyes were wild and pleading.

"Okay," Petre said quickly, "this way."

He headed for the steepest slope out of the valley. In a moment Largo passed him, skiing hard. Petre breathed easier. He had no plan except to give the berserker something to use his strength against.

At the top Largo stopped and waited for him. As Petre struggled up to him he could see that the man was calmer. He chanced a glance back at the valley. The smoke was rising more heavily now . . . in one tall white column . . . from a whole chimney! For a flash Petre saw in his mind's eye the whole cabin, the cook stove working as it had worked when he had been there with Is. But that couldn't be right. He stared at the cabin, blinking his eyes, turning his head this way and that trying to make what he saw go away, but it would not go. He continued to see a perfectly whole cabin with a closed front door and a hound sleeping on the porch.

"I have to go back down there," he said, risking his life. "You can stay up here. I won't try to leave without you."

Petre turned his skis and shoved off. Three strokes later he was still alive. No one knocked him from his skis. No massive hand closed around his throat. He listened, but Largo wasn't following.

At the bottom of the valley there was barely enough snow to ski. He took his skis off and walked, carrying them. Before he had even crossed the stream, the dog sat up. It was young and lean with a long whip thin tail, the way Is had described seeing it when she had been here with John. The hound regarded Petre for a full minute before it tipped its head back and howled. The man who opened the cabin door was a younger version of Amil, sandy haired and without the white beard and eyebrows that would distinguish him in his old age. The dog silenced at his touch.

Petre forded the stream on stones, on knees that didn't work properly, accompanied by the roaring of a heart overworking itself. He tried to think what to say, how to explain to Amil that he had just walked out of his future, which was actually the distant past. His ability to think seemed inaccessible, all circuits locked on one overwhelming message. "Danger! Get out!"

He forced himself to walk forward until his legs simply refused and he fell. For several more heartbeats he continued instructing his body to crawl, but he had lost the coordination of a movement that he had known since infanthood. After that he could only keep his eyes open in short flashes. Indelible images etched into his brain in those flashes. Amil's eyes boring into his own with the extreme attentiveness he remembered. The set of a particular rafter with a white stain running down it. The glow of red coals in the cook stove as a draft of air shimmered over them. Each time, Petre had the feeling he had been talking but did not know what he had been saying. When he finally got his eyes to stay open, it was Largo's face he saw.

"Are you well now?" the berserker asked.

Petre felt all the previous images fading from his mind like a dream. He sat up. They were up on the ridge top where he had left the berserker. "Why am I here, not at the cabin?"

"I brought you back."

"Why?"

"It is bad down there," Largo said firmly.

Petre remembered the time Largo had gotten lost trying to follow him through a different time disruption. "How did you find me?"

"A dog barked and barked. I never saw it but I saw you by the creek with your skis off."

"I wasn't in the cabin?"

"What cabin?"

Sitting down made Petre feel too helpless. He felt dizzy and weak but he tried to get to his feet anyway. Making his body obey him was his only means of fighting whatever it was he was fighting. Insanity probably.

Largo put his arm around Petre and helped him stand. Suddenly Petre felt the man tense. A moment later a stallion's loud, challenging whinny split the evening air.

Then Petre heard the horse's heavy breathing as it struggled to gallop uphill in deep snow. *No!* Petre pleaded, *No!* The snow erupted as a war stallion lunged over the ridge in front of them. He came to a halt, rearing, and throwing a cloud of snow into the air. His massive hooves pawed the sky. His eyes were white rimmed, ears pinned, distended nostrils flaring red. He was black with sweat. Steam rose from him and gushed from his open mouth. His mane whipped back as he reared again. There was no one on his back but he was saddled and bridled, the reins and stirrups neatly tied up so they wouldn't get caught on anything.

Neck arched, stepping high, he advanced on Petre. His powerful legs and enormous hooves were all the weapons he needed, but his teeth were also bared, his ears pinned against the huge curved muscles of his neck.

The berserker thrust Petre aside with so much force Petre was flung to the ground, skidding on the snow. Then Lark was blotted from his view by Largo's bulk as the berserker placed himself between the stallion and Petre. Petre saw Largo reach his arm forward and heard the horse's breath come in short excited snorts as he took in the man's scent. Moving very carefully, Petre edged around to where he could see.

There was no sign of Is. But the way the stirrups and the reins were tied he knew she had not been thrown from Lark's back. She had sent him here alone and ready for the berserker to ride. Lark stood as square and still as a small building while Largo mounted. Then they were off, plunging down the slope without even a glance at Petre.

Petre had dreaded this encounter so much and now it was over. Relief flooded him. He leaned against a tree for support then slid down to sit with his back against it.

Some time later he moved restlessly and a pain in his neck woke him. He turned his head, cautious to determine the extent of the crick he had given himself by falling asleep sitting in the snow under a tree. Not too bad, he decided. He let his head roll back, and found himself staring into the large yellow eyes of a great white owl. For a moment he couldn't move while his heart pounded wildly and he tried to tell himself it was just a bird.

The owl shifted from one foot to the other, lifted its wings slightly and resettled them, and finished off with a wagging of its tail before Petre could look away. Just an owl. Not even unusual to see one at this time in the late afternoon, getting ready for its night hunting. They lived in this area; he'd seen one when he'd been here before. This one was probably a descendent of that one, or perhaps a predecessor depending on how time was behaving right now.

Then he remembered that Largo had the stallion and time should be back to normal. As he strapped on his skis, the bird flew like any wild owl would. When it landed nearby, Petre skied toward it until it flew again, to prove to himself that it was just a wild bird. But again it didn't go far. Petre felt vacant, no longer driven by a mission, he followed the bird, which continued to fly only short distances. One direction was as good as any other. Lark and Largo were on their way to the Mirror which would kill them. Is was probably already there, maybe already dead. Sooner or later he'd better try to connect with his people. But right now he wasn't sure what he could tell them. He wasn't sure how much was real.

Some things, like skiing all the way to Sacred Grounds from South Pass in one day and a night, were verified by other people, so that must be true. But while that was unusual and he would have said impossible, it was not supernatural. Probably someone else would go and try it and break his record. It would become a race and every few years someone would set a new record until they got tired of using that for the standard and moved on to something harder.

Then he realized that he was assuming that his people would still be around and their way of life undisturbed. He stopped dead in his tracks. How much of the rest of what he remembered was relevant?

The Alliance army moving through the land must be real, only maybe they'd turned back after what the Blueskins had done to them. But it didn't matter because now Largo would put an end to the Mirror, and suddenly Petre was struck with a strong desire to go to the Mirror too, which made absolutely no sense. He did not want to see Lark lying dead in the snow, or Largo, and certainly not Is. Yet he knew he would go there.

He was grasping wildly to make some sense of his thoughts when the owl flew past him so close its wing buffeted the side of his head. He hadn't heard it coming because owls fly silently. He ducked far too late, heart in his throat. The owl landed on the ground not ten strides away and faced him, mantling and popping its beak at him with a most impressive noise.

"Okay, I'm coming." He spoke out loud and at the sound of his voice the bird sprang into the air and banked away, but again it didn't go far, landing on a low branch in plain sight. Some of the memories Petre wanted most to discount had to do with owls – a great white owl swooping out of Is's cell, an owl crashing into the wall and drawing the guard's attention the night he'd escaped from Center.

He followed the bird down into the valley. It had gotten quite dark, but he could see the white flash of the owl's wings when it flew, and it never went very far. Suddenly it swooped out of a tree and took off, flying in a businesslike way that took it out of Petre's range of vision in seconds. He had just time to think what a fool he had been to follow an owl, when his eyes picked up the warm golden glow of a lighted window. Confused, he stood staring at it, his reactions so worn out that he hardly felt anything.

He unstrapped his skis because there wasn't enough snow here, and walked toward the cabin, walked right up on the porch. This time no hound bayed warning. He rapped on the door and heard a chair slide as if someone had stood up. A moment later the door opened. Amil's white hair, backlit by the glow of the cook stove, could have been the ruffled feathers of an owl. His face was in shadow. Petre could not see his expression. He could only guess at his own. "Come   in," Amil said after a long moment, moving aside as Petre walked past him toward the stove. The special herb scent of the place caught at his memory. Surely if he turned around he would see Is at the table, her side still bound. He didn't turn.

Amil closed the door. "My apologies. I will need a moment."

Petre watched red and gold shimmer through the coals and thought, *a moment. A moment to become completely human again?*

"How is this place here, now, when the stallion is gone with his berserker, maybe dead?" Petre asked, his thought trailing away into the impossible. He didn't turn when Amil spoke again.

"I think you know, this is a greatly disturbed spot. It will not stay long. We have things to say to each other and perhaps not much time."

Petre breathed shallowly intent on listening. He didn't dare turn or speak. He needed the answers this man might give him and he didn't want to do anything that might disrupt this moment.

"First, I would thank you," Amil said. "You set me on the right path long ago. You do not remember?"

When Petre didn't respond Amil continued. "You came, once, not long after I had set up here." His sudden deep chuckle filled the room. "You really gave me a start. You arrived on skis, dressed for winter when it was early spring and there was barely enough snow to warrant skis. The dog, who had never barked about anything before, set up such a baying. You seemed ill and delirious. You spoke with an accent I had never heard before. It was hard to understand the things you said."

"What did I say?" Petre's voice came out flat and forced, the words enunciated with careful attention while his heart screamed wildly for answers.

"You do not remember?"

"You said I was delirious."

"At the time I had no other explanation."

"And now you do." Petre addressed the stove, not daring to risk turning around.

"Yes. I think you stepped through a bubble of time that the war stallion left disturbed. You told me of things that would happen to me. You told me things I must do."

"The things I said came true?"

"As far as I am able to tell."

"What things?"

"You told me of a woman who would be riding a war horse and a man who would seem crazy. You begged me to help them," he said, with a short breath of a laugh. "No, you made me swear I would help them. You begged me to help your people but I could not understand what kind of help you thought they needed. As I said, you seemed . . . ill, delirious. And if all that wasn't strange enough, you kept returning to one question. 'Why couldn't John see the dog?'

Petre's knees threatened to give way. He reached out and took support from a post. "What did you answer?"

"I could only guess from your babbling that John was the crazy-seeming man who would come some day, but the dog is a perfectly ordinary dog. Anyone can see him. But you insisted he would follow John, and that John would not be able to see him. When you finally quieted I went out for a moment to get more wood for the fire and when I came back you were gone. I hunted for you and the dog barked like he was barking at someone but no one was there. After several days I gave up the search. I thought you must have died."

Amil paused briefly before continuing. "It was many years later that a woman on a war horse and a man who seemed crazy arrived on my doorstep. That was when I first began to believe that you might have been something more than ill and delusional. I helped them the best I could, just as you had asked. When they rode out of here the dog followed them. It was obvious that the man couldn't see him, yet the woman could. She kept trying to make him turn back and stay with me.

"It must have been at least twenty years after that when you came again, this time with the same woman and the stallion, and John's mare but without John."

Petre let go of a breath he had not been aware he was holding and turned to face Amil. "That's why you looked at me like you did. But you didn't tell me I had been here before. Why?"

Amil hesitated. "Try to understand it from my perspective. You walked into my life, that first time, apparently ill and delirious. You said crazy things that I may have mistaken partly because of your accent. Then, when my back was turned you stumbled out of here again. I thought you had died. Then one day, twenty-some years later, you rode up looking exactly as you had looked that first time. I convinced myself that you could not be the same person."

"For me," Petre said, "that encounter happened a few weeks ago, and the first visit happened earlier today."

Amil shook his head in wonder, his beard and hair resettling one over the other like an owl resettling its wings. "For me, perhaps since I live here and I'm bound to live one day at a time, in order, it happened in its proper sequence in my life."

"I see." Petre felt exhausted and overwhelmed as Amil went on talking.

"I have learned some very important things since your last visit."

Petre went to the table and sat where he had sat next to Is. He thought if he looked just right he would see her there, her side bound, a red stain on her borrowed shirt. An intense emotion went through him that was beyond name. His attention came back to Amil, mid sentence.

". . . so your people are an experiment, but not the way you believe, not an experiment in utopian living. They were given that false history and turned loose with their horses until such time as they will be needed."

"Needed?" Petre's mind seemed to work slowly. "For what?" he asked, wishing only to lose himself in the sweet rosin smell of the memory of the place he had shared with Is.

"That's not clear. But one thing the Alliance does not do is waste any line of research that may some day be of use. They can move a star ship through light years, but moving through time with nothing more sophisticated than a horse, that must have intrigued them."

"So they bred the horses," Petre said, remembering the words of Don Fey. "But the people were lost."

"Almost," Amil said intensely. "Apparently it wasn't just anyone who could form the sort of link with the horses that don Bocher was investigating. The people who had the most indigenous genes did best. He discovered it by accident, as those people tended to be of the lowest class, so they ended up in menial jobs, like cleaning stalls. By the time the Alliance realized the importance of the native people there were almost none of them left. The ones they could find were brought to the Bocher Stud. They tried to genetically re-engineer them. But it didn't work. It was more than a matter of getting the right gene sequence. It seems there had to be a certain synergy between the people, the horses, and the land. So they did the best they could with line breeding them."

Petre felt sick, atrocity piled on atrocity. He could not form the next question: What happened to them?

But Amil was answering anyway. "Some of them were destined to train the horses in the area in which don Bocher was working. But I have also come across some references to the 'wild' genes being incorporated into the new berserker line. They were just beginning the second berserker line then. They already had the Blueskins but at that time they were beginning the eternal life experiment and creating the second line of berserkers – the ones who would face the Mirror. Perhaps they needed those wild genes to give those berserkers that extra quickness, that . . . well, wildness that the Alliance people had lost over millions of years of civilization. Or they may have thought it would help them connect to the stallions. Whatever the case, they got more than they realized.

"For many years there was a small group of carefully selected people and horses at don Bocher's Stud. When those experiments fell out of favor what was left of the indigenous people he had collected there were turned loose in a place where they would breed true and continue to breed their horses true. Your people are their descendents and your horses are descended from the original horses of this world."

At Amil's words Petre had a vivid flash of rearing horses, their hooves raking at the destruction in the air, their riders equally helpless and terrified. He pulled himself away from the memory and the feeling of abject betrayal the horses had radiated.

"So they gave us a false history," he said harshly. "Did they think that we would never find out?"

"Who could tell you? I was long dead," Amil said. "The records were burned. You did not know the potential of your horses and you could not make them perform. Until Lark."

"No wonder they were so desperate to get him back."

"Yes."

"Still, it seems so risky for them to have turned us loose like they did."

"They had to. The land is part of the synergy they were trying to recreate. You could not develop completely in their cities. Anyway they keep track of you. I suspect that is why they tolerate Hluit spies. I suspect they pick one up every now and then and the strange medical procedures that get reported as torture might actually be tests to see how the Hluit are progressing."

It was a lot to absorb but Petre felt it in his guts, the connection to the horses, the land. The way he had been drawn to follow Is and Lark, even the way he had felt about Largo – a man he should have hated and feared – made more sense. All of it came from deep inside him. A secret known, and not known. Yet he still had to ask, "Are you sure?"

"Yes," Amil affirmed. "I am sure."

"If they realize we've found out . . ?"

"They'll either cage your people somehow, or exterminate them."

"Yes." That fit exactly.

"So what will you do?"

"I have to tell my people. They have to know the whole story."

"And when they know? What will they do?"

"I don't know."

"Yes you do. In your heart you know, they must take over the Alliance. Now. Now, in your time, while they have the chance."

Petre shook his head. "We are not conquerors. We have no desire to rule."

"But the Alliance will not let you live."

"They have their own problems right now."

"Yes, I know. The Mirror may destroy them."

"But now Lark is taking Largo to the Mirror and he will shut it off."

"But there is still John. He may yet get through their defenses at Center."

"You know about John?"

"Is told me."

"When?" The numbness that had begun to form broke wide open and pain seared through Petre. Is had been here, talking to Amil, perhaps sitting where he was sitting . . . and he may never even see her again alive.

"She came here after the Blueskins reclaimed Lark for her. She said you ordered them." Amil tipped his head, birdlike, and regarded Petre with bright feral eyes until Petre answered.

"It wasn't quite like that."

"No? I had hoped . . ."

"What?"

"You know your people cannot deal with the Alliance. It is too corrupt. Your only hope is to take over their government and change it."

"We have no desire to govern a large, complex and technologically-oriented society," Petre said.

"You must learn. This is the best, and probably only, opportunity you will get. The war will be fought for you by the Blueskins. You will only have to take over afterward and rebuild."

"I'm sure it will not be so clean and bloodless as that."

"No. But it is your best opportunity. You must try to convince your people of this."

"Why do you care? You won't even be alive when it happens."

"No, of course not."

Amil's quick response stirred feelings of distrust in Petre.

"You are lying," he said bluntly. "You will be there. You were there. Whatever. Your damn owl, or its descendent, was with Is in her cell and with me on the wall."

"What exactly did that owl do?" Amil asked quietly.

"You don't know?" Petre was suddenly suspicious.

Amil sighed. "You are speaking to me so many years before you were even born. If you suspect me of somehow becoming an owl and being able to help you in that form in your lifetime, the least you can do is tell me what you think I did."

Put like that it was too outrageous for Petre to believe. "All I know is that a great white owl brought me here tonight, and one created a diversion when I was trying to escape from the Alliance, and one was in the cell with Is when the Alliance held her prisoner. And one roosts on that beam," he said, gesturing accurately without having to look, "who has stained it white with its droppings."

"It is a companion," Amil said carefully. "Somewhat tame."

"I don't believe you."

"I have found that sometimes it is hard to know what to believe. In those instances it has usually proven to be a good idea to behave as though one accepted the more acceptable of the possibilities."

"You do not intend to tell me the truth?"

"No. But I will make you a promise. I will not tell anyone else either."

Petre considered. "Is the truth that dangerous."

"The opportunities to abuse this . . . are enormous."

"But I can trust *you* not to abuse it?" Petre said with a harsh laugh.

"Your trust is not really necessary," Amil said slowly, "but for some reason I desire it. Perhaps I will tell you. Then I think you will reach the same conclusion that I have. There are probably very few people who could learn to do this anyway." And he launched into a tale.

"It was you who started me on this research when you came here that first time, on skis when there was no snow, delirious, I thought, but really speaking words from my own future. In those days I was following my own line of research. I was born with empathy for the wild animals of this world. Of course, growing up in the Alliance I was not allowed near any animals. But there were always the little creatures that could not be kept out, birds and mice and rats.

"I was born one of the lucky ones for I was slated to be taught to read and to become a librarian. That was fine with me because it gave me access to many old records and research and I was curious about my empathy with the creatures. I thought I might find some answers in books. I had a peculiar talent, I would always know where the little creatures were around me – a mouse behind the bookshelf, a bird trapped in the attic. I seemed to feel what they felt, to see through their eyes. Imagine my delight when I learned about the indigenous people and their horses.

"Of course what the Alliance had done to those people was being hushed and forgotten, but I found old accounts of the many strange incidents that seemed to point to the same sort of connection between those people and their horses as the connection I had with other animals. When I learned that they intended to destroy those records I managed to steal them and hide in the Boundary. There I followed my own line of research undisturbed.

"Animals came to me. I graduated from rodents to owls. And the dog, the dog found me and I don't know how or from where he had come but he was lonely and he taught me so much. It was with him that I first truly left my body behind.

"I was happily puttering along with my research when you showed up. The dog obviously knew there was something very strange about you. The way you left, it was almost like he knew where you were even when I couldn't see you. I think he could have gone with you if he had wanted to. And then there were your words, 'Why couldn't John see the dog?' And then I couldn't see you but I think the dog could.

"After that, I really paid attention to that dog and I got so I could get inside his mind and travel out of my body and in his, sometimes for three or four days at a time before I had to come back. And then John and Isadora showed up and I went with the dog and followed them and that is probably why John couldn't see the dog. It connected to Is and crossed time with her and Lark, but John was more loosely connected into all that.

"True to your words John couldn't see me, nor could his mare, but Isadora and Lark could. In that different time I met the Dark Bodies. They taught me about being dead. Then I knew that I didn't have to have a body to be alive. I could move from one animal to another or just 'be' somewhere like them, like a ghost. I was, potentially, immortal."

Amil paused and shook his head, remembering the incredible joy and power he had experienced. Petre sat transfixed, waiting patiently for him to continue.

"The Dark Bodies made me realize that I was in a time way far in the future. Is and Lark had shown me that it *could* be done. I came back to my cabin and my body and my time and then applied myself to learning how to travel properly."

"But I don't understand how you did it," Petre said. "Just knowing it was possible? Then anyone could do it."

"No. There is much more to it. But your ancestors and their horses, and some of the other beasts native to this planet have this ability."

"The owls," Petre said, understanding.

"Yes."

"But how did you learn?"

"The Alliance documented a lot of things without ever really understanding them." Amil gave a small chuckle. "They were limited by their knowledge that certain things were impossible. I was not so handicapped."

"So you . . . after they burned your cabin, you lived on in the owls?"

"I do not know yet, but I think from what you say, that might be so."

"You are still alive when . . . when I live. You helped me escape on the wall?"

"If you say so. Remember, you have come back in time. I have not yet lived that."

"So you might be a ghost sometimes, or an owl sometimes, or a dog. Could you . . . use the body of a man?"

Petre was thinking how the Mirror had taken over John's body and was "forcing" it to do things that John would never have done. And he was beginning to wonder if maybe it wasn't the Mirror that had taken over John's body, but this man.

After all, Amil wanted the Hluit to stop the Alliance and take over governing the people. Would he go so far as to use John that way?

"No, I doubt that I could use a man," Amil answered. "I seem to have this synergy only with certain animals. And if you're implying that I might forcefully take over a person, like John, and make him do my bidding, no. I would not do that even if I could. I am not a murderer, in this body or any other."

Petre met Amil's eyes coldly. "The owl kills."

"Yes, the owl kills its appropriate prey," Amil answered. "It has to. If I inhabit the owl's mind, I must allow that mind its space."

"And when you have no human mind to return to, won't you long for a human mind and a human body?"

Amil laughed. "Have you ever flown? Have you ever galloped as a deer does? Smelled the scent rising from the ground as a dog does and known it secrets . . .?" His eyes glowed with secret joy that made Petre wish for those sensations.

"But you must come to miss thinking as a human. Speaking? Interacting with humans?"

"Perhaps. I do not yet know."

Then Petre remembered that for this man the cabin had not yet been burned, his body had not yet died.

"Yet you wish me to trust that this will not happen?"

Petre saw the flash of anger in the old man's eyes but when Amil spoke it was civilly.

"What you fear is not possible. Even putting my morals aside, I would never be able to 'take over' a human mind or body. It is not something I do to a hapless victim. It requires a synergy between me and that animal and forces I do not even name. I suspect the deep empathy between the natives and their horses was like this."

Petre remembered the feeling he had had seeing the horses being killed, a feeling of deep betrayal.

"The horses stopped allowing it," he said without forethought.

"Yes." Amil was looking at him oddly. "How did you know?"

Petre shrugged the question away. "The people tried to get their horses back, to make it up to them, but the Alliance was too strong for them. The horses didn't understand. They found themselves with people who didn't understand and they stopped . . . they stopped doing whatever it was. They withdrew their empathy. It wasn't until they were crossbred with Alliance horses that the ability resurfaced maybe because those horses didn't know, didn't *remember*, what had happened.

"Yet our horses let us ride them without bridles. They empathize that much, but no more." The sadness Petre felt brought tears to his eyes. "Will they ever forgive us?"

"It may not be so much a question of forgiving," Amil said softly. "It may be that they *can't* reach you on that level. You are *not* the original people after all. Close, but not completely true."

"But you formed this synergy . . . this connection . . . with the owls, the dog . . ." Petre began.

"But not with the horses. They don't allow it."

"But I still don't understand how you could have learned to do this?"

"I believe that it is largely because of who I am," Amil said and began to explain. "There is some mystery surrounding my lineage. I believe that my grandparents might have been pure indigent. But my grandmother was forced to give my mother away as a child. It may have been to save her from being a slave that she was given to an Alliance woman to raise. That Alliance woman had just lost her child and she raised my mother as if she were her own child. This was illegal of course, but documents were altered. No one cared if another indigenous child had died, so that part was easy. A birth certificate was altered and my mother was raised in an elite household. Someone forgot to change the baby's eye color on the birth certificate but that mistake was never caught until I found it many, many years later. My mother was accepted as a full citizen. She married and her firstborn (me) was slated to become a scholar because everyone believed she was a well-placed Alliance citizen, and so of course was I.

"My odd talent with animals showed up when I was a young child but I quickly learned to keep it secret. I did not like to be called Rat Boy, or Mouse Turd, or any of the other names kids called me. But my mother knew about my gift, and when I was still very young she took me aside and explained to me. She told me that while I must hide my talents I should also be very proud of them because they were given to me by my real people not by my Alliance parents."

"The Alliance man my mother had married was not really my father; my biological father must have been indigenous or at least a part-breed. I think my mother sought out an indigenous man to produce a child that was as pure of genes as possible.

"There was a lot of that going on, very quietly behind the scenes. It was the only way our race could survive. But because I had such an iron-clad, albeit false, lineage with such an important family, I was never successful in trying to find other people like me. And when I had to flee from the Alliance . . ." He shrugged, expressing how the whole thing had ended.

Grief welled up in Petre for what had been lost, destroyed by the Alliance. The native people must have been very different from the Alliance people. The world must have been so different, where humans and animals existed in empathy. Perhaps time had been mutable and even death might not have been final. But no one would ever know for sure now. It was lost, destroyed. The injustice of it all threatened to overwhelm him. He had to move, had to do something. He went to the cook stove and opened the door. Air rushed in, shimmering over the coals. In places a blue-white flame sprang up as he added a piece of wood. The cabin was flooded with light as the wood burst into flames.

"So you think that we should use the means at our disposal to overthrow the Alliance government, take over and govern in their place?" Petre said coldly.

"Yes. They took so much from you, from your people, and they will finish the job if you do not stop them."

"I can only advise my people of this. I cannot control what they do."

"But you will tell them?"

"Yes. If I get out of here. If I ever find any of them again."

"That is all I can ask."

"What about you?"

"Evidently I will go back to Center. There may be things I can do."

"To bring about the fall of the Alliance government?"

"Yes. With an eye to having the Hluit take over."

"I wouldn't count on that."

"You still do not trust me?"

"No."

Amil accepted Petre's response with a slight dipping of his head. "Perhaps time will prove you wrong." And after a moment, "Will you keep my secret?"

"I don't know. I think I need to talk this over with a few people."

"I guess that will have to be good enough."

"Unless someone finds these records."

"They will be, or were, burned with my cabin."

Were burned. Petre looked around at the room – that was really ashes – full of books that were burned a hundred years ago.

"Barring someone stumbling into one of the time bubbles, like I did."

"You didn't come by accident, the owl brought you here. But I guess it could happen that someone would find this place. It has not happened yet, in my life, and I am quite old.

I just think it is better if no one knows, for now. There will be enough problems without misunderstanding over this too."

"I don't know. That is the way the Alliance operates, not the Hluit," Petre said, uneasy with the secrecy and implied dishonesty of the whole thing.

Amil tipped his head in consent, his gaze keen and intent, the way Petre remembered. "Perhaps I am more tainted by the Alliance mindset than I wish to believe," Amil finally conceded. "Anyway, you will do what you will do. I would not even attempt to control that if I could."

Petre felt the tension ease between them.

"I can tell you where Isadora went," Amil said.

"To the Mirror?"

"Yes."

"Why did she send the stallion back?"

"She came to understand that she could not properly control him and she saw how dangerous that was for everyone."

"The earthquakes. The time bubbles, he *does* cause them?" Petre needed to hear it said concisely and positively.

"Yes."

"So, Is had Lark take her to the Mirror and she is waiting there for the berserker to return with him. Do you know what she intends to do?"

"No, only that she felt compelled to be there."

Petre understood. The moment his thoughts turned to Is he felt the same compulsion to follow her again. He rubbed at his face, trying to scrub some sense into his brain.

Amil brought a book from the shelf and held it open to Petre. "I want you to see something."

Petre saw a crude line drawing but dread rushed through him with the quickness of a flush of adrenaline and the finality of death.

"What do you see?" Amil's voice seemed far away.

"I see a dozen or more horses pulling an island," Petre answered, his voice dead of its usual tone.

"Ahhh . . . so you already know."

The drawing was a stylized depiction of horses all in the same stance, a foreleg lifted high, and their hindquarters low as though they were pulling hard. They did not seem to be wearing any sort of harness but were attached to the island by lines, perhaps symbolizing traces, perhaps something else. Beneath their hooves were jiggly lines that might be water. Though the island itself was nothing more than a few lines representing the rolling hills of the land behind the Boundary, Petre was sure of his interpretation.

In the foreground the water smoothed into lines that might represent land, or might be a person's cupped hand. At the top of the picture there were lines that might be clouds, or might be a corresponding hand, as though a giant cradled the scene in his palms.

"This is a reproduction of a drawing from the cave at Morv. It is more recent than the other drawings but done in the same style. Morv was not found until a hundred years after the Alliance landed. The meaning of the drawing was not correctly interpreted even in my time."

"And perhaps not even in mine," Petre said.

"What do you mean?"

"Oh, they know – or the ones who are allowed to know – know that the indigenous people and their horses moved the island through time. But what do these lines represent? They look like hands cupping the whole thing in their palms." He fixed Amil with a hard stare. *"Who* do the hands represent?"

Amil came within a heartbeat of breaking eye contact before he found the proper balance of boldness and deception.

"They were a superstitious people. They may have believed in a god, or an *overbeing* of some kind."

"I don't consider anything superstition if it works," Petre said. "There may have been a god."

Amil chuckled, breaking the tension. "Perhaps, or perhaps a very strong shaman."

Petre's thoughts came fast. *The power was just lying around. In the land, in the people, in the horses. What if someone found out how to connect it, focus it?* Again, he felt the familiar pull of his muscles as he skied all day and all night with the energy flowing through him, tireless and inexhaustible. For a short while he had known how to connect to it, how to weave it, or unweave it. He felt Is's ropes parting in his hands, fibers turning each other loose . . . cellular bonds breaking apart.

And then he felt the wind across his face and he was just one small being again. Attached, but not attached. Alone and filled with craving. One step removed from the realization of perfection. Human. Aware, but unable to cross a critical boundary.

He felt the wind cross his face again, freezing the wetness of his tears against his skin. Cold. Small. Frail, to let a freezing wind be important to him. To let it re-crystallize him in one spot.

The wind brushed his face with a sprinkle of snow. He looked up. The cabin was gone. He turned around with care and keen awareness. There was nothing left for him here. As he skied away he heard the hunting cry of an owl. He didn't look back.

Chapter Twenty-One

"This body feels . . . gratitude." The words echoed in Ondre's mind. Standing in the suddenly pitch black room with his brother's blood wet on his hands Ondre heard the whisper of a breeze. The Dark Bodies closed around him. He did not know how to fight them. He did not expect to be alive much longer. In the murmur of the breeze he thought he heard a voice.

"John promised to releasse them. Can hyou . . . can hyou do it?"

It wasn't quite a human voice. It reminded Ondre of the sound of wind in the tall dry grass his people cut for hay. He wondered if he'd imagined it. He turned slowly around, encircled by the dark disorienting wall of whispering breeze in a room where no breeze should exist. While he stood trying to decide if he should answer, there was a dull explosion outside.

"Answer," the voice demanded in the low "whop" of sound that shook the building under Ondre's feet. "Can hyou help them?"

"I don't know how." Ondre's voice sounded strangely too substantial in the unreality of the moment. The breeze whispered and the dark wall flowed to one side. A red flickering glow from a fire outside became visible in the window. The light gave dancing edges to the shadows in the room, almost human, almost real.

"Are you going to kill me?" Ondre asked levelly.

"I ha asked them not to," the voice said in a burst of crackly static as the flames leaped higher outside.

"Who are you?"

A chuckle reverberated in the air seeming to come from all directions at once. "You might sssay I am the ghosst captain of an army of ghostsss." The wind blew as though somehow feeding the flame outside with a voice.

"Are you Hluit?"

"No."

"But you have stopped them from killing me."

"I have *asked* them not to," the flame snapped. "They have sssome hope," the wind hissed, "that hyou will find a way to releasse them. You *are* John'sss brother."

"Yes. I will help them if I can, but I really don't know how."

"Then lissten."

"I am listening," Ondre answered the sighing wind stirring the tops of pines far from this room.

"Wee will get hyou into the casstle. Wee will make hyou rhuler. Hyou will put Alliancce ssscience to work to releassse usss," the wind whispered.

Ondre took a few seconds to decide on the best answer. "I do not want to rule the Alliance."

The chuckle filled the air again. "That isss why I trussst hyou to do it."

"Who are you?" Ondre asked again.

The air stirred and Ondre felt space open around him. In a moment the room became lighter, orange lit by the fire raging outside. He looked around. The body of his brother lay sprawled near his feet. Ondre was glad it was too dark to see John's features and the awful wound in his stomach

---

There were bodies by the door too, bodies of Alliance troopers on which the Dark Bodies had "fed."

Behind Ondre an almost human voice spoke. "I asked them to loan me some . . . energy." He spun, crouched, heart racing. A man stood silhouetted by the window. His beard and hair gleamed in a way that reminded Ondre of one of the great white owls.

"The name you will know me by is Amil. I cannot sustain this energy level very long. I have asked the berserkers to leave so we can talk. But we don't have long. Either they will 'feed' on everyone nearby or they will wander off. It took me too long to collect them; I don't want to do it again."

The light flickered and the man receded into shadow until Ondre could only see the glow of his white hair and the shine of his eyes.

"That's better," the man said. "We have too much to do to squander energy on illusions. At the moment I am bodiless, but at times I inhabit a great white owl." He paused watching the effect of his words.

"You helped Petre?"

"Yes. I have lived by passing from one small animal to another. I like the owls best, but dogs have helped too."

"And what happens to these . . . hosts?" Ondre asked, his voice much more level than he felt.

"They benefit from increased intelligence. I do not harm them."

"And people? Do you 'inhabit' them too?'

"No." And he told Ondre what he had told Petre. "They do not have the right . . . empathy."

Then Amil continued to tell Ondre a story of horror and deception that made what Ondre already believed about the Alliance pale in comparison.

"So," Amil concluded, "your people are what could be salvaged of the indigenous people and your horses *are* the indigenous horses. You have more right to a say in how this land is governed than the Alliance outsiders who came here and disrupted everything."

When Ondre didn't respond immediately, Amil continued. "All around us right now people are killing each other, hurting and destroying for no better reason than that they have been hurting all their lives and it is all they really know. Not a mile from us the highest Alliance people sit in fear and impotence, unable to stop the riots and uncaring of the suffering. This is the moment to act. This is the moment to change all the future history of this planet and your people. *You* are the man in the position to act."

Amil paused, perhaps waiting for a reaction. But when Ondre remained silent, Amil went on. "With the help of the Dark Bodies you can make a successful coup. Then you can stop the riots. Simply bringing the lights back on line would be a big step. You know it is safe to do that because you have stopped your brother, while DeFroe sits quaking in his office. He is afraid to touch anything to do with computer systems and so he lets the people die. With a little help from us, you can get the people behind you. You can end this suffering, and institute a new government with a new direction."

"How do you propose that I do that?" Ondre asked.

"You have three good Hluit men waiting in the castle to advise and help you. You have an army of dead berserkers who will bring DeFroe and his followers to their knees. You have the opportunity of confusion and chaos. You must act. You do not have to rule for long. But you are the one in the position to oust the corrupt government – a government that is surely going to exterminate your people if it survives tonight. You are in the position to lead an interim government until the right things can be done and the right changes can be made in the right way." At last, he fell silent.

"You make a very convincing argument."

"Then you will do it?"

"I do not believe it will be so easy, or so . . . bloodlessly accomplished."

"No, they are already killing each other outside, and the Dark Bodies will kill to get you into the castle. But if you do not act all the people who die will die for no reason."

"I know," Ondre admitted. "But I have to be sure of one thing. I have to be sure that you are not somehow the next mutation of the Mirror's intellect. Can you prove that to me?"

"I am not part of that horrid thing!"

"But you consort with its creations."

"They are no more under its control than I am."

Ondre's momentary silence resounded with unspoken suspicions. "So tell me what *you* expect to get out of this?"

"I am an old rebel. If you will recall I stole books from the Alliance long before you were born. I always resented their high handed methods. When they burned my books they destroyed their real history, plus what is known of the history of the native people. I am the only one who knows what really happened. And soon, with Petre's help, your people will know. But the Alliance will destroy them too, if it can." He sighed. "I am in the business of preserving true history. Once that history resided in the books in my cabin, now it resides in your people. I do not want them to be destroyed too." He hesitated. "Besides, I have a fondness for those of your people that I have met."

"You have no desire to rule? To perhaps take over DeFroe's body?"

There was a slight pause and Ondre felt the man's anger before hearing his words.

"Think what you have just said to me." Amil's voice grated with the effort to control anger. "You have just asked me if I would like to be intimately in touch with one of the most evil minds imaginable. You have asked me if I want to intimately know every detail of every vile act and every corrupt thought that man has had. You have asked me if I want to immerse myself in a body that knows the 'pleasures' of forcing itself on women and watching, perhaps taking an active part in, the mutilation and the physical and psychological torture of men." Anger overwhelmed Amil's control and he stopped speaking.

"I apologize for an insult that was not intended," Ondre said quickly. "But I find myself more inclined to believe you now."

There was a pause during which the energy in the room seemed to change somehow, as though an electrical charge left the air.

"Then it was worth it," Amil finally said. "No insult is taken. You could not be expected to understand how it is to share a body and a brain."

"So you have taken up with these . . . dead berserkers. Are you sure you can control them?"

"In all honesty I believe they will obey me, except perhaps in the matter of feeding. I was a Scholar and they were created to be told what to do, but . . ."

"If they want to die why don't they just stop feeding?"

"Starvation can not kill them, it only makes them weak and useless."

"I do not want more people killed."

"People are being killed right now while we stand talking."

That was true, and it was good reason to make a decision. There was another explosion, within the hospital this time. The sound of running feet and voices raised in anger reached Ondre. Right or wrong, for better or worse, he made his decision.

"I have to make sure there is nothing left of John first."

"Good. We will wait for you. But understand. They were berserkers. They never had much patience and the energy from the riots is affecting them."

"I understand. But I must do this first."

Steeling his heart, Ondre bent over his brother's body and gathered it in his arms. It was too dark to see the wound but he could feel the slippery wetness of John's blood, cold now against his arms, soaking through his clothes, covering his chest, his heart. He carried his brother out a side door and no one tried to stop him.

Fire raged in the building next to the hospital. Ondre carried John's body as close as he could but the heat was too intense for him. He could not get near enough to put John's body into the flames. Then suddenly a breeze swept across him. It whipped into the flames, gaining in strength, driving the flames back. Quickly Ondre rushed forward. The flames bent away from him at their base, but towered overhead like a gigantic wave about to crash down on him. The roaring they made was deafening as the wind that pushed the flames back also fed their intensity. Heat scorched the hair on Ondre's arms and singed his eyebrows. He forced himself to go to the very base of the flames before setting John's body down. Then he retreated from the writhing wall of flame as fast as he could.

As soon as he was clear the wind withdrew and the flames leaped forward. He watched the fire engulf his brother's body. Then he turned and ran back to the sewer where the boy had told him there was a way to get through the wall. A breeze at his back raised the hair on his neck. He could not tell if the horror he felt was caused by the ghosts whispering behind him or by the vision of flame and blood that haunted his eyes.

The tunnel wasn't very big. Ondre had to crawl through part of it and then climb another part with his back pressed against one wall and feet against the other – the way he would climb a chimney, a skill he'd had to learn to keep up with John when they were boys. He did not know if the updraft he felt was natural or the locomotion of Dark Bodies.

Finally he got past the part that had been blocked and found himself back in a well-maintained sewer system again. Now he was on the inside of the wall. He jogged, breathing the foul air, harried by shadows until he came to a ladder.

The ladder brought him up in the basement of a service area. The castle had its own power source and the lights were on beyond the doorway. Ondre had only a moment to make out the plumbers' tools that lined the walls before the light dimmed as the Dark Bodies flowed around him.

He had no choice but to move or be overwhelmed by the darkness. At the door he heard voices, but they were just the voices of bored guards playing some card game. He slipped through the door and turned away from the voices his dark army following soundlessly. He wondered if they had spared the guards or if they had fed.

A stairway led him up to the ground floor. The ceiling vaulted high overhead. Stone pillars stood in orderly columns. Little clumps of guards were at each door. Darkness eddied around Ondre as he began to walk across the open floor. Silently, desperately he prayed that no guard would notice him and no one would cry out a warning so that no one would have to die.

He kept going, one step after the next, not too fast. He could see nothing surrounded by the soft whisper of death.

Then the darkness parted and in front of him was a stairway. He began to climb. Behind him wind shifted through fallen leaves. Ignoring the prickling of the hairs on the back of his neck, he jogged the stairs in a steady rhythm.

The top floors were living quarters. But with the city burning around them, DeFroe was likely to be with his advisors in one of the council chambers. A door opened above Ondre, stopping his thoughts and his heart. He froze, expecting the worst, and then suddenly he was engulfed in blackness.

"Shit!" a voice said. "What's wrong with the lights? Well, I'm not going down in *that*."

Another voice murmured agreement and Ondre heard the door close. In a moment the Dark Bodies flowed away and he could see again.

"Thanks," he whispered and began to ascend again.

During his stay at the castle Ondre had met with DeFroe or his advisors in various rooms, formal and informal. But there was one that stuck in his mind as the one where DeFroe felt the most comfortable.

The stairwell opened into a corridor. The room Ondre wanted was at the end of the corridor and could only be approached by passing through an open "sitting" area first.

DeFroe's ever-present honor guard was lounging around the sitting area. Ondre started to walk, trying not to be concerned about their weapons. Weapons hadn't done the guards in the hospital any good.

He walked until someone caught sight of him and shouted. He heard the crackle of weapons as he took off running. In a moment the disorienting dizziness that had affected him so badly at the hospital slapped his spine like a giant whip stroke down the center of his back. He fell hard against the door. The door slammed open and he plunged into the room.

People froze in various postures of twisted disbelief at his sudden entry. He saw DeFroe, round eyed, mouth gaping. Around him were some people Ondre recognized, other people he didn't.

Ondre was aware of himself the way they must see him – limbs spread wide, eyes wild, covered with his brother's blood, streaked with soot from the fire and smelling of the sewer.

"Don't move!"

That was Stevens. Ondre had forgotten that Stevens, as Chief of Security, would be armed. He wore a wrist attachment that Phol had identified as a weapon. Ondre had no clue what the thing could do.

Before he could contemplate further, a smashing blow to the back of his knees sent him sprawling. He regained his footing just in time to see Stevens disappear into darkness.

Ondre yelled. "Get away from him! Get on the other side of the room!"

The people obeyed, except for the two men who had been on one side of Stevens and one man who'd been on his other side.

Ondre put his back to whatever was happening to them and shouted over the rushing of the wind. "Don't move! Don't anybody move! If you want to live through this, don't move."

His plea was hysteria driven. But he could see by their terror-stricken eyes that they would obey him. With only a moment to adjust himself, he went to wipe hair out of his eyes and saw his own blood-coated hand. He ran his hair back, wondering at the blood that similar gestures had left streaked across his face. He made his voice match the way he looked.

"You," he said to DeFroe, "are about to make some very difficult decisions."

Chapter Twenty-Two

Petre didn't push himself very hard. The second day out from Amil's he met Hluit scouts and told them all that had happened. He even spent a day and a night making a written account for the elders, but the spoken word would travel more quickly. In a surprisingly short time all the Hluit would know about their true ancestry and the truth about their horses. Along with that message went Amil's urging to action, now, while there was a chance to check the Alliance in its inhumane and unethical ways.

Petre supposed he would add his voice to that urging and his body to whatever fighting was required to make it happen. He had no illusions that change would be cleanly and bloodlessly accomplished. He did not want his people sullied by these decisions and actions, yet there seemed no other way.

If they went to war he did not particularly want to survive it. He would find the most dangerous position possible and carry out that job to the best of his ability. And if he died, at least he would be done with pain, for he was sure that both Is and Lark were dead. John was either dead or would be soon, or else Ondre would be, and many more of his people would be lost before it was over.

But for now he was doing what he had come to hate himself for doing – following Is again. There was no good reason for this futile pursuit. She had undoubtedly gone to the Mirror to die. Either the Mirror had killed her, or Largo had been unable to keep his promise and had struck her down, or Lark had attacked her.

Petre could not bring himself to hurry. Whatever he was going to find there would not be good. Even so, he could not turn away. He imagined finding the magnificent stallion lying dead in the snow and not far from him, Largo, as cold as the snow drifted around him, used and discarded by the people who had made them. And maybe that was part of why he had to go – so at least someone would stand by that man and that horse and grieve. At least they would have that. And then he would find Is . . . his thoughts shied away from that image as he slipped into a numb state where the motion of skiing engaged his entire being. Each step of a glide, each turn on a slope, or the exact placement of each ski as he herringboned up a steep place consumed him. Surprisingly he was free from pain, free from fear. He felt as though nothing could cause him more pain than he had already felt over Is. And now he had made a pact with death.

So he skied, not fast but perfectly, hypnotized by the fullness of each moment.

On the fifth day he reached the vicinity of the Mirror. He had encountered no herd fogs, no earthquakes, no Dark Bodies, or avalanches. No manifestation of either the stallion's or the Mirror's existence had marred his progress. By this he was certain they were both dead in their separate ways, and that Largo and Is were dead with them.

No one knew where the Mirror really was. It had appeared to different people in different places and had left the dead of those encounters strewn about a radius of many miles.

Petre decided that if he felt no hunch about where to go he would ski a search pattern. It could take him days or even weeks to find what he was looking for. He was in no hurry. Although he had no hope of finding Is alive, he knew that once he saw her dead, something would change within him and pain would come out of the place of abeyance to which he had temporarily banished it.

The first night he camped under a tree his people called The Guardian. Its girth was enormous and although it wasn't much taller than the other pines at this altitude where fierce winds did the pruning, it was obviously ancient. The spread of its dense branches allowed no other trees to grow near it, so that it was set apart in its own shrine of deep needles. Even the snow hadn't penetrated here.

Petre felt he needed to ask the tree's permission to camp in that hallowed glade. He looked up at boughs bigger around than his own torso and offered a silent apology for his need to make a small fire in a spot he cleared in the pine needles. As he leaned his back against a trunk that would take him twenty strides to walk around, something of the tree's solidness seeped into his soul. The rightness of the way time progressed when it was not disturbed and a sanity that went deeper than just being a member of a quick-living human society entered him. He slipped into sleep as though slipping down into the tree's roots and rested there, deep within the ground of that sanity.

He woke, what seemed a millennium later, like leaves unfolding to the sun after a winter's sleep. But all too soon, his memories and the reality of his mission returned to him.

Then he heard the sound that had awakened him, a horse blowing rhythmically with its steps, reassuring itself in the slick snow beyond the tree. Petre stood up slowly so as not to startle the horse.

The war stallion watched Petre disengage from the tree and stopped, ears pricked, alert to treachery. From his back, Is spoke some nonsense syllables of reassurance to the horse. Petre heard her voice like a caress on his own nerves.

"Hello," he said. Just that. As though he'd seen her yesterday, as though he'd been expecting to see her alive.

"Petre," she said, beyond surprise.

A dream, Petre thought, *I am still asleep in the embrace of the tree.* Then Lark lowered his head and came forward. He reached out his massive neck and sniffed Petre's hand with his gentle chocolate-brown nose. His warm breath gusted over Petre's hands. His limpid eye looked into Petre's with intelligence and kindness. Petre's knees went weak. He had two choices: take support on the neck of what should be a killer stallion, or crumple right where he was.

He found himself hanging onto Lark's mane, leaning against the stallion's shoulder. Is said something he couldn't take in. A moment later she was down from the stallion's back standing beside him. "Petre," she said, demanding his attention.

"I wasn't expecting to see you alive." He spoke into Lark's mane while demanding of himself simultaneously, *don't be dreaming* and *don't wake up*. He breathed the smell of horse and sweat, felt the heat of Lark's body and the coarseness of his mane. He turned to find Is studying him. Her dark hair spilling from under a winter cap was as twisted and tangled as the horse's tail. She watched him with the ever-so-slightly-slanted eyes he had seen so many times in his dreams, her emotions hooded behind dark lashes. Her skin was darker than his people's, appearing tanned even in winter, and so soft looking he could hardly resist the urge to touch her. He took in every detail of her face, comparing her to his memory, re-memorizing her in case he never got another chance. Her lips parted and moved in complicated ways. He tried to concentrate on what she was saying.

". . . so I had to bring Lark back. And this . . ."

As she turned away, he watched her face in profile while her gloved hands undid the flap of the saddlebag. Then she struggled to lift something out and he moved to help her just as any other man might help a person of lesser strength accomplish something that required raw muscle power.

He found himself holding an almost featureless black rectangular cube about half a meter tall and less than that wide, but incredibly heavy for its size.

"That's all the Mirror ever was," she told him. "*This* little box."

Petre set it on the pine needles and looked at it in disbelief. He could see the coals of his fire glowing in its deeply reflective surface, as detailed and real as if he were looking directly into the fire itself. This "box" had cast illusions as big as a house, peopled by every berserker and every horse it had ever killed. It had cast illusions across the land, herded people with its disorienting fogs, killed, possessed . . .

"The berserker deactivated it," Is said. "I thought your people should have it before the Alliance got it."

"Yes." Whatever it was, truly dead, destroyed beyond all ability to reactivate it, or only deactivated, it was imperative that the Alliance did not recover it.

"Lark wouldn't attack the Mirror," Is continued. She had waited as close to the Mirror as she dared until Lark had come, carrying his berserker, galloping hard, stained black with sweat, red nostrils blowing out clouds of fog. She would never forget how he had looked, fully mature in his moment of glory.

"The meadow was suddenly full of berserkers and horses, but I think Lark could tell they weren't real." She let it trail off.

"And Largo, Lark's berserker?" Petre had to ask. He had to know if Largo had kept his word.

"He . . ." Is shook her head not wanting to remember. "He saw me."

She explained how he had stepped down from the massive war horse and come toward her. He had towered over her, stripped to his waist, unaffected by the cold and carrying the short sword in his left hand. "His eyes . . .he was ready to kill . . . to die. But he just stood and looked at me. And suddenly I knew he wasn't going to harm me. Then he turned away and screamed as he attacked . . . something. I think . . . I think he was . . . happy?"

"Yes," Petre confirmed, imagining the scene and Largo's scream of fury, challenge, joy. The berserker had fought hard and well. "It was all he wanted to do."

They were quiet, each in their own thoughts until Is spoke. "I knew the moment he died because the meadow went still. All the illusions disappeared at once and there was just this little black box and the berserker lying there dead. And Lark came over to me and I could see he was all right.

"I didn't want to just leave him there, like that," she said of the dead berserker she should have feared and hated. "I couldn't bury him. The ground was frozen solid, so I got rocks. It took days.

"I thought the Mirror would kill Lark," she confessed softly. Her hand stroked Lark's neck saying all the things her voice did not. How she loved him. How she had not wanted him to be killed. How she had been forced to make the decision to return him to his berserker.

"I didn't think I could save him. He'd gotten unmanageable. At times it was as if he could hear his berserker, or something. He'd . . . it would feel like he'd reared, or plunged off a cliff I couldn't see and then we'd be in some other place. Sometimes it was a nice place with herds of horses grazing, and people who were fair like the Hluit, yet different, smaller. But they could not hear me, and the horses could not see Lark although sometimes they seemed to sense something strange.

"One time . . ." her voice choked down to almost nothing. "Lark took me somewhere and they were killing the horses." Her eyes grew enormous, her skin white, seeing again the carnage. "The riders were trying to run away but the Alliance had some sort of weapon that knocked the horses down." Her hand stopped its stroking. Her fingers trembled against Lark's dark shoulder.

Petre reacted without organizing his thoughts. "I saw . . ." he began, his voice so husky he had to clear it to continue. "I saw a massacre. The horse people were surrounded. The Alliance fired a huge blast into the middle of them, again and again until they were all dead. And the horses were screaming. They didn't understand, and they felt . . . "

"Betrayed," Is said, cold voiced.

"Yes," Petre agreed. "Betrayed."

"That's why they quit," Is said after a moment of silence in which they shared that sense of absolute, terrible betrayal. "That's why the horses would never travel through time for anyone ever again."

"I think you're right," Petre said. "That would explain why the Alliance didn't understand what they'd captured when they took the people's horses. And that's why the horses won't do it for us, even though we're as close to the original people as the Alliance could make us."

"They might forget some day," Is said. "They might forgive."

She was talking about horses who had not forgotten something that had happened so many generations ago, but Petre could feel the rightness of her guess. The Hluit horses had not forgotten, they had not forgiven. Perhaps the passage of time meant nothing to that sort of memory.

"But the half-breeds like Lark either don't 'remember' or they're more obedient, or something. They can be made to do what the descendents of the wild horses cannot."

"But that's wrong," Petre said harshly, feeling the knot of anger in his guts. "We shouldn't take from them what they don't know any better than to give us."

"Yes," Is agreed. "But will your people understand?"

"Yes. Even without knowing why, the Hluit have been working to restore the horses' trust for generations. That's why we ride without bridles and our whole lives revolve around taking care of the horses."

"Then you will take that," she said, pointing to the box, "to them? And you will take Lark?"

He wanted to say no. He wanted to say, where will you go? Why can't you bring them yourself? But he knew the answers. She wasn't coming back. She had come here to die, and that was still all she wanted.

"It's going to be different now," he said. He wanted to say that the Alliance would be overthrown, the Hluit would be safe. She should come back with him and all would be well. But he could not, because he did not know that for sure. And even if it eventually came to pass, there would be rough times to get through first. He knew his own reluctance to fight and kill, and to face what that would do to his soul and his people. He could not pretend for her that it would not be bad.

Is understood his silence, she understood what he could not promise. She wanted to be done. She had seen enough, suffered enough.

"Will you watch out for Lark?" she said. "If he can stay with Celeste he'll be happy. He'll stay home." But they both knew that if that didn't happen, if Lark kept disrupting the land, the Hluit would have to kill him. And, even if Is were there, she had already shown she could not completely control him.

"I will watch out for him," Petre said. His voice was an octave lower than he had ever heard it before. He wanted to say, no he would not look out for her horse, she would have to come and do it herself. He wanted to take her by the shoulders and shake her. He wanted to scream at her. 'Everything's going to change now. We need you. We need everyone who understands, for only they can keep the balance. We have a chance to make things better. We owe it to ourselves, our horses, our children's children, and the children of the Alliance.' But he could not say that to her. If she could not feel that, if she refused to take it upon herself to be part of what would happen, he could not force it upon her.

He watched her hand run along Lark's neck.

"Thank you." Her voice caught. "I'm sorry. I know you love me. I know I haven't been fair to you. I know I shouldn't ask you for anything."

You don't know anything, Petre thought. She could ask anything of him, even this, and he would do it.

He wanted to tell her: *You don't know how it is to be loved. Yes you loved John, and he loved you but it wasn't enough to erase all the years of pain and all the wrongness of what the Alliance did to you. You don't know how to be whole and well, but you could learn if you would give yourself a chance.*

But he held back, uncertain that it was true. She might not be able to recover from what had been done to her. She was the only one who could answer that question, and if she did not even *want* to try he could not force her. And he realized that she *had* tried to some extent.

"I appreciate what you did," Petre told her. "I know it was hard. I know you were suffering."

Petre was amazed by the steadiness of his voice. It didn't break until the last word, and then only a little. But Is heard it.

"I'm sorry," she said, her voice flat, depleted. "I really am. I know you love me, and all I can do is hurt you. I wish, for you, that it was some other way."

He couldn't speak. He couldn't say it doesn't have to be this way, because he had finally given up that belief. He should say something to give her solace or forgiveness, but he couldn't find the words for that either. And then it was too late.

When she pressed Lark's reins into his hands, his fingers took hold of them without his permission. He listened as she walked away while he stood unable to move, unable to think, unable for the moment even to feel. He knew that if he did move he would break wide open. The pain would make him crazy. He would do something for which he would never forgive himself.

She didn't look back. She had already left a long time ago. She had only allowed him to borrow her, animate her and cause her to do one more thing for his people, for John's people.

Is had done her part. Now he was doing his. It took every bit of his strength to resist calling out to her, running after her.

When he could no longer even imagine hearing her footsteps, he turned swiftly and began to tie the great war stallion to a branch. His hands worked methodically, without need for thought, tying the halter rope, removing Lark's bridle and saddle. And then there came a moment when all the tasks were done and his hands hesitated and total desperate aloneness closed in on him. Then he lost control. He managed a few steps before falling to his knees, grabbing at the tree by reflex he clung to it very hard because he had to hold something together. Had to . . .

He was lost for a while in that struggle. The pain that seemed to come from his core was too vast for a single body to hold. It was infinite. It was more than the loss of Is. It was more than the horror of John's death. It was everyone's anguish. Forever. Every injustice. Every broken heart. Past, present, future.

Its intensity swept him and eventually exhausted him. When he became aware of himself again he was just one small broken person in one small body huddled against a tree. But inside his body was a vast, bottomless hole. For the rest of his life that gaping hole would be waiting for any unguarded moment, any small unexpected memory.

Now he believed he could truly understand what Is had felt. "I'm sorry," he begged her forgiveness silently, finally. "I'm sorry. I didn't know what you felt. I thought I did, but I didn't. Not really."

He had asked her for a great sacrifice – to continue living, to continue trying, hoping. And now she had asked him for something – to let her go, to let her quit. He turned back to the stallion. Lark stood patiently, tied as Petre had left him.

Petre stroked his neck, offering comfort to the horse who could not understand that he would never see Is again. And he thought of what Largo had told him. "You are connected to the stallion the same as me."

With deepening insight Petre realized how Is had been an essential piece of the whole that he and Lark and Is were intended to make. He felt the shattered pieces of the gestalt and understood how Is must have felt after losing John – broken in some way that was much more than losing a loved one. Irreparable.

Chapter Twenty-Three

It was the same meadow where Is and John had found the Mirror. Where she and John had lain together, linked by that Mirror in a way other lovers had never been linked. It was the place.

It looked different in the snow. It looked different without the large square-sided reflective building that had been the Mirror's illusion.

The snow wasn't deep here, windswept as this place was. Is didn't let herself think about Petre. He was of the past. Her crimes against him were unforgivable in her own eyes. Soon even that would not matter.

She took the knife from her belt. She had killed rabbits with this knife, taken their lives so hers could continue. She had used this knife to skin them. She knew exactly how it would slice through her own skin, her artery. Already engulfed in agony, she was not concerned about pain. As she held the knife before her, its silver blade caught light from the bright moon rising over the tops of the trees, the white snow. Cold colors. Death's colors.

She lay the blade along her wrist. One quick movement and there would be no turning back.

Petre sat with the tree at his back, his eyes staring but seeing nothing, his heart stunned into silence. And then Lark, who had been standing quietly, tied to the tree, threw up his head snorting as though something had frightened or pained him.

Is! Peter's heart screamed. He was sure the war horse had felt her die.

An instant later, Lark reared back against his rope. The strong cable snapped like a string and Lark spun on his heels and took off at a gallop. Petre lunged to his feet and raced after the horse, his heart stabbing. He didn't need Lark's tracks in the snow. He honed in on the spot like a magnet.

Is hesitated, the knife against her skin. She was not afraid – the pain she had already endured would make the sting of this cut seem small in comparison. She had given all that she had to give, and more. She wanted out. She wanted to be done.

But Petre's eyes haunted her. *I can't love you,*" she thought angrily. *"I have nothing left to give.* Yet he had given his love to her. "You can't accept it," he had once told her, "because you don't understand what it is. You don't understand that you can't reject love – it is already given. You have no control over that. You never did."

She looked at the knife lying silver and cold against her wrist. Taking her own life should be her own decision, one that should not involve anyone else so deeply. But it was not that way.

The pain of being without John seemed nearly unbearable. She wondered if Petre would miss her in the same way. Would her death cause him as much pain as John's death had caused her? She didn't want that, she truly didn't. She could not wish that kind of horrible aching on anyone. But she and Petre had not been lovers. Perhaps he would not experience as much pain as she had over John. Yet she could not deny the feeling of deep connection with Petre.

Still, he had let her come here. He had not tried to stop her. But Is knew it was not because he didn't care. Rather, he believed in her right to make her own decisions even when those decisions held the power to hurt him deeply.

She turned the knife so the edge touched her skin. *You do not have to face any of this,* she told herself. *You do not have to try to figure out what is right.*

She felt the sharp edge of the cold steel press her warm flesh, so simple . . . and so wrong.

She took the knife away and slipped it back into its sheath on her belt.

For a moment she was stunned by her decision. She had not thought she would change her mind. And then she felt deeply, terribly afraid. *What if I don't have enough courage? What if I am always going to hurt this badly? What if I try and I can't do it?* But she knew her decision had been made.

Then she heard Lark's whinny, not the loud blast of a war stallion, but a call, a question.

"Yes, I am here," she called back to him. And a moment later he burst from the woods at a gallop. He saw her and came toward her in great high bounding strides that threw the snow into the air in a spray of silver mica. His lethal hooves flashed in the moonlight, his mane flowed from his arched neck. A piece of broken rope dangled from his halter. He skidded to a stop in front of her, his breath billowing over her in great gusts.

As she reached out and touched his face, her legs went weak and she pitched onto her knees in the snow. He lowered his head to her and she clung to his mane.

Petre ran into the clearing, saw Is kneeled in the snow, her back to him, bent in pain. *But not dead yet. Not dead yet.* His heart pounded as he slammed to a stop. He was afraid to approach, afraid he would see her blood gushing from her unstoppably.

Lark stood beside Is, his head lowered to her, docile and tame. She wrapped her arms around his neck and her tears ran into his mane. Lark accepted that calmly and then slowly raised his head. Still clinging to the stallion's neck, Is was lifted to her feet, her back toward Petre.

Petre stood frozen, overwhelmed by emotions – despair, hope, love. And with the final letting go of any resistance, he acknowledged his connection to Is, Lark, the land, and whatever would happen next. Lark turned his head to look back over his shoulder at Petre, curling his neck around Is so she faced Petre too. Unashamed of her tear-streaked face, stripped of her usual armor, she took one arm off Lark's neck and reached out toward Petre.

His feet moved of their own volition. He gripped her hand, her arm, and then she was in his embrace. He held her as if he could draw her right into him, through skin and bone and into every muscle, every sinew of his body where she already resided.

She laid her cheek against his and her grief eased. She felt her connection to him, the horse, and the world she would not leave. They stood like that a long time, interwoven, with the great horse wrapped around them.

Chapter Twenty-Four
Epilogue

The colt raced by them going as fast as he could. His short flag of a tail beat up and down against his hindquarters as he sprinted, small hooves kicking back clods of the rich spring soil. Then realizing he had gotten too far from his mother he tried to turn, but he was going so fast that his feet went out from under him. For a moment he was sliding on his haunches on the slick green grass, front feet running to keep in front of his hind end, a very surprised look on his face. In the next moment he regained his feet. He shook himself all over like a dog as though to ascertain that he really was all in one piece. Then suddenly he leaped in the air, twisting his young body to kick at the offending spot on the ground that had caused him such indignity.

Is laughed, sending a trill of good feeling through Petre. He smiled but did not look at her. Such moments when she forgot herself like this were still too rare. Instead, he looked out at the land through which they were riding. Spring flowers were everywhere, pushing up between the short green shoots of grass, clinging to rocks, tinting the gravel by the stream purple. Above, the sky was impossibly blue. Ahead, in the distance the white peaks of the Boundary waited for them. It would be cold there, but it would take weeks to get there traveling at the colt's pace as they were. And here it was spring! Glorious spring!

The colt came to a walk, momentarily subdued at his mother's side. But soon he noticed Petre's boot right there at the height of his face and he had to taste it, see what it was made of, and see if biting it was as forbidden here as it was when Petre was standing on the ground.

Petre shooed him off and spoke an affectionate rebuke to the mare. "Celeste, where *did* you get such a colt?"

"Lark was just like that," Is said. "He had to see everything and get it in his mouth. After all that's the only 'hand' he has. And you see how well he's turned out."

She ran her hand along the crest of Lark's neck. He had matured this last year and come into the stateliness that only a fully mature war horse could project. She rode him without a bridle now, the way the Hluit rode their horses.

She didn't speak of the fact that this trip was partly a test to see if she could control him. They could not allow him to disrupt the flow of time ever again. The damage to the land had been severe. There were still places, pockets, where time was not yet right and people could get lost. But Is had insisted on riding Lark.

"I think I know how to control him now and I have to find out for sure," she had said. Petre understood her need. She could not live wondering if the stallion would leave her or perhaps have to be killed if he continued to disrupt time. But there had been no incidents all winter and Petre felt a growing certainty that there would be none.

"Do you think Ondre will like the colt?" Is asked.

"You know he will. He'll love him."

"But he may not have time for him," Is worried. "You know it takes a lot of time to raise a colt properly."

Petre laughed, imagining Ondre indoors at a desk or in one conference after another *not having time for a colt*. "The colt is exactly what Ondre needs."

Ondre had been at Center over the winter *administering* the new government. Even with Ellie at his side he must be very homesick by now.

"What Ondre needs more than anything in this world is an excuse to be outdoors and be with a horse. Felice doesn't demand his attention that way. She is mature and well trained and there are many other Hluit in Center now who can take care of her. But this colt! He is a handful. He will need just the right touch. Ondre will see that immediately. It will be the perfect excuse."

"But *can* Ondre take time from his work just for a horse?"

"For Lark's colt!" Petre gave her a grin. "He will have to." It was not known what abilities Lark's descendents might have.

Is and Petre were returning to the Alliance to deliver the colt to Ondre but Petre also suspected that Is needed to see how much the Alliance had changed. The perversity that had ruined her childhood was no longer allowed to ruin others. Of course the job was not complete by any means, but the groundwork was laid and the process of re-education, which would make the changes stick, had begun. Fortunately, the people were behind Ondre, especially the children. To them he was already a hero. Change was happening. Change for the better. Petre could not think of a better way to help Is heal than for her to see how the part she had played had led to positive change.

But there were things that still worried Petre. The research that was supposed to free the Dark Bodies from their eternal half-life was difficult and dangerous. As a result, the Hluit were probing into directions they would otherwise have left alone. But Ondre had promised the Dark Bodies that he would try to free them and so they must try. Petre thought of Amil who had overcome both death and time, and he wondered if his secret would become known. The power inherent in such knowledge and the temptation to pervert such power made him uneasy, and his distrust for that man ran deep.

But for now . . . for now there were the rolling hills, the spring grass, the birds singing. He could not ask for more than what he had – a good horse, the company of the woman he loved and an open trail.

Lisa Maxwell lives on a farm in Weaverville, North Carolina, Where she teaches riding and trains horses when she isn't traveling to teach horsemanship clinics. She also holds a second degree black belt in aikido.

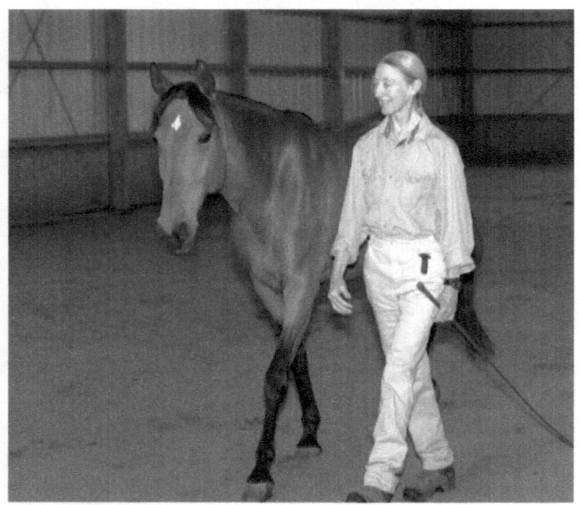